DEATH ON A SUMMER NIGHT

Nerine Tarrant lay sprawled on her back on the wide stone terrace, limbs splayed, neck at an unnatural angle, feet pointing away from the house. She must have been in her early thirties, Thanet thought, and even now, in death, was one of the most beautiful women he had ever seen: classic oval face, high cheekbones, and a Dallas-style tumble of long dark expensive curls. Already, in mid-June, her skin was tanned to a rich honey (sunbed? he wondered), and her simple linen dress the colour of an unripe lemon enhanced the slim youthful body, the long shapely legs. A second, closer look told him that he had underestimated her age. The faintest lines at the corners of eyes and mouth reminded him that Damon Tarrant, aged eighteen, was her son. Late thirties, then, he decided. But exceedingly well preserved. He would guess that a great deal of money had been spent on maintaining that youthful façade. And to what end? To die only half-way through her allotted span in the garden of her own home on this tranquil June evening. No one deserved an end such as this.

Bantam offers the finest in classic and modern British murder mysteries. Ask your bookseller for the books you have missed.

Agatha Christie

Death on the Nile
A Holiday for Murder
The Mousetrap and Other Plays
The Mysterious Affair at Styles
Poirot Investigates
Postern of Fate
The Secret Adversary
The Seven Dials Mystery
Sleeping Murder

Dorothy Simpson

Last Seen Alive
The Night She Died
Puppet for a Corpse
Six Feet Under
Close Her Eyes
Element of Doubt
Dead on Arrival

Sheila Radley

The Chief Inspector's Daughter
Death in the Morning
Fate Worse Than Death
Who Saw Him Die?

Elizabeth George

A Great Deliverance
coming soon: A Payment in Blood

Colin Dexter

Last Bus to Woodstock
The Riddle of the Third Mile
The Silent World of Nicholas Quinn
Service of All the Dead
The Dead of Jericho
The Secret of Annexe 3
Last Seen Wearing

John Greenwood

The Mind of Mr. Mosley
The Missing Mr. Mosley
Mosley by Moonlight
Murder, Mr. Mosley
Mists Over Mosley
What, Me, Mr. Mosley?

Ruth Rendell

A Dark-Adapted Eye
  (writing as Barbara Vine)
A Fatal Inversion
  (writing as Barbara Vine)

Marian Babson

Death in Fashion
Reel Murder
Murder, Murder Little Star
Murder on a Mystery Tour
Murder Sails at Midnight

Christianna Brand

Suddenly at His Residence
Heads You Lose

Dorothy Cannell

The Widows Club
coming soon: Down the Garden Path

Michael Dibdin

Ratking

Antonia Fraser

Your Royal Hostage
coming soon:
Oxford Blood
A Splash of Red
Cool Repentence
Jemima Shore's First Case

ELEMENT
OF
DOUBT

Dorothy Simpson

BANTAM BOOKS
NEW YORK • TORONTO • LONDON • SYDNEY • AUCKLAND

This edition contains the complete text of the original hardcover edition.
NOT ONE WORD HAS BEEN OMITTED.

ELEMENT OF DOUBT
A Bantam Book / published by arrangement with Charles Scribner's Sons

PRINTING HISTORY
Charles Scribner's edition published February 1988
Bantam edition / July 1989

ISBN 0-553-28175-5

Published simultaneously in the United States and Canada

Bantam Books are published by Bantam Books, a division of Bantam Doubleday Dell Publishing Group, Inc. Its trademark, consisting of the words "Bantam Books" and the portrayal of a rooster, is Registered in U.S. Patent and Trademark Office and in other countries. Marca Registrada, Bantam Books, 666 Fifth Avenue, New York, New York 10103.

PRINTED IN THE UNITED STATES OF AMERICA

O   0 9 8 7 6 5 4 3 2 1

To Keith, again

ONE

As he swung into the drive Thanet felt distinctly smug. Joan
had asked him to try to be home by six and it was one minute
to. He was still smiling to himself at the thought of her
surprise at his almost unprecedented punctuality when the
front door was flung open and Ben came racing down the
path.

"Dad! You just had a phone call. There's been a murder out
at Ribbleden!" At twelve Ben was still young enough to relish
the more sensational aspects of his father's police work and to
enjoy parading his imaginary inside knowledge before his
friends.

Thanet groaned. The fantasy of the long, lazy, thoroughly
self-indulgent evening he had planned lingered tantalisingly
in his imagination for a moment or two longer before fading
reluctantly away. He gave Ben an accusing look. "And you
shouldn't have been listening, anyway."

"Oh come on, Dad! I can't just go deaf every time the
phone rings."

"You know perfectly well what I mean. But as you did
listen, not a single word about it at Scouts tonight, do you
hear?"

"Oh, *Dad*!"

"I mean it, Ben. I don't want rumours flying around. If
that's all it turned out to be, a rumour, there could be all
sorts of complications."

"Oh all right. If I must . . . On one condition . . ."

1

"Condition, my foot! If you think I'm going to submit to blackmail . . ."

"Blackmail?" said Joan, as they reached the front door. She looked harassed.

Thanet shook his head. "A joke." He kissed her. "We've got a problem, I gather."

Joan, a probation officer, was due at a meeting at six thirty and it had been arranged that Thanet should do the Scout run and, later, pick Bridget up from Doc Mallard's, where she and Mrs. Mallard were having one of what they called their "creative" evenings. Helen Mallard was a well-established writer of popular cookery books and Bridget's love of cooking had forged a strong bond between them.

"Not any more. It's all organised." Joan was fishing in her handbag for her car keys. "If you could manage to take Ben and the others to Scouts, as arranged, Jane Orton will fetch them home. And Helen will bring Bridget back when they've finished their session."

"Fine. Thanks. Ben, disappear for a few minutes, will you? Go *on*. Your mother's in a hurry." Thanet waited until Ben had gone into the living room and shut the door, then turned to Joan. "So, what's it all about? Ben said something about a murder out at Ribbleden."

"That's right—well, a suspicious death, anyway. I don't know the details, but here's the address. I hope I didn't jump the gun, but as I had to ring Helen Mallard anyway, I arranged for you to pick up Doc Mallard on the way, as she'll be needing his car to bring Bridget home. Hers is in for servicing."

"Thanks, that's fine. Off you go then, love." Thanet paused. "What's the matter?"

Joan was hesitating.

"That address. High Gables, Ribbleden . . . Damon Tarrant lives there."

"Damon . . . ? Ah . . . Possession of drugs, right?"

Joan nodded.

"The poor little rich boy."

"I wish you wouldn't call him that!"

Thanet held up his hands in apology. "All right, I'm sorry. But why so uptight?"

Joan hesitated. "He didn't turn up for his appointment this afternoon," she said reluctantly.

"I see . . . And now you're worried in case he had something to do with this . . . suspicious death."

"Well, not worried, exactly, not in that sense. Concerned would be a better word. He is only eighteen, after all."

"Were you told who the victim is?"

Joan's mouth turned down at the corners. "His mother . . . Of course, his not turning up for an appointment could be purely coincidental."

"True. But in any case, there's absolutely nothing you can do about it at the moment, so you'd better get off. You're going to be late as it is. I'll let you know what the situation is when I get home. OK?"

Joan nodded. "I suppose you're right. But . . . Oh goodness, it's twenty past already. I must fly."

Thanet gave her a quick kiss and a gentle push towards the front door.

"Ben?" he called. "Ready?"

Doctor Mallard, the police surgeon, was ready and waiting when Thanet's car pulled up outside the bungalow transformed since Mallard's recent remarriage by fresh paint, new curtains and a garden full of flowers instead of weeds. Every time he passed it Thanet would marvel at the difference this marriage had made to his old friend after the years of sadness and depression which had followed the death of the little doctor's first wife. The man himself had also taken on a new lease on life. Gone was the irritability which had made him so uncomfortable to work with, the scruffy, down-at-heel clothes and unpolished shoes. Watching him now as he walked briskly down the path to the car Thanet offered up a brief prayer of gratitude on his friend's behalf.

Helen Mallard and Bridget appeared at the front door, waving. Thanet got out of the car. "Thanks for helping out, Helen," he called.

She smiled and made a dismissive gesture. "Any time."

"It's very kind of Helen to take so much trouble over Bridget," said Thanet as they moved off. "Joan and I really appreciate it, and I know Bridget does."

"Nonsense. She really enjoys having someone to share her ideas with. It's a relief for me to get out tonight. I'm definitely persona non grata on Thursday evenings." But Mallard's indulgent smile belied his words. "She says Bridget is very talented."

"The admiration is mutual, I assure you."

"Anyway, tell me a bit more about this case. Joan didn't say much on the phone."

"I don't suppose I know much more than you. A suspicious death at Ribbleden. A Mrs. Tarrant."

"Of High Gables? Good grief!"

"You know her, then?"

"I have met her a few times. Know *of* her, would be more accurate."

"Well?"

"Well what?"

"Don't be tantalising. What do you know of her?"

"Far be it from me to pass on gossip," said Mallard, primly. Glancing at his companion Thanet caught the mischievous glint about the lenses of the half-moon spectacles. "Don't be infuriating, Doc. If this turns out to be a murder case . . ."

"It's just that she has something of a reputation, that's all."

"For what?"

"Promiscuity." Mallard was no longer smiling. "And as a matter of fact, it's not just gossip. I know of at least one marriage she destroyed. It's a number of years ago now, but the husband was a friend of mine. What I found so hard to swallow was the fact that she'd just been playing around with him. He thought it was the great love of his life, but when it came to the crunch and his wife left him, taking the children with her, and he suggested to Nerine Tarrant that she get a divorce and marry him, she just laughed at him. He was left with nothing."

"His wife didn't come back?"

Mallard shook his head. "Said the whole experience had been so humiliating and so disillusioning that she could never trust him again."

"So what happened to him?"

"He left the area, soon afterwards. Last I heard, he was thinking of emigrating."

"Nerine . . . It's an unusual name."

"Just what I said, when I first heard it. Apparently Mrs. Tarrant's father was very fond of flowers and named his daughters after two of his favourites, Nerine and Daphne. He owned a nursery, but he died some years ago and Daphne now runs it—very efficiently, I believe."

"A real mine of information, aren't you, Doc?"

"I get about . . . And don't forget, Luke, I've been living in the area since before you drew your first breath. Turn left here."

Ribbleden lay at the heart of an unspoiled area of countryside south of Sturrenden, the country town in Kent where Thanet lived and worked. Protected from coachloads of tourists by the maze of narrow twisting country lanes which surrounded it, the village was a sight to gladden the heart of any photographer in search of calendar material. Village green, pond with ducks, picturesque pubs and period houses, they were all there. At this hour of a fine June evening the place was deserted. Presumably the entire population was either eating its evening meal or glued to its television sets.

A moment or two later Thanet was kicking himself for being so naive. As they rounded a bend he saw that the entire population of Ribbleden seemed to be clustered around some tall iron entrance gates.

Mallard frowned. "The ghouls are out in force I see."

"As usual," said Thanet grimly.

The crowd parted reluctantly to allow the car through, closing behind it like the Red Sea behind the Israelites. Ahead, a curving drive led to a substantial Victorian red-brick house ornamented with the gables, pinnacles and turrets so beloved of that era. A number of police and private cars were parked on the gravel near the front door.

"Lineham's here, I see," said Mallard, nodding in the direction of a red Ford Escort. "How is he these days? He seems a lot more cheerful, I must say."

"Yes, he's pretty buoyant at the moment."

"Recovered from not getting his promotion last year, has he?"

"I think so, yes."

"Is he going to try again?"

"No, he seems pretty determined not to." Privately, Thanet thought this a wise decision. Mike Lineham was a first-rate sergeant, but he lacked the extra flair essential for the higher rank. In Thanet's opinion Lineham would never have made the application in the first place if it hadn't been for his wife. Louise was both determined and ambitious.

"That'll suit you, I should think."

"True. There's no one I prefer to work with."

Thanet got out and stood for a moment taking in his surroundings. The drive continued around the left side of the house and disappeared, presumably in the direction of the garages. The whole place had an air of complacent prosperity. The gravel was weed-free, the lawns and flower-borders well maintained, the house itself, despite its size, in excellent order.

"What does Mr. Tarrant do?"

"He's a surgeon at Sturrenden General, with a prosperous private practice."

Thanet grinned. "You're in the wrong branch of your profession, Doc."

Mallard smiled back. "Bit late to do anything about it now."

"Ah, there's Lineham."

The detective sergeant had appeared round the right-hand corner of the house. He raised a hand in greeting, then beckoned. The two men began to walk towards him.

"Evening Mike. Not inside?"

"Evening, sir, Doc. No. This way. She fell," the sergeant explained, "from a first-floor balcony onto a stone terrace. Broke her neck, by the look of it."

"And you don't think it was an accident, presumably?"

Lineham shrugged. "Difficult to see how. The balcony rail is just that little bit too high for her simply to have overbalanced."

"I see." Thanet's tone was abstracted and unconsciously his pace had quickened. They were approaching the corner of the house and he was steeling himself for the moment he dreaded, that first sight of the corpse. He wanted to get it over with as quickly as possible.

"Here we are, sir."

It was the familiar scene of disciplined activity. Sketches were being made, measurements and photographs taken. Trace, the Scenes-of-Crime Officer, was waiting for the police surgeon officially to pronounce death before launching on the painstaking task of taking his samples. And at the heart of it all lay the inanimate object that had once been the miracle that is a live human being. Thanet took a deep breath and moved forward to look as Mallard dropped to his knees beside the body.

Nerine Tarrant lay sprawled on her back on the wide stone terrace, limbs splayed, neck at an unnatural angle, feet pointing away from the house. She must have been in her early thirties, Thanet thought, and even now, in death, was one of the most beautiful women he had ever seen: classic oval face, high cheekbones, and a Dallas-style tumble of long dark expensive curls. Already, in mid-June, her skin was tanned to a rich honey (sunbed? he wondered), and her simple linen dress the colour of an unripe lemon enhanced the slim youthful body, the long shapely legs. A second, closer look told him that he had underestimated her age. The faintest lines at the corners of eyes and mouth reminded him that Damon Tarrant, aged eighteen, was her son. Late thirties, then, he decided. But exceedingly well preserved. He would guess that a great deal of money had been spent on maintaining that youthful façade. And to what end? To die only half-way through her allotted span in the garden of her own home on this tranquil June evening. No one deserved an end such as this.

Thanet's gaze swung upwards. A white-painted wooden balustrade edged the covered balcony which ran right along this side of the house at first-floor level. An unusual feature for a Victorian house, surely? Perhaps this section had been added on later. On the ground floor two sets of french windows led out onto the terrace and stepping back he could see that there were two matching sets on the balcony above, one open, one closed.

"Her bedroom and sitting room," said Lineham's voice in his ear. The two men had been working together for so long that the sergeant could gauge to the second the right moment to break into Thanet's thoughts. "The open windows lead into the sitting room. The bedroom windows are locked."

"And there's no other access to the balcony?"

Lineham shook his head.

"Have you looked at the sitting room yet?"

"Only a quick glance. There's no sign of a struggle, if that's what you're thinking. And the balcony rail is about three foot six high. At a guess, Mrs. Tarrant was around five seven, so the rail would have come roughly to the top of her thighs."

Thanet glanced from balcony to body and back again. "From the way she's lying it looks as though she came over head first, wouldn't you agree?"

"Yes. Did a somersault, I'd say."

"Did you bring up the question of suicide, with her husband?"

"Touched on it, that's all. He's pretty shocked, of course, I thought it could wait. But he dismissed the idea out of hand."

"They always do," said Thanet. "All the same, in this case I'd think it a pretty remote possibility. If you really want to kill yourself there are far more certain ways of doing it. That balcony can't be much more than—what?—fifteen feet from the ground?"

"Something like that, yes."

"If you threw yourself from that height you'd quite likely end up in a wheelchair for the rest of your life . . . No, I think we can safely rule out suicide."

"Or accident, sir, surely. I mean, if she'd been leaning on the rail and just fallen, either because she was dizzy, or drunk, or even drugged . . ."

"Are there any indications, up there, that she had either been drinking or taking drugs?"

"No, sir, not that I could see. But as I said, I only took a quick look . . . I was just speculating."

"Right, sorry, go on."

"Well, if she just toppled over, for whatever reason, surely she would be lying closer in to the house."

"I would have thought so, yes. She could have been sitting on the rail, I suppose."

"Most unlikely," said Lineham promptly. "It's too narrow, only about three inches wide."

"Hmm. Well, it looks as though you're right, and she was helped on her way. If she was leaning on that rail, all anyone would have to do would be to bend down, lift her legs off the ground, give one hard shove, and that would be it."

Mallard closed his bag with a snap and stood up.

"Well, Doc?" said Thanet.

"I'd be very surprised if the PM shows she died of anything but a broken neck. One never knows, of course, the unexpected is always a possibility . . . But there seems to be no sign of a struggle. Difficult to see how she could have fallen over of her own accord, though."

"That's what we thought . . . If she'd taken any drugs, would you be able to tell?"

"Here and now, you mean?"

"Yes."

"Unlikely—though it would depend on what they were and how and when they were taken. Most tablets dissolve pretty quickly and are absorbed into the bloodstream, so it's impossible to tell until the analyst has had a go at some samples."

"What about constriction of the pupils?" said Lineham.

"Unreliable. It's quite normal for pupils to be either dilated or constricted after death, and you sometimes even get irregular dilation, with one pupil much larger than the other. Anyway, this woman's look all right to me."

"And injection marks?" persisted Lineham.

"There are certainly no obvious punctures, but as you know, they're not always visible. Is there any suspicion that she was involved with drugs?"

"No, none, at the moment," said Thanet. "It's just that her son was up on a drugs charge recently."

"Hard drugs?"

"No. Cannabis."

"In that case, in the present economic climate, I think you'll find it difficult to make a case for drug tests to be done."

"I doubt that we'd even suggest it, at the moment. We're just looking at possibilities. We might ask for an alcohol test, though."

"Fair enough. Right, well if that's all . . . Any chance of getting someone to run me home, Luke?"

"Yes, of course. Er, just one more question, Doc . . ."

"I thought you wouldn't let me get away without asking. Time of death, of course . . . When was the body discovered?"

"Five forty-five," said Lineham.

"Yes, well I'd put it at any time within the last four or five hours."

"From two o'clock onwards, then," said Thanet.

"Something like that."

The two men escorted Mallard to a car and then turned back to look up at the house.

"Have you had a chance to find anything about the household yet, Mike?"

"Mr. Tarrant, Mrs. Tarrant, their son, Mr. Tarrant's mother and her companion." Lineham was ticking off his fingers. "And Mrs. Tarrant's sister lives in the coach house at the back of the premises with another woman. I'm not sure of her connection with the family, but the local bobby is here, PC Driver. He'll be able to fill us in, I'm sure."

"I'll have a word with him later. You've been busy, Mike. Well done. Who discovered the body?"

"The husband."

"Ah."

The two men exchanged glances. There was no need to say what they were both thinking. In a domestic murder, the police always look first at the husband, then at the person who discovered the body. When the two were one and the same . . .

"And he's very cut up, you say."

"Certainly seems it, yes."

"Where is he?"

"In his study."

"Right, we'll go and have a word with him. But we'll take a quick look at Mrs. Tarrant's sitting room first. I just want to get the geography clear in my mind."

As they set off briskly for the front door Lineham said, "Surprising how often the old chestnut comes up, isn't it, sir? You know, 'Did she fall, or was she pushed?'"

"Yes. Though in this case there doesn't seem to be much doubt about the answer. The point is, why?"

TWO

The massive front door of High Gables was surrounded by
panels of stained glass depicting the four seasons. The house
faced west and as Thanet and Lineham entered the sun
streamed in, creating a brilliant multicoloured archway on
the white-tiled floor of the hall. Had this been the magical
effect the architect intended? wondered Thanet as he and the
sergeant paused for a moment to exclaim. Then Lineham led
the way past tall green plants in huge white ceramic pots, up
the green-carpeted stairs and along a corridor to Nerine
Tarrant's sitting room.

Here, the predominant colour was blue: powder-blue carpet, pale blue curtains with deep blue patterned borders, and
an entire wall covered with a collection of blue-and-white
plates. The room was saved from coldness by touches of a
deep vibrant pink in upholstery and cushions, and by the
lavish arrangement of summer flowers in a glossy pink bowl
on a table near the open french windows.

Thanet crossed to the balcony, which was about five feet
wide and furnished with white cane chairs and table. Lineham
was right. The rail was around three foot six high and it was
difficult to see how Nerine could possibly have fallen over
without being pushed, even if she had had a sudden attack of
vertigo.

Thanet turned back into the sitting room and wandered
around, hands clasped behind his back to remind himself to
resist the urge to touch. It was an attractive room, yet now

that he looked at it more closely there was something subtly wrong with it. What was it? Pondering the question, he stooped to examine a photograph: Nerine Tarrant and her husband on their wedding day, posed against a background of silver birches and daffodils naturalised in grass. Tarrant was gazing adoringly down at his bride, while she... She was directing a brilliant, seductive smile at the photographer. Was he being unfair? Thanet wondered. Was this impression of her unjustifiably coloured by what Doc Mallard had told him? He looked again, noting the determined tilt of the chin, the proprietorial hand laid casually on her new husband's arm. There was no doubt, looking at the photograph, who was going to be the giver and who the taker in this marriage.

Greedy whispered a little voice in his brain, and he thought, that's it, that's what's wrong with this room. It was too crowded, too cluttered with objects, as though Nerine hadn't known when to stop, how to say no to herself. Had this attitude carried over into her relationships?

"A real looker, wasn't she?" Lineham was peering over his shoulder.

"What's her husband like?" said Thanet. According to the photograph, tall and slim, as fair as Nerine was dark. How had the years dealt with this young man so patently in love with his fairytale bride? "No," he went on as Lineham opened his mouth to speak, "don't tell me. I'd rather judge for myself."

Down the stairs again, across the hall and around a corner. As they entered a corridor a young woman with long brown hair caught up in a ponytail closed a door half-way along, glanced at them, then hurried away in the opposite direction.

"Who was that?" said Thanet.

Lineham shook his head. "No idea. Old Mrs. Tarrant's companion, perhaps? In any case, she was coming out of Tarrant's study."

It was a square, masculine room furnished with club-style leather chairs, tall bookshelves filled with leather-backed volumes and an impressive antique kneehole desk in glowing mahogany. There were two people in the room, a man and an older woman. Tarrant was sitting at his desk, head in hands, in an attitude of despair, the woman standing beside him, hand on his shoulder. He glanced up as the door opened. He looked dazed.

Thanet immediately experienced a painful wave of empathy. How would he feel, in Tarrant's position? And how could he possibly question a man in this state, and at such a time? It was the part of his job that he hated most, tormenting people when they were at their most vulnerable. Many of his colleagues, he knew, disagreed. They took the view that now would be the time to press home the advantage. The end, they argued, justified the means, and in pursuit of the truth all other considerations should be put aside. Thanet was equally determined to get at the truth—but not in such a way that he wouldn't be able to live with himself afterwards. *What is a man profited, if he shall gain the whole world, and lose his own soul?*

"This is Detective-Inspector Thanet, Mr. Tarrant," said Lineham.

The man nodded. "Do sit down," he said, waving his hand at some chairs.

Thanet and Lineham complied, Thanet pulling a chair up to the other side of the desk, Lineham retreating to one against the wall.

"I'd better be going, then, Roland," said the woman.

"Oh, Beatrix, forgive me..." Tarrant rubbed a hand wearily across his eyes and forehead. "Inspector, this is Mrs. Haywood, who has been kind enough to keep me company. She lives in the coach house, with my wife's sister. She..." He shook his head as if to clear it, preparatory to giving some apparently complicated explanation.

"I don't suppose the Inspector wants to hear about me," said Mrs. Haywood. Tall and angular, with untidy greying hair escaping from a bun, she was wearing what Thanet privately labelled "arty" clothes: long flower-sprigged skirt with a wide flounce at the hem, shapeless white blouse, a felt waistcoat with flowers appliquéd down the front and several indian cotton scarves, loosely tied and floating around her as she moved. She was, understandably, looking pale and shaken. "I'll be back later, Roland."

"Perhaps we could have a word with you afterwards, Mrs. Haywood?" said Thanet.

"Oh... Yes, of course."

Thanet waited until she had gone, then turned back to Tarrant. "I'm sorry to trouble you at a time like this, Mr. Tarrant, but I'm afraid that I really shall have to ask you a few questions."

Tarrant waved a hand, wearily.

"I quite understand. Yes, of course I do." It sounded as though he was trying to convince himself. "You'll want to know when I found her..." His voice thickened and he swallowed, hard.

"That's right. And one or two other details..."

"Of course, of course." Tarrant made a visible effort to pull himself together, sitting up straighter and squaring his shoulders.

The surgeon had not worn as well as his wife, Thanet thought. Although well groomed, there was a visible paunch beneath the expensive dark suit, and the abundant fair hair had receded and thinned to little more than a token covering of the scalp. The dryness which is so often the bane of the fair-skinned had created a network of fine lines on his forehead and around the pale blue eyes. He looked a good ten years older than her.

Thanet sat down again.

"Perhaps we could begin by asking you to tell us exactly what happened when you got home this afternoon, sir?"

"Yes..." Tarrant frowned and massaged the side of his forehead for a moment or two with tiny circular movements, as though trying to erase a pain—or perhaps reactivate a memory he had tried to blot out?

Behind him, through the open window, the garden stretched serene, the trees at the far end washed with an almost eerie crimson glow from the setting sun.

"I got home at about, oh, twenty to six, I suppose. I went straight upstairs. Nerine—that's my wife—was usually in her sitting room at that time of day. But she wasn't there, so I knocked at her bedroom door. It was locked, so I knew she couldn't be in there, either..."

"I'm sorry to interrupt," said Thanet. "But perhaps you could just clarify that statement?"

"Clarify...?" Tarrant looked puzzled, then his brow cleared. "Oh, I see what you mean. Well, my mother lives with us, and she has a passion for clothes, jewellery and make-up—especially my wife's clothes, jewellery and makeup, I'm afraid. She is suffering from Alzheimer's disease—senile dementia—so she's rather confused and finds it difficult, after living here all her life, to understand that some parts of the house are out of bounds, so to speak, and that everything in the house is not hers to do what she likes with. Once or twice she's made rather a mess of my wife's bedroom and eventually my wife got into the habit of locking the door whenever she left the room. So this afternoon, when I found the bedroom door locked, I knew she wouldn't be in there."

"I see. Thank you."

"So I went downstairs, looked in the drawing room and the kitchen, but I couldn't find her anywhere... Then I thought, it's a lovely afternoon, perhaps she's still sunbathing in the garden. So I went out onto the terrace and... and found her."

Abruptly, Tarrant swivelled around in his chair to gaze out of the window.

Thanet guessed that he was fighting for control. "I'm sorry, I don't suppose I can even begin to imagine how painful this must be for you."

Tarrant swung back. "At least you didn't say 'I *know* how painful this must be for you.' God, when I think of how often I've said those very words myself, to people whose relations had died... You just have no idea, no conception of what it's really like, until it happens to you—and of course, you never really expect it to. Tragedies are things that happen to other people." He shook his head despairingly. "I'm sorry. You don't want to hear all this. Please, go on. Ask me all the questions you want." *Then go, go and leave me alone, for God's sake.* The man's unspoken cry was almost audible.

"Look, I'm not sure that you're really in a fit state to be questioned at the moment. Perhaps we could go away for a while, come back later, when you've had a little more time to recover from the shock..."

"Recover!" Tarrant gave a harsh, bitter, laugh. "Oh, make no mistake about that. I'm never going to recover from this, Inspector. Never. I can't even begin to imagine life without her... So you might as well ask your questions. Now is as good a time as any."

The outburst seemed to have helped. Tarrant was looking much more in command of himself.

"Very well... When you went into your wife's sitting room, did you go out onto the balcony?"

"Not actually out onto it, no. I did walk across as far as the french windows, just to see if she was out there."

"So how long, in all, would you say this process of looking for your wife took?"

"Five minutes?"

Lineham made a note. Thanet could visualise it. *Body found 5:45 p.m.*

"Did you see anyone during this time?"

Tarrant shook his head. "No."

"I understand that your mother has a companion?"

"Marilyn Barnes, yes. Perhaps I should explain that, contrary to the impression I may have given just now, we lead separate lives, Inspector. Fortunately this house is constructed in such a way as to make that possible. It is, broadly speaking, shaped like an H. The hall and staircase form the central section; my wife, my son and I live in one of the long, vertical arms, my mother, Miss Barnes and her small son in the other. My mother, as I said, does tend to wander, rather, but part of Miss Barnes's job is to try to prevent that happening."

"What about your son? Was he home at the time?"

"No. I noticed his car was missing, when I parked mine."

Thanet did not betray his quickened interest. For the first time there was something not quite straightforward in Tarrant's tone... Nothing as definite as a lie, but a reservation of some kind...

"Has he come home, since?"

"No."

"So he doesn't even know about his mother's death yet?"

Tarrant shook his head.

"Do you know where he is?"

An uneasy laugh. "You can't have any teenagers or you wouldn't be asking that question, Inspector. When he goes out, I never know where he is, how long he's going to be or who he's with."

Then you have been far too lax with him. Battles or no battles, Thanet was determined that his children's adolescence was going to have some kind of positive framework, however long they had to spend hammering out the rules together. Freedom should be a common goal, independence something to be worked for by parents and children alike, not a dangerous weapon carelessly bestowed upon those too immature to know how to handle it.

"How old is he?"

"Damon? Eighteen."

"He's still at school?"

"No. He's very bright, and took his A levels early, last year. He's having a year out while he tries to decide what to do."

"He has a job?"

Tarrant shook his head, regretfully. "Not at the moment."

Thanet was thinking of that missed appointment with Joan.

"So you have no idea whether he was at home, earlier in the afternoon?"

"None, I'm afraid. Look here, Inspector, why all this interest in Damon? If he'd been here earlier, and seen his mother fall, do you seriously think he wouldn't have reported it, or rung me, immediately?"

"I'm just trying to get a clear picture of the situation in the house, this afternoon," said Thanet evasively.

"But why?" Tarrant's suspicions were aroused now and he was staring at Thanet as if trying to read his mind.

"In the case of a sudden death we have to investigate the ciucumstances as thoroughly as possible."

"Now wait a minute. You're not suggesting—you *can't* be suggesting that my wife's death was anything but a simple accident? My God! That *is* what you're suggesting, isn't it?"

"I'm not suggesting anything at the moment, Mr. Tarrant. I'm merely trying to find out what happened. But I think it only fair to tell you—and I'm sorry, because I know that this will cause you additional distress—that we have to take the possibility into consideration."

Tarrant jumped up out of his chair and stood glaring down at Thanet, running a hand over his head. "I don't believe I'm hearing this! You surely don't think she was..." But he couldn't bring himself to say the word and for a moment there was total silence in the room.

"Mr. Tarrant, please, do sit down again. I assure you that at the moment I have a completely open mind. Nevertheless, you must see that I have to consider the possibility."

"But why? Who could possibly want to...?"

"That is one of the questions I have to ask you."

Tarrant shook his head in bewilderment and subsided into his chair. "The idea is preposterous. There's no one, no one..."

"Well, perhaps you could help us by giving us some idea of what your wife was going to do today."

But Tarrant was still staring at Thanet, trying to adjust himself to this new and appalling idea.

"Mr. Tarrant?" said Thanet, gently.

"Sorry... I... What did you say?"

Thanet repeated his question.

Tarrant made an effort to concentrate, blinking and again pressing his fingers into his temples.

"Nothing special, so far as I know. She always has . . . had her hair done, on Thursday afternoons."

"Where?"

Tarrant told him, and Lineham made a note.

"But apart from that, you had no idea of how she was going to spend her day?"

"Sorry, no."

"When did you last see her?"

"After breakfast. I went up to say goodbye to her. She always has a tray in her room."

"And she seemed perfectly normal?"

"Yes." Tarrant shook his head. "If I'd only known that was the last time I'd see her alive . . ."

How often, Thanet wondered, had he heard these words from shocked and grieving relatives, anxious to have bestowed upon that final encounter some special significance. But he knew that this is possible only if one always treats one's loved ones as if seeing them for the last time, an impossible counsel of perfection.

"And she was well? No complaints about dizziness, for example?"

Tarrant hesitated and Thanet could almost hear him thinking. *If I say yes it would be such an easy way out* . . . "No." The regret in his voice was evident.

"She wasn't taking any medication?"

Tarrant shook his head.

"Or drugs of any kind, in fact?"

Thanet hoped he had slipped that particular question tactfully in, but Tarrant reacted strongly.

"Drugs? What do you mean? What are you implying?" But he didn't wait for a reply. "Oh, I see . . . Now look here, Inspector, just because Damon had a spot of trouble over cannabis, it doesn't mean that this is a household of junkies. My God, you never miss a trick, do you?"

"I only meant . . ."

"I know damn well what you meant, and you're wrong. If Damon had been dabbling in the hard stuff, believe me, I'd know. I've been keeping a pretty close eye on him for any symptoms, I assure you, and as for Nerine . . . The idea is ludicrous . . ."

"Very well. I'm sorry. But I had to ask, you must see that."

Tarrant glared at him for a moment or two longer, then

sank back into his chair, his expression softening. "Oh, I suppose so. But you must see..."

"Believe me, I do. And I don't like asking these questions any more than you like answering them."

Tarrant gave him an assessing look. "Then perhaps it's my turn to apologise..." He rubbed the back of his hand over his forehead. "I don't usually lose my temper like that."

"These are not usual circumstances."

"No, thank God. Anyway, carry on, will you? I'd like to get this over with."

"Right. Well, if we could go back a little... You spent the day at the hospital?"

"Sturrenden General, yes."

"And you left at what time?"

"At around 5:15."

"And you got home at about 5:40, you say?"

"That's right."

"Did anyone see you arrive?"

"Not to my knowledge."

Was there a hint of reservation there?

"You're sure?"

"Well I didn't see anyone myself. But with several other people living here I can't speak for them, naturally."

"Apart from your mother, Miss Barnes and her son, does anyone else live in the house?" A reasonable question, in the circumstances. Nerine Tarrant could scarcely have run an establishment of this size without help.

"We have a housekeeper who comes in from eight in the morning until four in the afternoon. And a woman who comes in to clean three mornings a week."

Their names were duly noted by Lineham.

"And your wife's sister lives, I gather, in the coach house. Where is that? I'm afraid I haven't had time to look around yet."

"At the back of the house, near the garages. Yes, she bought it some years ago, when their father died. Daphne had lived with him until then, but it was a large house, much too big for one, and the coach house was empty... We offered it to her rent free, but she preferred to buy."

"And Mrs. Haywood...?"

"Ah, yes. Well, Daphne is unmarried, but she was engaged, once. Her fiancé was killed in a car crash and she kept in touch with his mother, Mrs. Haywood, who was at the time living in a rented house. When that was pulled down for a motorway project she had nowhere to go and Daphne suggested she come and live with her." Tarrant shrugged. "I must admit I wasn't too keen on the idea. I could see Daphne being saddled with an ageing woman who was strictly speaking no relation of hers, but she was very set on it and Mrs. Haywood moved in. They've lived together— quite harmoniously, I might add—for some years now. Mrs. Haywood runs the house, and with Daphne working full-time it seems to have worked out very well for both of them."

"Fine. Well, I think that apart from one more question, that's about it for the moment, Mr. Tarrant. Thank you for being so cooperative."

"You're wrong, you know," said Tarrant. "Thinking that my wife might have been..." He steeled himself to say it. "might have been...killed, deliberately."

"I didn't say I thought that. I said, if you remember, that it is a possibility we have to take into account. But it does in a way lead on to my final question. And I apologise in advance for causing you pain by asking it."

"What?" said Tarrant, warily.

"Your wife..." Hell, there was no way to cushion the impact. "Did you have any reason to believe that she was not faithful to you?"

Tarrant stared at Thanet for a moment, his expression unreadable. Then he said quietly, "I see that I was mistaken, Inspector. I thought that, contrary to my expectations, you were a reasonably civilised human being." His voice rose. "Get out, will you?" He made a violent, dismissive gesture. "Just get out!"

Without another word, they left.

THREE

Outside the study door Thanet and Lineham grimaced at each other.

"You'd no option. You had to ask," said Lineham.

"Yes, I know. Especially after what Doc Mallard told me about Mrs. Tarrant." Briefly, Thanet filled Lineham in.

"Ah, so you're saying that Dr. Tarrant's reaction . . ."

"Mr."

"But . . ."

"Up to consultant status, doctors are 'Dr.' After that, they're 'Mr.'"

"But why? They're still doctors, aren't they?"

Thanet shrugged. "No idea. I've always assumed it's because when they become consultants they're so obviously important that they don't need a special form of address."

"Stupid sort of system, if you ask me."

"Anyway, what were you going to say, Mike?"

"I can't remember now."

"Something about Mr. Tarrant's reaction."

"Ah, yes. Are you suggesting, then, that he reacted as strongly as he did not because he considered your question an insult to his wife but because you'd hit the nail on the head and he hated to admit it?"

"The thought had crossed my mind. Ah, here we are."

They had arrived at a green baize door.

"I've only ever seen these in stately homes," said Lineham. "I didn't know they had them in houses like this."

"Any house where there were lots of servants, I imagine. To cut off noise and cooking smells . . . and I suppose also to draw a symbolic line between upstairs and downstairs."

"Just as a matter of interest, where exactly are we going?"

"To see Mrs. Haywood. And Mrs. Tarrant's sister too, of course. I imagine she's home from work by now. Come to think of it, she should have been home from work some time ago . . ."

"That's a point. I wonder why she wasn't the one to rush over and give Mr. Tarrant moral support."

"Too upset, perhaps? Anyway, I just thought it would be interesting to go out the back way, see a bit more of the terrain."

They were now in a short passage with doors along one side. Thanet glanced in: storeroom, flower room with sink and shelves of vases, and finally a large square kitchen. This was a sight to gladden any woman's heart, with custom-made pine units, acres of work surface and cupboard space and every imaginable gadget. It was immaculately tidy and spotlessly clean. On the pine table was a note, weighted down by a salt cellar. Lineham picked it up and they read it together. "THURS: *chicken mayonnaise, potato salad, green salad, strawberries and cream, all in fridge*."

"Note from the housekeeper?" said Lineham. "Tonight's supper, I presume. Very nice, too. Just the job for a warm summer evening."

"Mmm . . . Mike, I've just realised . . . When we get back from seeing Mrs. Haywood I want to take a look at Mrs. Tarrant's bedroom, but presumably it's still locked. Go and tell one of the men to get hold of a key in the next half an hour or so, will you? I'll wait for you outside."

Thanet saw the coach house as soon as he stepped out of the back door, some fifty yards away on the far side of a gravelled yard. A sleek Porsche was parked in front. Daphne's, he presumed. He didn't know her surname, he realised. The nursery must be doing well.

He could understand her wanting to own this place rather than live in it by grace and favour. Solidly built of stone, with a steeply pitched slate roof and dormer windows, it was an attractive little property by any standards. Ideally situated, too, away from the road and surrounded by the extensive gardens of High Gables. Over to the right were the garages for the main house, obviously converted from another outbuilding. Room for three cars, Thanet noted. One of the spaces was empty.

Lineham appeared around the corner of the house, predictably gazing in the direction of the garage. "A Mercedes and a Jaguar XJS!" he said. "And a Porsche 844! Not exactly short of a penny, are they?"

"I don't suppose that's much consolation to Mr. Tarrant now."

Lineham pulled a face. "True. Bentley's going to track down the key, sir. Oh, and one interesting thing I noticed. There's a path which goes in the direction of the garden boundary, leading off the terrace where the body was found."

"And there are french windows downstairs . . . So anyone wanting to get in unobserved . . ."

"Exactly, sir."

Beatrix Haywood must have been watching for them; as they approached the front door, it opened.

She put a finger across her lips, adjuring silence. "Come in," she whispered. "This way."

She led them through a narrow hall into a large square sitting room and closed the door behind them. "That's better," she said, in a normal voice. "I didn't want to disturb Daphne—Miss Linacre. She has a migraine . . . Sit down, won't you?"

She perched on the edge of a hard-backed chair.

She was getting on for seventy, Thanet estimated, and it was scarcely surprising that she was still looking upset. A sudden brush with violent death is liable to shake the hardiest of constitutions.

"Thank you. I'm sorry to hear that. Miserable things, migraines, aren't they? She suffers them regularly?"

"Oh yes, as far back as I can remember."

"Brought on in this instance, I suppose, by the shock of her sister's death?"

"Oh no. That's just made it ten times worse. She came home from work early with it this afternoon, and went straight to bed."

"What time would that have been?"

"Around twenty to five, I suppose."

During this brief conversation he had been glancing around the room. It was comfortably and conventionally furnished with fitted carpet, chintz curtains and chair covers. On a small table near the fireplace pride of place was given to the photograph of a young man with a weak, rather effeminate mouth and a quantity of untidy brown shoulder-length hair. Mrs. Haywood's dead son? he wondered. But the most striking feature of the room was the number of pictures, which covered every available inch of wall space.

"Yours?" he said.

"No, my son's."

He had been looking for a way to put her more at ease and the pride in her voice told him he might have found it.

"He was an artist?" A somewhat fatuous question, in the circumstances, but it would serve. The tense he had used, however, made her frown.

"How did you know he was dead?"

"Mr. Tarrant told me of his accident. I'm sorry."

"Yes." Mrs. Haywood shook her head and sighed. "It was a tragedy, as you can see." And she waved her hand at the paintings, which she evidently considered a mute testimony to her son's talent. "Such a *waste*. It was said, you know, that if only he'd had the opportunity to fulfil his potential, he could have been one of the world's great artists."

That, Thanet thought, was a matter of opinion. Personally, he couldn't see that Haywood's work had an ounce of original-ity in it, in terms of composition, execution, or use of colour. Not that he was an expert, of course, but still... "He was very prolific."

"Jocelyn was devoted to his work." She was warming to her subject. "Absolutely devoted to it. How different things would have been, if he had lived to marry Daphne... She under-stood him, you see, recognised his genius. She would have allowed him to dedicate himself entirely to his work, instead of being forced to prostitute his talents..."

Thanet's look of mild enquiry was enough to encourage her to continue. This was clearly her favourite theme, the subject nearest her heart, and her natural diffidence and hesitant manner fell away as she became engrossed in talking about her son. Listening to the enthusiasm in her voice and noting the sparkle in her eyes, the mounting flush on those pale cheeks, Thanet reflected that it must be rare for her to have so rapt an audience. Most of the people she knew must long ago have grown tired of listening to these exaggerated claims of his genius. His attention sharpened as she began to talk about his romance with Daphne.

He had met her, it seemed, when he had been commissioned

to design a cover for the 1969 catalogue for Linacre Nurseries. Daphne was then nineteen. After leaving school she had done a business studies course and had gone straight into the office at the nurseries. Listening carefully to what was not said, Thanet deduced that by the time she met Jocelyn it was already obvious that one day she would be taking over the business.

"It was love at first sight," sighed Mrs. Haywood. "Daphne has never even looked at another man. Not like . . ." The flow of information broke off abruptly and she looked embarrassed, the temporary spell broken.

"What were you going to say, Mrs. Haywood?" said Thanet gently.

Pause.

"Mrs. Haywood?"

Again he waited for a reply, but she merely shook her head.

"Not like her sister, perhaps?" said Thanet, softly.

Another shake of the head, lips compressed.

Thanet rose, began to wander around, studying the paintings. A closer view did nothing to alter his opinion of them. "Perhaps I should tell you, Mrs. Haywood, that there does seem to be some question as to whether or not Mrs. Tarrant's death was an accident."

Her head snapped around, eyes stretched wide. "Not . . . not an accident? What . . . what do you mean?"

Thanet did not reply and she was forced to break the silence.

"You don't . . . You can't . . . You're surely not implying that . . . someone killed her, deliberately?"

"It's a possibility we have to take into consideration."

"But why? She fell . . . From the balcony . . . I always did say that rail was dangerously low . . ."

"But perhaps not low enough for an accidental fall . . ." Thanet returned to his chair and sat down. "I'm sorry, this has obviously been a shock to you. And I must stress that we haven't made up our minds, yet. But you must see that if there is even the remotest possibility that Mrs. Tarrant was murdered, we can't waste time by assuming that her death was an accident. If, later on, it is proved to be otherwise, well and good, but at the moment we have no choice but to proceed as if this were a murder investigation."

Silence. Mrs. Haywood's hands were clasped tightly together in her lap as she considered what had just been said.

"Yes," she said at last, hesitantly. "Yes, I see that . . . But why are you saying all this to me?"

"Because we need your help. Unlike Mr. Tarrant and Miss Linacre, you are here all day. Even though you don't live in the house, you overlook the garages. You must know a lot more about Mrs. Tarrant's movements than they do."

Mrs. Haywood chewed at her lower lip. Clearly, she was trying to reach some decision.

"We really would be grateful for any information you could give us."

She sighed and shook her head. "There's no point in pretending I had much time for Nerine . . . But it seems so wrong, to gossip about the dead."

"We are not gossiping, Mrs. Haywood. Far from it. We are merely seeking the truth, trying to find out who killed her—if indeed she was killed. I can understand your not wanting to discuss her when she can no longer defend herself, but try to look at it this way. Could you come to terms with your conscience if you refused to help bring a murderer to justice?"

He was laying it on a bit thick, Thanet knew, but you had to adapt your approach to the personality of the witness concerned.

And he had struck just the right note. He could see the lines of indecision in her face already beginning to harden into conviction.

"I suppose you're right," she said at last. "Of course you are . . . What is it you want to know?"

But there was still a reservation in her voice.

"Perhaps we could begin by going back to the point at which you broke off. You *were* going to say, 'Not like her sister', weren't you?"

A reluctant nod.

"Perhaps you could explain what you meant?"

Mrs. Haywood pulled one of the floating scarves from her neck into her lap and began to tug it, twist it around one hand.

Did she know, Thanet wondered, how revealing these movements were? She could not have mirrored the conflict in her mind more clearly if she had tried.

As if she had read his thoughts she laid the scarf down, smoothing it out across her knees, and raised her head to look

Thanet straight in the eye. "She was not a good woman. She... It was upsetting, the way she carried on."

"Carried on?" echoed Thanet.

She lowered her eyes and murmured, almost inaudibly, "With men."

"You're saying that she was often unfaithful to her husband?" She nodded, lips compressed.

"And at present?"

She glanced up at him quickly from beneath lowered eyelids, and shook her head.

Mrs. Haywood, please... This could be very important, you must realise that."

She hesitated a moment longer and then mumbled something.

"I'm sorry, I didn't quite catch that."

She sighed again, and raised her head, capitulating. "Speed," she said. "Lance Speed."

"He's local?"

She nodded. "He runs the garage—in the village."

"And this has been going on for... how long?"

"A few months." And then, in an uncharacteristic outburst, added bitterly, "Judging by her past record, I should say that any minute now Mr. Speed would have found himself supplanted."

"Was this affair general knowledge?"

"Oh yes." She gave him a shamefaced look and said, "I'm afraid Nerine's affairs always were. She never took the slightest trouble to hide them from anybody."

Which, Thanet thought, was no doubt why Mrs. Haywood had finally decided to be so frank now. If Nerine Tarrant's promiscuity was common knowledge, it wouldn't have been long before he had heard about it from other sources.

"From anybody, Mrs. Haywood? What about her husband?"

Mrs. Haywood shook her head so vigorously that a few more wisps escaped from her bun. "Not even from him. I don't know how he stood it. In fact, I used to think, sometimes..."

She hesitated, then stopped.

"You were saying?"

"Nothing."

"You were going to say, perhaps, that you sometimes wondered if Mrs. Tarrant used deliberately to flaunt her lovers in front of her husband?"

"I didn't say that!"

But he had been right, he could tell.

"But in any case, you are saying that her husband had full knowledge of her behaviour?"

She inclined her head.

"And what was his reaction?"

She hesitated for a moment, then said earnestly, "I can tell you this, Inspector. Mr. Tarrant would never have hurt a single hair on his wife's head. He adored that woman, and didn't care what she did as long as she stayed with him."

So that spurt of anger just now had been on Tarrant's behalf. She was obviously fond of him, thought highly of him.

"How did Mrs. Tarrant get on with the rest of the household?"

"Well..." She hesitated. Discussing Nerine, whom she had disliked, and who was dead, was obviously one thing; talking about the other people with whom she lived at close quarters was another.

"I understand, for example, that there were... certain difficulties with Mr. Tarrant's mother."

"That's true, yes..." she said reluctantly. Then she added defensively, "There are always problems, having parents living in the same house. And Lavinia—Mrs. Tarrant senior—well, it's not her fault. It's her illness, you see. She can't help it if she's become a little, well, eccentric, as the disease progresses."

"She is suffering from senile dementia, I understand?"

"That's right." A sigh. "Such a shame. When I think how lively and active she was only a few years ago..."

"But I understand that she and Miss Barnes, her companion, have what is virtually a separate establishment."

"I know. But Marilyn, Miss Barnes, can't keep an eye on Lavinia twenty-four hours of the day. Lavinia has lived in that house for over forty years and genuinely forgets that she is not still mistress of it. It used to drive Nerine mad, especially when Lavinia used to get into her—Nerine's—bedroom and try her clothes on as if they were her own. Like..." She stopped, abruptly.

It was obvious that she wished that last word had not slipped out. No doubt she didn't want to get the old lady into trouble.

"Like when?"

"I..." She shook her head. "Nothing."

"Like this afternoon, perhaps?"

She was still hesitating, but now she gave a little shrug. "I suppose if I don't tell you, someone else will... Yes, there was a row this afternoon."

If so, how had she come to overhear it? Thanet's puzzlement must have shown in his face and she forestalled his next question by adding, "I only know because I went over to the house to look through the attic for some stuff for a jumble sale in the village on Saturday. With permission, of course."

"I'm sure... What time was this?"

"Let me see. I went over just before two. I waited until I saw Nerine leave for the hairdresser's. That must have been about ten to two. She always has—had a two o'clock hair appointment on Thursdays. I intended finishing before she got back—she was usually gone about an hour—but there's so much stuff up there..."

"Mrs. Tarrant was a compulsive hoarder?" Yes, thought Thanet. That would fit with the impression he had got from her sitting room.

Mrs. Haywood grimaced. "Yes."

Thanet grinned. "In that case I'm surprised she agreed to let anything go at all. People like that can't usually bear to part with a thing."

She responded with a hesitant smile, her first. "I know. She only agreed this time because the attic was getting so crammed with stuff that Roland absolutely insisted she part with some of it."

"But a house of that size must have an attic as big as a warehouse!"

"Ah, but most of it has been converted into a flat for Damon—Mr. Tarrant's son. So there's only a small space left for storage, about the size of an average room, I suppose."

"I see."

Mrs. Haywood passed her hand across her forehead and rubbed her eyes. "I'm not sure how we got onto this, surely it isn't relevant..."

"You were explaining how it was that you came to overhear the row between Mr. Tarrant and her mother-in-law."

"Ah, yes... Well, the point was, I became so engrossed up there I didn't notice the time. Not until I heard Nerine shouting at Lavinia."

"And that was at what time?"

"Just after half past three. I looked at my watch. I didn't want to get caught up in the argument, so I waited until things had quietened down and then crept out, as quietly as I could."

"I understand from Mr. Tarrant that Mrs. Tarrant usually kept her bedroom door locked, to prevent that particular problem occurring."

Mrs. Haywood shrugged. "She must have forgotten, this afternoon. She would, occasionally. And Lavinia always seemed to know, when she did. She seemed to have a sixth sense about it. Extraordinary, really. The ideal solution would have been for Lavinia and Marilyn to have a separate establishment. I suppose, if this house had been free, they could have come here, but of course, at the time when Daphne bought it, there was no hint of the way Lavinia's mind was going to deteriorate. It's so sad... As it stands, well, High Gables belongs to Lavinia and she steadfastly refuses to leave. Why should she, after all? It's her home. She was there for many years before Nerine came on the scene."

"But if she is becoming senile?"

"You cannot make people do things against their will, Inspector." Mrs. Haywood was reproachful. "Lavinia's illness is erratic. She still has long lucid periods when, although she is forgetful, she can converse quite rationally. And Mr. Tarrant is far too fine a person to trick his mother into signing away her home..."

"And Mrs. Tarrant?"

Mrs. Haywood sighed. "Would have been delighted to see her go. She made no bones about it. I think it's the only issue over which I have ever known Roland refuse to give her what she wanted."

"So, did you by any chance see young Mrs. Tarrant after the argument with her mother-in-law?" Thanet had spotted a photograph which interested him, over by the door. A woman, holding hands with two little girls, one on either side. Daphne and Nerine, as children?

"No. I came straight back here and started preparing supper. I usually try and do that in the afternoon, so that I'm free when Daphne gets back."

"Which is usually at...?"

"About twenty to six. But today, as I say, she was an hour or so early, because of the migraine."

"Did you happen to see Mr. Tarrant arrive home?"

"No. After Daphne got here, I'm afraid I was pretty

occupied with looking after her. Until, of course, Mr. Tarrant came across to tell me about the . . . about Nerine."

"I understand that the Tarrants' son, Damon, whom you mentioned just now, has no job at present. Was he about at all during the day, do you know?"

"Oh, yes. He was working on that old car of his this morning, in the end garage."

"And then he went back over to the house?"

"I don't know. I assume so."

"Did you notice if his car was in the garage during the afternoon—when you went over to the house, for example?"

"No, I didn't, I'm afraid."

"Or when you came back?"

She shook her head. "Sorry . . . Oh, wait a minute. I do vaguely remember hearing him drive out . . . There's something wrong with the exhaust of his car. It makes a terrible din, we all complain about it. I think he likes the noise and keeps "forgetting" to get it attended to."

"What time was this?"

She frowned, thinking. "I'm not sure. Where was I, at the time? I think I was . . . yes, that's right. I was crossing the hall. I'd just come downstairs to fetch some ice for Daphne. She finds a really cold compress helps. And that was . . . yes, that was only five or ten minutes before Roland came across with the news."

The memory clearly distressed her. Her lips began to tremble and she pressed the back of her hand against her mouth as if to hold in the potentially embarrassing sounds that might escape. Thanet judged that she had had just about as much as she could take, and that it would be best to bring the interview to a swift conclusion. But she was speaking again.

"He . . . he didn't know what he was doing," she whispered. "Like . . . I saw someone once, who'd been in a car accident . . . He looked just like that. In a complete daze."

"What did you do?"

"When I realised what he was saying, I went to look at . . . at Nerine. Then I rang the police. By then I was beginning to feel a bit dizzy myself, what with the shock, and Daphne being ill and Roland in that state . . ."

"I suppose Miss Linacre still isn't well enough to be interviewed?" As soon as the words were out, Thanet could have kicked himself. Lesson number one in how not to phrase a question, he thought.

"No," said Mrs. Haywood, predictably.

Should he insist? What if Daphne Linacre didn't have a migraine? What if she had killed her sister then rushed across to her loyal friend and begged her to keep the police away until she'd had time to pull herself together? He ought at least to have some independent corroboration of her illness. "You've called her doctor?"

"There's no point. We know exactly what to do when she has one of these attacks, by now."

She was being unexpectedly firm. All her considerable maternal instincts were evidently now directed at Daphne.

"All the same . . . With the additional shock over her sister's death . . . Don't you think it advisable?"

"Possibly . . . We'll see."

Thanet hesitated. But Mrs. Haywood looked exhausted and he didn't want to put further, unnecessary strain upon her. No, he'd leave it for the moment. He could always come over later, if it became essential to talk to Daphne tonight.

"In that case, I'll see her in the morning."

"Well . . . She usually has to have twenty-four hours in bed before the worst of the attack passes."

Best not to press the point at present. Tomorrow would be a different matter. "Well, thank you very much, Mrs. Haywood. You've been most helpful." Thanet stood up and Lineham closed his notebook and followed suit. On the way to the door Thanet paused, nodded at the photograph. "Mrs. Tarrant and Miss Linacre, as children?" he asked.

"Yes."

The woman was middle-aged, smiling, good-natured, the girls aged perhaps six and nine. But surely she was too old to . . . "Their mother?" said Thanet.

"Oh no. That's Mrs. Glass, their housekeeper. Mrs. Linacre died when Daphne was born. Poor little thing, she never knew her mother."

Poor Nerine too, thought Thanet. It can't be much fun having your mother snatched away and a squalling new infant thrust at you, all on the same day. He studied the solemn faces of the two girls, Nerine beautiful even then, slim as a willow wand, and as graceful. And Daphne . . . Oh, dear. It couldn't have been easy for plain, lumpy Daphne, with a sister who looked like that.

"Mrs. Glass is in a home now, in Sturrenden. Well, not a home, exactly. Sheltered accommodation. She's absolutely amazing for her age. She's well into her eighties by now."

Thanet recognised in Mrs. Haywood's tone the need to reassure herself so often displayed by elderly people seeking to allay the spectres of old age. Look, they seem to say: so-and-so has managed to avoid dependence, sickness, and its attendant indignities, so surely so shall I?

He opened the door and was at once aware of sounds of retching from upstairs.

Mrs. Haywood pushed past him. "Oh, dear," she said. "Daphne. I must go..."

"I should give her doctor a ring... Don't worry about us, we'll let ourselves out."

Thanet waited until they were a few paces away from the front door, then turned to Lineham. "Well, what did you make of all that, Mike? You were very quiet in there."

Lineham grinned. "Too busy listening, watching and scribbling." He tapped his notebook. "You always say..."

"Yes, yes. I know what I always say... So tell me, what do you *think*?"

"Several interesting things, sir."

Lineham's face was eager, bright with interest, and Thanet experienced the familiar sense of warmth and satisfaction which these discussions with the sergeant invariably gave him. He'd never found anyone else to work with whose mind was so in tune with his own.

"Such as?"

"Well, first of all, we guessed right about Mr. Tarrant. He obviously knew about this affair his wife was having. So he was lying, back there."

"Not exactly, Mike. He didn't actually say he knew nothing about it. He just refused to discuss it."

"Well, it's the same thing, isn't it?"

"Not quite. After all, put yourself in his situation. Would you want to discuss your wife's infidelities if you loved her and had just found her dead, perhaps murdered?"

"Well, if I suspected her lover might have done it..."

"I don't think he's got as far as that, Mike. In fact, I doubt if he was thinking rationally at all. No, I suspect that when we do tackle him about it, he'll suggest precisely that."

"Mrs. Haywood certainly seems to think a lot of him," conceded Lineham, grudgingly, abandoning that line of argument for the moment. "And then there was what she said about the son, Damon."

"Yes, the timing there was quite interesting, wasn't it? It sounds as though Damon left just a few minutes before his father got home."

"Did you notice," said Lineham eagerly, "that when we were talking to Mr. Tarrant, he was a bit, well, off, when we mentioned his son?"

"Yes, I must say I had the impression he wasn't being quite frank with us."

"Say the son did it," said Lineham. "Say he has a row with his mother, shoves her over the balcony and then panics, decides to run for it . . ."

"Let's not get carried away, Mike. We'll probably find that he turns up as innocent as a lamb, later on this evening."

"And if he doesn't?"

"Then we shall have to reconsider. But I think it's too early to jump to conclusions yet."

"What about Miss Linacre, sir? D'you think that migraine's genuine?"

"She was certainly being sick, up in the bathroom."

"Could have been guilt. Or remorse?"

"Slow down, Mike. We'll soon find out, when we do a bit of checking. I could hardly force myself into the sickroom, could I? We'll have a word with her doctor, if he comes, and first thing tomorrow you can send someone over to Linacre Nurseries, to ask a few questions."

"Right, sir."

Bentley appeared around the corner of the house.

"Ah, Bentley's found the key," said Lineham.

"It was in her handbag, sir," said Bentley, handing it over. "In the sitting room."

"Good."

The key was smooth and hard in Thanet's hand, a symbol of secrets withheld, of revelations to come. Over the years, if his investigations into domestic murder had taught him anything, they had taught him that it is in the character of the victim that the seeds of his own destruction lie. A woman's bedroom can reveal much of her personality. Anticipation began to fizz through his veins.

"Let's go and take a look, then, shall we?"

FOUR

As the door of Nerine Tarrant's bedroom swung open two impressions were paramount: opulence and chaos.

Lineham gave a low whistle of astonishment and admiration as they stepped inside. "Louise would love to see this. But what a mess!"

The bed dominated the room. An elaborate canopy was suspended from the ceiling, swathes of material cascading down to the four corners, creating a four-poster effect. In this room, too, the theme was blue and white. The flowered chintz of the bedhangings had also been used in the quilted bedhead and bedspread, and the two tones of blue in the floral design exactly matched the pale blue carpet and the deep blue range of fitted cupboards which stretched the length of an entire wall. Filmy white curtains hung at the tall french windows. The effect was both dramatic and romantic—clues to Nerine's character?

Clearly, much thought had gone into the designing of this room and no one could blame Nerine for being angry with her mother-in-law for making such a mess of it. Clothes were strewn everywhere—tossed on the bed, draped over the elegant blue velvet chaise longue, lying about in careless disorder all over the floor. And what clothes! Thanet didn't know much about fashion, but he could recognise quality when he saw it: silk, satin, velvet, lawn, wool, suede, leather, fur...

Also... "Can you smell something, Mike?"

"Like what?"

"I'm not sure. Something..." Thanet shook his head. It had been a whiff, no more, of something familiar, yet alien to this room.

Both men stood still, sniffing.

"No, it's gone..." Thanet shrugged, moved on. He and Lineham were being very careful not to touch or move anything.

"I bet she spent more on clothes in a year than I earn," said Lineham, stepping gingerly over what looked like a mink coat. "You think Mrs. Tarrant senior really did this?"

"Sounds as if it was a regular occurrence. Anyway, it doesn't look to me as though it's the result of a struggle, wouldn't you agree?"

The clutter of open jars and bottles, some overturned, on the dressing table, the gaping wardrobe doors and half-open drawers, told their own story. They had been rifled by an eager, impatient hand, searching—for what? For some exquisite garment that would transform the ravages of age into an illusion of youth and beauty? Or, more sinister thought, for revenge? Had the old woman been seeking to strike where it would hurt most at the daughter-in-law who regarded her as nothing more than a nuisance?

Lineham was obviously thinking along similar lines. "D'you think this really was just an old lady having fun, or d'you think she might have done it on purpose?"

"Just what I was wondering myself."

"It doesn't sound as though they were exactly on the best of terms, does it? Sir, you don't think..."

"I sincerely hope not!" To have to arrest a senile old lady was the last thing Thanet wanted.

"Old people can be very difficult, when they're suffering from dementia," Lineham persisted. "I know a chap whose mother went like that and he said that if she was crossed, she used to go quite beserk. She'd be beyond reason, he said, and she was amazingly strong. It took two of them to hold her back, once, when she wanted to go shopping in the middle of the night, in January, in her nightdress!"

"Hmm... It was around half past three, wasn't it, when Mrs. Haywood said she heard Nerine Tarrant start shouting at her mother-in-law?"

"Yes. I imagine the companion, Miss Barnes, will be able to verify that. Doc Mallard put the earliest time of death at two o'clock, but it looks as though we can push that back at least an hour and a half... And another thing... Surely Mrs. Tarrant must have been killed either during or soon after that row, or she would have tidied up in here?"

"Not necessarily. She might well have blamed Miss Barnes for allowing the old lady to give her the slip, and told her she expected her to do the clearing up. But I suppose you could be right... We'd better go and have a word with them."

They relocked the door, gave the key to Trace, the SOCO, who would need it when he had finished working on the sitting room next door, and set off in search of old Mrs. Tarrant's quarters. They were crossing the landing when Thanet put out a restraining hand.

"Wait," he murmured.

He had glimpsed a flicker of movement ahead of them and now a figure appeared at the far end of the landing. The two men exchanged glances of astonishment. Nothing they had heard about old Mrs. Tarrant had prepared them for this. The slack, puckered flesh of arms and neck, the knotted veins on the hand that now went up to her throat in a dramatic gesture of surprise, betrayed her age. But she was dressed like a young girl, in flowing white muslin skirt, very high heels, an off-the-shoulder blouse and, the final grotesque touch, a white velvet ribbon tied in a large bow on the top of her scanty curls. She had attempted, and failed, to conceal the deeply scored wrinkles of her face with heavy, garish make-up: thick, deep blue eyeshadow, symmetrical circles of rouge on either cheek and a scarlet cupid's bow of a mouth. Thanet experienced a powerful shaft of compassion as she gave them a brilliant, coquettish smile. Mrs. Tarrant might appear to them to be a bizarre, almost clownish figure, but in her own eyes she was clearly beautiful. He and Lineham watched in painful silence as she dipped to gather up the hem of her skirt in her right hand and, wafting it backwards and forwards in rhythm with her steps, began to descend the stairs with an exaggerated, swaying walk. Half-way down she paused to cast the same smile back at them, over one shoulder.

"Now what?" said Lineham, in a low voice.

Thanet shrugged. "We can but try. Mrs. Tarrant?" he called, as they began to descend the stairs behind her.

She had reached the bottom now and she paused, putting one hand on the newel post to steady herself. When she looked back at them this time that terrifyingly flirtatious rictus had been replaced by a look of terror.

"Mrs. Tarrant?"

She made a little choking sound in her throat and in a swirl of movement, a diminishing clatter of high heels along the passageway beside the stairs, was gone.

"This isn't going to be easy," said Thanet grimly. "Come on. With any luck, she's run to Miss Barnes."

He was right. The sound of voices—or rather, of a voice— led them to a half-open door, and they paused outside.

"Come on, Lavinia, you tell Marilyn." A coaxing tone. "How can Marilyn help you, if you won't tell her what's the matter?"

Thanet knocked and pushed the door further open. "Miss Barnes?"

It was a kitchen which had obviously been converted from a former sitting room; a heavy marble fireplace still dominated one end of the room. Seated in a rocking chair beside it crouched Mrs. Tarrant, moaning, face in lap, hands clasped at the back of her neck, as if defying anyone to make her raise her head. The woman they had glimpsed earlier, coming out of Tarrant's study, was kneeling on the floor beside her, stroking her hair. It was, Thanet thought, a remarkably touching picture. He suspected that not many paid companions would in privacy treat their charges with such compassion.

The young woman scrambled to her feet, pushing long lanky brown hair back off her face.

"Who . . . ? Oh, you must be the policemen."

"That's right." Thanet made the introductions. No one would give Marilyn Barnes a second glance, he thought (and yet, someone had—the child existed, to prove it). She was neither pretty nor ugly, dark or fair, fat or thin, tall or short, but always somewhere in between. Even her eyes were an indeterminate bluish-greyish-greenish brown. "I'm afraid we gave Mrs. Tarrant a fright just now, appearing upstairs like that."

Cautiously, the old woman raised her head, revealing eyes still drowning in tears, cheeks streaked with mascara.

"That's better!" said Miss Barnes with genuine pleasure in her voice, unconsciously displaying her best feature, a wide generous smile which illuminated her face and briefly gave an illusion of attractiveness. And to Thanet and Lineham, "Perhaps you'd like to sit down? I won't be a minute." Snatching up a box of tissues she tenderly wiped the old lady's eyes. "There, that *is* better, isn't it?"

Mrs. Tarrant's eyes, fixed until now on her companion's face, flickered briefly in the direction of the two policemen. She beckoned her companion to come closer. Her whisper was quite audible.

"Have they come to take me away?"

Miss Barnes laughed and patted her employer's hand. "No, of course not. They just want to talk to us about Nerine, I expect. You remember, I told you, she's had an accident."

The old lady's eyes clouded with incomprehension. "An accident?"

"Yes," said Miss Barnes patiently. "She fell, from her balcony. I told you."

Mrs. Tarrant shook her head. "I don't remember." She clutched suddenly at Miss Barnes's arm. "You won't let her send me away, will you?"

A firm shake of the head. "No. No, of course not. No one is going to send you away. You're going to stay here with me."

Mrs. Tarrant gazed doubtfully at her companion. "She said she was going to." Her face puckered. "She shouted at me." It was the whining, petulant tone of a child.

"I know. But it's all right now. I promise." Taking up a shawl which hung over the back of a nearby chair, Miss Barnes draped it around the old lady's shoulders, covering up the unsuitable blouse, the scrawny, knobbly shoulders. "There, that's better isn't it?" Then she sank down into a chair at the table, facing Thanet. "I'm sorry, I'm afraid she's rather upset."

"Because of the row with young Mrs. Tarrant, this afternoon?"

Miss Barnes sighed. "You heard about that, then. Yes. She's been very unsettled ever since."

The old lady seemed to have withdrawn into herself. Rocking gently to and fro, she was stroking the soft, fine muslin of her skirt.

Thanet glanced at Lineham. *Your turn.*

"What time was this, Miss Barnes?" said Lineham. "The row?"

"About half past three. Lavinia—I hope you don't mind if I call her that, but it's so confusing, with two Mrs. Tarrants in the house, that we decided it was the sensible thing to do—Lavinia usually has a rest in the afternoon, from two until three thirty, then I get her up so that by the time

Nicky—my son—gets home from school at a quarter to four, I'm free to attend to him."

"So what went wrong, this afternoon?"

"How did Lavinia get into young Mrs. Tarrant's bedroom, you mean?" Miss Barnes shrugged. "Just an unfortunate combination of circumstances. I did look in on her at a quarter past two, to make sure she'd dozed off, but she must have been faking." Miss Barnes shook her head and sighed. "The trouble is, she absolutely adores dressing up—well, you can see that for yourselves—and Mrs. Tarrant has such beautiful clothes . . . That room is like a magnet to Lavinia. I don't know how she does it, but it's uncanny, she always seems to know, every time Mrs. Tarrant leaves the door unlocked— which is rarely, I can tell you. Anyway, that hour and a half is the only time of the day that I get to myself, so once I'd satisfied myself she was settled I came back down here, made myself a cup of tea and read a magazine. Just before half past three I made a cup for Lavinia, and I was on my way upstairs when I heard Mrs. Tarrant shouting."

Marilyn Barnes broke off and glanced anxiously at the old lady, who was still rocking gently, stroking her muslin skirt and gazing blankly into space. She lowered her voice. "I don't want to upset her again, now she's settled down."

Thanet and Lineham leaned closer.

"Mrs. Tarrant was dragging Lavinia along the corridor towards the stairs. She was really livid.

'You bloody woman. You ought to be put away, you know that? Locked up, where you can't be a nuisance to anyone. And where the hell d'you think you've been, Marilyn? Lazing the afternoon away in the kitchen, I suppose, while this wretched old woman has been busy turning my bedroom upside down again. What d'you think we pay you for, that's what I'd like to know?'

'Don't cry, Lavinia. I'm sorry, Mrs. Tarrant, I thought she was asleep.'

'You thought. You thought. Well, it's not good enough. I've had enough, I really have. I've told you, over and over again, you ought to lock her in, in the afternoons . . .'

'But I can't do that. I have no right . . .'

'You have every right. We have every right. We employ you and I'm telling you, you lock that bloody door or I'm warning you, for the last time, you'll be finding yourself out of a job

*and my dear mother-in-law can take herself off to a nursing
home. Or the loony-bin, which is where she really belongs.'*

'She can't help it, Mrs. Tarrant. It's her illness.'

*'Don't make excuses to me! Ill or not, no one in their right
mind would put up with this sort of performance for a
moment longer than they had to ... Oh, do stop snivelling,
Lavinia. Here, take her away, for God's sake. But you needn't
think you've heard the last of this. I shall speak to my
husband tonight.'"*

They all glanced at the old lady as Marilyn reached the end
of her story, but there was still no change. Old Mrs. Tarrant
had, consciously or unconsciously, decided that it was more
comfortable to blank out reality for the moment.

"Do you think she meant it?" said Thanet. "About the
nursing home?"

Marilyn shrugged. "Oh, she meant it, all right. Whether
Mr. Tarrant would have agreed is another matter. The house
belongs to his mother, you see. She wants to stay here and so
far he has always refused to try to get her committed. You
may not think it, looking at her now, but sometimes you can
have a perfectly rational conversation with her. And she's
really a very sweet person. So appreciative. And the rest of
the time ... Well, I just tell myself to treat her as if she was a
child, and it usually works."

"You don't find it very frustrating, at times?"

"Well of course. But what job isn't? And I can't be too
fussy." She glanced down at her left hand. "I'm not married,
as you'll have gathered, and jobs aren't exactly thick on the
ground. Especially ones that keep school hours and allow you
to be at home during the holidays. And this one pays bed and
board for Nicky and me, too, so ..." Again she shrugged.
"I've always thought, well, he's only got one parent, so I must
try and be available when he needs me, to make it up to
him ... This suits me very well, until he's a bit older."

"How old is he?"

"Ten."

"Where is he now?"

"I've arranged for him to spend the night with some friends
in the village."

"Good idea." Though if Nicky were anything like Ben, he'd
be furious at being summarily removed from the scene of the
action, thought Thanet.

"Of course," said Marilyn, "the trouble is that every time

this sort of thing happens, Lavinia lives in fear and trembling
for ages afterwards."

"In case she's sent away, you mean?"

"Yes. That's why she was so frightened when she saw you.
She thought you'd come for her."

Quite possible, thought Thanet. Though there could be
another, more sinister explanation . . . He glanced at Lineham.
Take over again.

"So what happened after all the fuss had died down?" said
Lineham.

Marilyn grimaced. "It was all a bit hectic. Lavinia was in a
state and Nicky was due home, so I brought her down here
and gave her a cup of tea, tried to calm her down, while
Nicky had a glass of squash and an apple. Then he went out
to play and I put Lavinia to bed for an hour—she hadn't had a
sleep this afternoon, and the fuss had worn her out. She went
up quite happily, and I sat with her until she dozed off.
Before I came downstairs I knocked at the door of Mrs.
Tarrant's bedroom and when she didn't answer I checked that
it was locked. I didn't want the same thing happening again."

"And was it? Locked?"

"Yes."

"What time was this?"

"About four thirty, I should think."

"Did you see anyone about?"

Marilyn shook her head. "Not a soul."

"So what did you do then?"

For the first time she hesitated.

"What's the matter?" said Lineham.

"It's just that . . . Well I suppose I'm wondering why you
want to know all these details."

Lineham glanced at Thanet, who gave an almost impercep-
tible shake of the head. "Its simply that whenever there's an
accidental death, we have to try to build up a complete
picture of the movements of all the people in the household . . .
In case one of them might have seen or heard something
significant, you understand."

"But I haven't. I didn't."

"The point is, you can never tell. It may not seem significant or important to you, but it can be very helpful to us."

Thanet was watching Marilyn closely. She seemed to be
taking Lineham's explanation at its face value. It was, after
all, true.

She shrugged. "Fair enough. What was it you wanted to know?"

"What you did after putting old Mrs. Tarrant to bed, and checking that her daughter-in-law's bedroom door was locked."

"I came down and got Nicky's tea ready. I usually cook him something simple and he has it about a quarter to five. I did pop upstairs to check on Lavinia before I called him in, but she was still fast asleep. I sat with him while he ate it, then I washed up, cleared away, and went back upstairs, to get Lavinia up."

"What time was it then?"

"About half past five."

"And did you see anyone about, either then or on the earlier occasion?"

"No."

"What about earlier in the afternoon?"

"I saw Mrs. Haywood, going upstairs, soon after lunch. She was going to look out some jumble in the attic, I believe."

"Ah, yes, she told us . . . Did you see her leave, later on?"

Marilyn shook her head.

"Anyone else?"

"I don't think so . . . Not in the house, anyway."

Thanet saw Lineham restrain himself from pouncing too eagerly. The sergeant was doing very well.

"And outside?"

"Well, I did see Miss Linacre come home, not long before I called Nicky in for his tea."

"Around twenty to five, then?"

"Yes. I noticed especially because I was surprised to see her home so early. She doesn't usually come until an hour or so later."

"She has a migraine."

"I thought that might be it. She goes down with them every few months or so . . . Miserable things . . . She looks like death warmed up for days afterwards."

"Anyone else, outside?"

"Only Damon. At least, I assume it was Damon. I glanced out of the landing window when I was coming downstairs with Lavinia, the second time, and I saw his car backing out of the garage."

"This was at half past five?"

"Well, five or ten minutes later, I should say. Because although I didn't have to dress Lavinia after her rest—I'd only slipped her shoes off, earlier—it took me five or ten minutes to coax her out of her room." She glanced at her charge, leaned forward and lowered her voice again. "She was very upset again. When I went into the bedroom I couldn't see her anywhere, and I almost panicked. I thought, Oh God, if she's somehow managed to get at Mrs. Tarrant's things again ... But she made a little sound, and I found her. She was sitting on the floor in a corner, on the far side of the bed. She was all ready to come back downstairs—she'd put her shoes and cardigan on ... but I think she'd been afraid that if she went out onto the landing, she might meet Mrs. Tarrant, and there'd be another scene."

Lineham glanced at Thanet. *I think you'd better take over now, sir.*

"She was frightened," said Thanet.

"In case there was another row, yes."

"Or," said Thanet delicately, "possibly because she had already been out of her room, before you came up to fetch her, and had seen something to upset her...?" Or done something to upset her, he silently added, mentally shuddering away from the picture of the old lady, with a strength born of desperation and dementia, grabbing the shapely legs of the woman who was threatening to lock her away forever and heaving, tilting, shoving and finally watching, as Nerine's body smashed down on the paving stones and lay still, still ... A moment of appalled clarity, as she realises what she has done, then flight, back to her room and into a corner to hide ...

Marilyn was looking horrified. "You're not suggesting she might actually have seen..." Her eyes swivelled to her employer, who was now frowning down at her lap. The blunt, varnished nails had scrabbled a hole in the gauzy material, Thanet noticed, and even as he watched, the old lady seized the torn edges on either side and with a twisting, rending movement ripped the skirt apart from waist to hem.

"Lavinia!" exclaimed Marilyn, springing up and imprisoning her employer's hands in her own. "Why did you do that? Look what a mess you've made of your pretty skirt..."

"I'm thirsty," said the old lady querulously. "I haven't had my Horlicks. Where's my Horlicks...?"

Marilyn stood up. "Well, there's no need to show off like that, to get my attention," she said, with understandable irritation. "All you had to do was ask, and I would have got it for you." Already she was pouring milk into a saucepan, spooning Horlicks from a jar.

But the old lady wasn't listening. Watching her, Thanet could see the beginnings of a tremor in her body, scarcely perceptible to begin with, like the first breath of wind stirring the topmost leaves of the trees in a forest, then gradually becoming more and more apparent. Marilyn, busy with the hot drink, had not yet noticed.

"Miss Barnes," said Thanet softly, calling her attention to her charge.

Shoving the saucepan hastily aside, off the heat, Marilyn swooped forward and seized the old lady's hands, in a very different manner from a few minutes previously. "Lavinia!" she cried. "What is it? What's the matter?" And leaning forward she gathered the frail, shaking body into her arms. "Don't worry," she murmured. "Marilyn isn't cross with you. Really. Hush, now. Marilyn's got you . . ."

Thanet was more certain than ever that the old lady had seen something, heard something, done something that had terrified her. Which? he wondered. And what?

Her next words confirmed this.

"I'm frightened," she quavered. "Death . . ."

Marilyn looked helplessly up at Thanet, then turned back to her employer and began to murmur soothingly again, rocking her gently and patting her back.

Thanet stood up. "She's obviously not up to being questioned now. Tomorrow, perhaps?"

Marilyn nodded. "She might be calmer then, after a good night's sleep. Though there's no guarantee she'll remember anything, of course."

"Just one more question . . . We noticed that no attempt had been made to tidy Mrs. Tarrant's bedroom . . ."

Marilyn's eyes were hard as she looked up again. "That was because she wanted her husband to see the grounds for her complaint. She told me she wasn't going to clear away a thing until he'd seen exactly what his mother had been up to."

"I see. Thank you."

They left.

FIVE

"Nice woman," said Lineham, when they were out of earshot.

"Very."

"I don't suppose there are many in her position who'd take so much trouble over a batty old lady like that. And she wasn't just putting it on for our benefit, was she?"

"I don't think so, no."

"What's the matter, sir?"

"I'm just hoping you're wrong, in your suggestion that old Mrs. Tarrant may have pushed her daughter-in-law off that balcony. Frankly, the idea appals me."

"She'd get off," said Lineham cheerfully.

"That's not the point."

"What is, then, sir?"

Thanet shook his head. "Never mind." If Lineham couldn't see it for himself, there was no point in explaining it to him. The sergeant's occasional lack of sensitivity was something Thanet had had to learn to live with.

"Anyway, even if she did do it, sir, there's no guarantee we'd be able to prove it, unless forensic come up with something useful."

"Well, it's early days yet," said Thanet vaguely. "Let's go and have a word with PC Driver, shall we? Where is he?"

"Down by the gate, holding back the ghouls."

"Right. Of course," Thanet added, as they headed for the

front door, "there's always the possibility that Miss Barnes did it."

Lineham's stride faltered. "Why?" Clearly, the suggestion didn't appeal to him.

"Well, she'd just been threatened with being thrown out on her ear, hadn't she? And for a woman in her position that's a pretty alarming prospect."

"I imagine she's very capable," said Lineham. "And people are supposed to be crying out for good domestic staff, house-keepers and such-like, these days. I shouldn't have thought she'd have too many problems in finding another job."

"With a ten-year-old boy in tow? Not as easy as you're making out, I suspect, Mike. Let's face it, like old Mrs. Tarrant, she had both motive and opportunity."

"For all we know, they could have been in it together," said Lineham sarcastically.

"Who knows? They say truth is often stranger than fiction." But Thanet didn't mean it. He could accept that both women had a powerful reason to be afraid of Nerine Tarrant—who sounded more and more unpleasant the more he learnt about her—and that either of them could, in the last resort, have lost her temper and given Nerine that fatal shove, but he simply could not see them sitting down and carefully planning the murder as conspirators.

Lineham gave a derisive snort. "There are limits."

Thanet enjoyed testing his sergeant occasionally. "To what, Mike? Our credulity? Their decency? Our gullibility? Their potential evil? I doubt it. On the contrary, I think that such limits are capable of infinite expansion and contraction. That's what makes people so fascinating. You never know where they're going to draw their particular line. I suppose," said Thanet, becoming interested in pursuing the idea, "it's what life is all about. Learning where to draw the lines."

Lineham was not interested in philosophising. He made a polite sound of assent but mentally he had switched off, Thanet could tell.

"Then, there's the son, sir. Damon." Lineham injected the name with the scorn of the conventional for the off-beat. "Didn't someone say he's on probation?"

"That's right. As a matter of fact, he's one of Joan's clients."

"Really? That could be useful."

Thanet wasn't so sure. He could foresee difficulties ahead. He had always dreaded finding himself in the situation where a suspect in one of his cases was also Joan's client. Thinking about it now he experienced a premonitory tremor of unease. Already he was in a slight dilemma: should he tell the sergeant about that missed appointment this afternoon?

There was no reason why not, so far as he could tell. Joan could hardly regard it as a confidence broken. In the circumstances it would be routine to interview Damon's probation officer and this information would have come out as a matter of course.

"As a matter of fact, she's already told me something interesting. Damon had an appointment with her this afternoon, and he didn't turn up."

"Really? What time was he supposed to have seen her?"

"I don't know the details. She was rushing off to a meeting, there was no time to talk."

"Was he in the habit of breaking appointments?"

"No idea. But I imagine not, or she wouldn't have been so concerned. In any case, the timing of his departure was interesting, didn't you think?"

"You mean, that was what his father was hiding? The fact that he met Damon driving out as he was driving in? So as to avoid implicating him?"

"It's quite likely, don't you think?"

"Possible, certainly. But I wonder why. So far there hasn't been any suggestion that Damon and his mother didn't get on, let alone that he hated her enough to kill her . . ."

"Perhaps it's just a natural paternal reaction—try to keep your offspring out of trouble if you can—and especially if they've already had a brush with the law. Anyway, it sounds as though Damon might well have been here over the crucial period."

"Yes. It'll be interesting to hear what he has to say . . . Ah, there's Driver, sir."

It was now just after nine thirty and the light was seeping out of the sky. Sharp-edged silhouettes of trees were etched against the pearly brightness which still lingered above the western horizon, and the crunch of their footsteps on the gravel sounded unnaturally loud in that strangely cathedral hush which falls over the land as day fades into night.

Most of the crowd had dispersed by now, resigned to the fact that there was to be no more drama tonight, and only five or six die-hards were still lingering on the far side of the tall gates. PC Driver was chatting to them through the wrought-iron scrolls and curlicues, his stance relaxed, a man at ease among old acquaintances. He was in his mid-twenties, tall and thin, with a hooked nose and a frizz of tight, fair curls. As Thanet and Lineham approached he turned, unconsciously stiffening to attention. Lineham made the introductions and the three men strolled a little way up the drive, out of range of all the eager ears flapping on the other side of the gates.

"We're hoping your local knowledge is going to be of some use to us," said Thanet. "How long have you been living in Ribbleden?"

Driver pulled a face. "A couple of years, sir. That's only five minutes—less—by rural standards."

"But you've got a good idea of what goes on here, by now."

"I make it my business to keep my ear to the ground, sir. And my mouth shut."

"Good. So tell us what you know about the people who live in High Gables. And especially about young Mrs. Tarrant."

Driver shuffled his feet. "She had a bit of a reputation, I'm afraid, sir." He looked uncomfortable, as if he felt it slightly improper to gossip about his social superiors. Thanet knew that in the country such distinctions were still more clearly delineated than in the town.

"She played around, you mean."

"She certainly did." Driver rolled his eyes, warming to his subject. "It's common knowledge that she'd have a new man every few months or so. You'd have thought she'd have run out by now, in a place this size."

"And the current candidate?"

"Lance Speed, sir. Owner of the local garage."

"What can you tell us about him?"

"He's married, with one son, Tim, aged eighteen, who's a friend of Damon Tarrant. Mrs. Speed is very popular, does a lot in the village organisations."

"She's aware of this liaison?"

"Opinion is divided, sir. But the majority view is that no, she doesn't know about it. Sometimes the wife is the last person to know, especially if she's well liked, and I'd guess that in this case there was a sort of conspiracy of silence, to prevent her getting hurt. Mr. Speed has a reputation as a bit of a lad with the ladies, but to my knowledge until now it hasn't gone beyond a bit of harmless flirtation at the petrol pumps."

"Where do they live?"

"In a bungalow at the entrance to the village. I expect you passed it on your way in. Shangri-la."

"What about the rest of the people in High Gables?"

"The son's a bit wild, Damon. Got put on probation a couple of months ago, possession of drugs. Mr. Tarrant is pretty well liked, I've never heard anything against him— except that most people think he's a bit of a fool to put up with his wife's behaviour."

"There was no talk that they were on bad terms?"

"Not to my knowledge, sir. Beats me how he stood it. She never made any attempt to be discreet." Driver shrugged. "He was potty about her, if you ask me."

"What about the old lady?"

"Eccentric but harmless. She did a lot for the village, in her time—ran the Darby and Joan club, chairman of the WI, that sort of thing, and there's a lot of goodwill towards her. The general feeling is that it's sad, the way she's gone downhill."

"And her companion? How long has she been looking after her?"

"Since just after I came. There was a drawing aside of skirts to begin with, on account of her being an unmarried mum, but she keeps herself to herself and people have accepted her by now. Seems a nice enough woman."

"What about Miss Linacre and Mrs. Haywood?"

"Miss Linacre is out at work all day, so we don't see much of her, but Mrs. Haywood helps out at church events—jumble sales, cake stalls, that sort of thing. She's regarded as harmless but a bit odd, partly because of the way she dresses and partly because of the way she goes on and on about that son of hers, the one who died, years ago. I don't think she has any close personal friends in the village."

"Right, well what I'd like you to do is see if you can find out anything more about the Speeds. DS Lineham and I are going to go along and have a word with them now, and I'd be interested to know what you can pick up. People in the village know you, they're more likely to talk freely. Also, I'd like you to compile a list of Mrs. Tarrant's previous boy-friends, with addresses if possible. Mark those with whom she is thought to have parted on bad terms, and those who were said to be jealous. Let me have a report, tomorrow morning."

"Right, sir."

"The pub'll be the best place for you, tonight. Mike, nip up to the house and arrange for someone to relieve PC Driver at the gate in, say, half an hour."

Lineham was back in a few minutes. "I assume you didn't want me to bring the car, sir?"

"No, we'll walk. Take a look around. Perhaps drop in at the pub ourselves, on the way. I don't know about you, but I'm starving."

"I could do with a bite. Haven't had anything since a sandwich, at lunchtime."

The hangers-on at the gate fell silent as the three policemen approached. Driver opened the gates, slipped through with Thanet and Lineham, then resumed his I'm-your-approachable-local-bobby attitude, leaning back against the gates with his arms folded. The people held back until Thanet and Lineham had gone a little way down the road, then turned back to cluster around Driver, eager for titbits.

"What did they say?"

"What's the news?"

"What's the latest?"

"Come on, Billy-boy, give!"

Thanet and Lineham exchanged grins.

"He's got his head screwed on the right way," said Lineham.

"Yes. Though in fact he didn't tell us much we hadn't learned already."

"No. But it was interesting to have it confirmed by an outsider."

"True." Thanet's tone was abstracted. He had come to a halt and was looking around, trying to absorb his surroundings. High Gables was on the edge of the village in what Thanet now realised was an interesting and unusual position: private yet not isolated, and not directly overlooked by any other house, it stood on what could be described as a peninsula of garden, between two sharp bends in the road. If this had been a main road no doubt it would long ago have been re-routed to cut across behind the house, but such alterations to minor roads in the country are always being shelved in favour of other, more urgent repairs or innovations.

Glancing back, by craning his neck Thanet could just see another chimneystack, poking up above and beyond the trees

in Tarrant's front garden. And on this side, once he and
Lineham had carefully negotiated the bend (there were no
pavements), the narrow country lane widened out and the
village began. The domestic architecture was typical of vil-
lages all over Kent, a picturesque juxtaposition of Tudor black
and white, mellow brick and tile, crisp white-painted
weatherboard. Thanet studied the houses with an appreciative eye as he walked by. He himself would have loved to live
in one, with its crooked walls, uneven floors and, above all,
individuality. Alas, such aspirations were not matched by a
policeman's pay. The price of houses like these had rocketed
over the last twenty years and the dwindling supply ensured
that such properties were certain to climb even higher in
value, as time went on.

"Pretty little place," said Lineham.

"Mmm."

Here, the road divided, the right fork going straight on,
the left sweeping round in front of the church to encircle the
village green. Thanet's men were hard at work on their
house-to-house enquiries.

"That looks promising," said the sergeant, nodding at a
colourful inn sign depicting a labrador with a somewhat
garish cock pheasant in its mouth. Inside the pub the excited
roar of conversation stopped abruptly as the two men entered,
only gradually resuming and at a much lower, more subdued
level.

"Oh, to be a fly on the wall," murmured Lineham in
Thanet's ear as they carried their sandwiches and beer across
to a small corner table which had miraculously become
vacant.

It was obvious that they weren't going to learn anything
useful by attempting to eavesdrop and it was impossible to
discuss the case; they ate their sandwiches, drained their
glasses and departed. By the time the door swung to behind
them, the noise level had already increased perceptibly.

"Let's hope Driver does better than us," said Lineham.

They walked on, passing in turn the post-office-cum-shop,
the village school (still functioning, Thanet noticed; the tide
of closures had been stemmed in recent years, owing to the
soaring cost of transport), the village hall and a seedy-looking
garage, somewhat pretentiously called Ribbleden Motors.
Three second-hand cars, none of them less than three years

old, were drawn up on the forecourt, price stickers on windscreens. There was a solitary petrol pump.

"I thought they went out with the Ark," said Lineham, nodding at the overhead swing bar and trailing rubber hose. "If this is Speed's place, it doesn't exactly seem to be thriving."

"Not enough custom, out here. Too far off the beaten track."

Another few minutes brought them to the far end of the village and Shangri-la, which had been squeezed into a narrow slot between the last of the older houses and the inevitable council estate. Thanet noted that this was undergoing the by now familiar transformation process. The original Airey houses, ugly dwellings hastily erected after the war and apparently constructed of horizontal pre-cast concrete strips, had recently been discovered to have some design fault which rendered them unsafe, and all over the country were in the process of being pulled down and replaced. The new houses, he noted with approval, were much more attractive and in keeping with their setting.

Unlike his business premises, Speed's home looked spruce enough. Paint gleamed, windows shone and well-tended flowerbeds full of newly planted summer bedding surrounded the close-cropped lawn. Mrs. Speed's handiwork, Thanet guessed.

"If she really doesn't know what's been going on between her husband and Nerine Tarrant," he said, "then this is going to be a bit tricky."

This was the part of his job that he hated, the damage done to innocent people peripherally involved in his cases. Mrs. Speed, by all accounts, was a nice woman protected until now by a consensus of goodwill from knowledge which would cause her considerable distress, and he, Thanet, was going to be the one to have to disillusion her.

"She's bound to wonder, if we ask to talk to him privately," agreed Lineham. "But what else can we do?"

Musical chimes sounded as he pressed the bell and a moment later a light went on in the hall. The man who opened the door stood back resignedly when Thanet introduced himself.

"Come in."

Geometric was the word which blinked on like a neon sign in Thanet's brain. Speed had a square head, and a square body, with oblongs for trousers and arms. The head was

adorned with thinning hair and a curly moustache which
drooped a little on one side, spoiling the symmetrical effect.
He was in his mid-forties, and was wearing designer jeans
and a shirt unbuttoned half-way to the waist. A gold medal-
lion winked coyly in the sparse hair of his chest. Thanet
spared a moment to marvel at the attractions between men
and women. What could Nerine Tarrant have seen in this
ageing Lothario?

The room into which he had led them was hazy with
cigarette smoke and rather too gaudy for Thanet's taste:
brown-and-white striped Dralon suite, multicoloured floral
carpet and fluorescent orange velvet curtains, which a woman
was drawing across the large picture window. She turned as
they entered.

"My wife."

If Speed was all straight lines, his wife was all curves. Short
and plump, with billowing breasts overflowing the tight bras-
siere clearly visible beneath the thin material of her dress,
she looked a prime candidate for Weight Watchers. Noting
the double—no doubt soon to be triple—chin, the sausage-
like arms and legs, Thanet wondered if PC Driver had been
wrong, if Mrs. Speed had known of her husband's affair
(affairs?) all along and had been stuffing herself with food to
compensate. But he had been right about the good nature.
Despite the anxiety in her face the lines were benign, the
mouth generous.

She watched the two policemen warily as they all sat down,
the Speeds side by side on the settee, Thanet and Lineham
in easy chairs facing them. Speed stubbed out his cigarette in
an overflowing ashtray and lit another.

"Actually, I was wondering if I might have a word with you
in private, Mr. Speed," said Thanet.

It was their very lack of reaction, their careful, frozen
stillness, which betrayed the unspoken message which passed
between them.

So Mrs. Speed had known of the affair, thought Thanet
with relief. The question now was, how long had she known?
For some time? Or just since this afternoon, when having
killed his mistress her husband had anticipated the possibility
of a murder investigation, and had decided to throw himself
on his wife's mercy?

"There's no need for my wife to leave," said Speed. "We
haven't got any secrets from each other."

Mrs. Speed's hand sought her husband's, squeezed it.

Thanet noted the stubborn line of her mouth, the defiant angle of her head. Good. Whatever happened, she was not going to faint or have hysterics. She was preparing for battle and he didn't mind that—welcomed it, in fact. He enjoyed a good fight. Better get on with it, then.

"As I expect you've guessed, we're looking into the death of Mrs. Nerine Tarrant. We..."

"Just a minute." The colour came up in Mrs. Speed's face and she shifted uncomfortably on her seat. "I'm sorry, but can I ask you something?"

She was not, Thanet guessed, a woman who was used to asserting herself in the presence of men. Her husband was watching her with surprise.

"By all means."

"How... How did she die? I mean, there's all sorts of rumours flying around the village but nobody really knows..."

No reason why the information should be withheld. "She fell from her balcony."

"Oh." A wave of colour again, stronger this time. She glanced at her husband, for the first time. "Then... Are you saying it was an accident, after all? We'd heard... We thought..."

"I'm afraid we don't know yet. And won't know for sure, until various tests have been done and we have the post mortem results. But as there is an element of doubt..."

"There is, then?" she pressed. "An element of doubt?"

"At this stage, in this particular case, yes, there must be. But," he went on, as Mrs. Speed squeezed her husband's hand and shot him a reassuring glance, "as there is a *strong* element of doubt, we can't afford to waste time doing nothing, we have to proceed as if the death were murder."

The word dropped into the conversation like a stone, and there was a brief, appalled silence on their part. Then they both spoke together.

"But..."

"So...?"

Thanet waited. Let them sort it out. It would be interesting to see who deferred. It was Mrs. Speed. From habit? he wondered.

"So what did you want to say to me, Inspector?"

"Can't you guess, Mr. Speed?"

Speed glanced nervously at his wife and Thanet could

guess what he was thinking. *There's a chance they don't know. If I assume they do, I could drop myself right in it for no good reason.* He cleared his throat. "I'm sorry, no, I can't."

"Oh, come on, Mr. Speed. Let's not play games." Thanet glanced at Mrs. Speed, who bowed her head as if to shield herself from the blow which she knew was coming. "Well, if you insist on making this painful for your wife . . . It is common knowledge that you have been having an affair with Mrs. Tarrant. Naturally, in the circumstances, there are some questions we would like to ask you . . ."

Speed shrugged and tried to look confident. "Like what, for instance?" He was beginning to sweat, Thanet noticed.

"Well, let's begin with an account of your movements today. From, say, lunchtime."

"Since lunchtime?"

Had there been a hint of relief in Speed's tone? If so, why? The testimony of both Mrs. Haywood and Marilyn Barnes confirmed that Nerine Tarrant had still been alive at half past three. But Speed ran a garage. Perhaps he had been up to something shady with second-hand cars this morning. Thanet knew that in the course of a murder investigation people often acted in a guilty manner for reasons which had nothing to do with the case, simply because they had some other secret to hide.

"That's easy," Speed was saying. "I was at the garage all afternoon—and all morning too, for that matter."

"You're sure?"

"Oh, yes. Absolutely." A thought struck him. "Oh, except for a test drive, late this afternoon. We'd changed a gearbox."

"What time was this?"

"Let me see . . ." Speed stubbed out his cigarette, leaned sideways and, with difficulty, extracted a handkerchief from the pocket of his tight jeans. He mopped his forehead. "It must have been about a quarter or twenty past five when I drove off. So it would have been around twenty to six when I got back. I usually take the same route for test drives, and the circuit takes about twenty minutes."

And Nerine's body had been found at a quarter to six. The garage was only minutes away from the Tarrants' house. Speed could well be in the running, then. "Which route do you take?"

Lineham took down the details. And yes, Speed's route had indeed taken him past High Gables.

"Did you see anyone at the house, as you passed?"

"I was doing a test drive, Inspector. I was concentrating on the car."

True, perhaps. But wouldn't it be natural for a man to glance at his mistress's house, however briefly, as he went by?

"There are two very nasty bends, near High Gables," said Speed, as if Thanet had spoken his thoughts aloud. "You can't afford to let your concentration slip. There've been a number of accidents there, in the past."

"Can anyone corroborate these times?"

This provoked a definite though almost undetectable reaction from both of them. A sideways flick of the eyes from Speed, a determinedly wooden look from his wife. What now? wondered Thanet.

"My son will bear me out. He's helping at the garage at the moment. He's just finished his A levels," Speed went on, forced to continue by Thanet's silence, "and they're allowed to stay at home if they want to. He'll tell you I was at the garage all day."

"And at lunchtime?" said Thanet, softly.

Again he picked up a tremor of reaction.

"My husband was at home for lunch," said Mrs. Speed firmly. "And a neighbour of ours can verify that. Mrs. Shrimpton. She called in to pick up some stuff for the jumble sale on Saturday."

Lineham noted Mrs. Shrimpton's address.

"And what did you do after lunch, Mrs. Speed?"

"Me?" She was taken aback.

"Just for the record," said Thanet, smiling.

"Well," she said, a little flustered, "let me see. From half past two till four I was at a meeting in the village hall. Afterwards I went to visit someone who is sick. I left there about five."

But she was holding something back. Thanet was intrigued; but he wouldn't probe any further at the moment, he decided. Better do a little digging and acquire some ammunition, first, in case he was met by blank stares and flat denials.

"Is your son at home? What's his name?"

And yet again he had touched a nerve, hard though they tried to conceal it. What on earth was going on here?

Speed cleared his throat. "Tim? Er . . . No, he's out, I'm

afraid." He gave an apologetic smile. "You know these young
people. The minute they've got some cash in their pockets,
they're out spending it."

"You know where he is?"

They shook their heads in unison, two clockwork figures.
"With friends," said Mrs. Speed. "That's all we know."

"Not to worry," said Thanet, rising. "I'll have a word with
him tomorrow."

This time they were even less successful in hiding their
consternation.

Lineham waited until he had closed the front gate behind
him before bursting out, "What on earth did she see in that
slimy little creep!"

"You're talking about Nerine Tarrant, I presume?"

"I mean, she was gorgeous, wasn't she? Really beautiful.
Surely she could have done better for herself than that."

Thanet forbore to point out that she had in fact done
better for herself than that; she had married Roland Tarrant,
who was handsome and successful and by all accounts as
devoted a husband as she could wish for. "Nothing better
around?" he suggested.

"All the same..."

"Interesting interview, though, Mike, didn't you think?"

"I bet he's our man," said Lineham enthusiastically. "It was
obvious that he was covering up, and I can just imagine him
creeping up behind her and shoving her off a balcony."

"Why?"

"Why what? Why should he shove her off?" Lineham
shrugged. "He was tired of her? Or, much more likely, she
was tired of him? That's probably it, sir. Mrs. Haywood and
PC Driver both said her affairs never lasted more than a few
months. Perhaps he nipped in to see her on the way back
from that test drive of his. She tells him to get lost, she never
wants to see him again. She stalks off onto the balcony and
leans against the rail, turning her back on him. He's in a
blind rage, determined that if he can't have her, nobody will.
He goes after her, bends down, lifts her by the legs like you
said, and gives a good shove. Then, naturally, he scarpers..."

"Maybe," said Thanet thoughtfully. "But I think there was
a lot more going on back there than just covering up a
murder."

"Just!" said Lineham. "Just! Now if I made a remark like
that you'd be having my guts for garters! *Sir.*"

Thanet laughed. "I stand rebuked, Mike. But you know what I mean."

"The way they nearly had heart attacks every time their son was mentioned, you mean? Yes, I noticed that, all right. I wonder what he's been up to."

"Something to do with Damon Tarrant, you think?"

"Could be. We'll have to find out, obviously."

"Along with a million other things," said Thanet.

Unconsciously, both men speeded up. There was indeed a great deal to do.

SIX

It was one o'clock in the morning before Thanet got home and he was surprised to see a light still burning in their bedroom. Joan was coming downstairs in her dressing gown as he entered the house.

"What on earth are you doing, still up at this hour?"

"I couldn't sleep."

"Worrying about your protégé, I suppose."

As soon as the words were out Thanet realised that he had been tactless; impartiality was the probation officer's golden rule.

"Don't call him that!" And then, more gently, "I left your supper in a low oven, if you feel like eating it." She went ahead of him into the kitchen and stooped to open the oven door. "Really, Luke, he's a client, nothing more, nothing less. But I was worried about him, yes. I was just about managing to get him onto an even keel, and now this happens... How is he?"

Thanet shook his head. "No idea. He hasn't turned up yet."

"Not turned up yet?" she echoed, turning plate in hand. "Do you want this?"

"Sorry, love, no. I'm past being hungry. I picked up a sandwich, earlier, so I won't starve." He sat down heavily at the kitchen table. "I'd like a cup of tea, though. No, Damon apparently left home in his car at about twenty to six, and hasn't been seen since."

"So does he know about his mother's death?"

"That's what we would like to know," said Thanet grimly. "Amongst other things."

"You're not suggesting he had anything to do with the murder, are you? It was murder, I gather, or you wouldn't be so late."

"We think it was, yes." Thanet explained about the balcony, the height. "But as far as Damon is concerned..." He shrugged. "Who knows?"

"But that's preposterous! You're not seriously suggesting he *killed* her?"

"Darling, you ought to know by now that at this stage I'm unlikely to be suggesting anything so specific. I'm just saying we don't know. How can we, if the boy isn't even available for questioning?"

"But..." Joan broke off to make the tea, maintained a thoughtful silence until she poured it. Then she sat down opposite him. "Look, Luke, I don't want to seem over-biased, but I really can't believe Damon would have had anything to do with it. He's just not the violent type."

"What is the violent type? You know as well as I do that everyone has potential violence in them, if they are pushed hard enough. Then there's the question of drugs..."

"But he's off drugs! That is, he was never really on them. It was only cannabis."

"Only cannabis! My God, I never thought I'd live to see the day when you said, 'only cannabis'! What would you say if we caught Ben smoking it? Is that what you'd say? 'Only cannabis'?"

"All right, darling, calm down. You know what I mean, I simply meant, it wasn't an hallucinatory drug. Those are the ones that are dangerous in the kind of situation we're talking about."

"We both know that once people get into drugs there's no telling where it'll end. Let's face it, he's just the type, isn't he? Rich parents, more money than love..."

"You're over-simplifying and you know it."

"No, I don't know it. I know very little about him. Why don't you tell me, then I can make up my own mind."

Silence.

With a shock, Thanet realised that Joan had no intention of doing so.

He had been right, then, to feel apprehensive. It had indeed come upon them, the moment he had been dreading for years, when their respective jobs would erect a barrier between them. He was appalled at how suddenly and stealth-ily it had arrived, catching them unawares, vulnerable, com-placent, even. He and Joan had never held anything back from each other before; there had never even been any need to discuss the matter, it was implicit in all they said or did. Thanet had seen too many of his colleagues' marriages eroded by resentment and mistrust to allow even a hint of such destructive emotions to creep into his own, if he could help it. Now, it seemed, he had no choice in the matter.

Joan looked up at him and their eyes met. She was thinking the same thing, he could tell.

He put out his hand to cover hers. "No," he said. "We mustn't let this happen. I know you can't talk about clients, especially in circumstances like this. I shouldn't have asked. And I'm sorry I snapped at you. I'm a bit tired, I suppose. Forgive me?"

She smiled, squeezed his hand. "Of course. Anyway, there's no need to apologise. I shouldn't have overreacted."

"And we're not going to allow it to come between us?" *But it had. It already had.*

She shook her head, smiled again. "No."

He only hoped their good resolutions would hold, if things became sticky. "I wasn't really saying we suspect him, you know. It's just that there is this unexplained absence..."

"I appreciate that. But there could be a dozen reasons for it. The most likely one is that he's gone to a party, some distance away, and he's simply late getting home."

"Quite." Or he could have had a row with his mother, and killed her.

They decided to call it a day. But in bed, Thanet couldn't sleep. He and Joan might have managed to build a temporary bridge over the chasm which had suddenly opened up be-neath their feet, but he could foresee all sorts of problems ahead. And his mind was crammed to the bursting point with all the information he had accumulated that day, with all the new people he had met and with endless speculation about the relationships between them. And at the heart of it all, an enigma yet, was Nerine, possessing everything a woman could want—health, beauty, a handsome successful husband who adored her, a son, a beautiful home, a life of ease, of luxury, even... yet restless, dissatisfied, apparently heartless and egocentric...

At least, this was the façade which she presented to the world. What had she really been like?

Thoughts of death and murder seemed singularly inappropriate when Thanet set off for work next day. It was a golden morning, with clear blue skies and brilliant sunshine gilding the feathery new foliage of the Gleditchia tree in the front garden. It was Thanet's turn to take the children to school and all along the suburban streets there was evidence that high summer had arrived at last: climbing roses in full bloom, early Dutch honeysuckle rioting over fence and porch, stately blue spires of delphinium towering over campanula and phlox, catmint and valerian.

Ben was in the back of the car, engrossed in last-minute revision for a History test that morning. Thanet glanced at Bridget.

"How did you and Mrs. Mallard get on last night?"

"Oh, it was great! We dreamed up this new chicken dish—chicken breast cooked in cider with onions, herbs and tomato puree. We're going to have it for lunch on Sunday."

"Sounds terrific." Thanet hoped he would be at home to enjoy it.

"And guess what, Dad! Mrs. Mallard said that the *Kent Messenger* had rung up the other day. They wanted to know if she would do a cookery corner for children—you know, something simple the kids could make for themselves. She said she didn't really have the time, as she's trying to finish her new book, but she could recommend someone..."

"You?" said Thanet.

Bridget nodded, face glowing. "They were a bit dubious at first, when they heard I'm only fourteen, but she reminded them about my winning the Young Chef of the Year competition last year, and told them about the column I'd been writing for the school news-sheet and they said if I sent some back copies they'd take a look at my stuff and let me know."

"Delia Smith, beware!" said Thanet. "That really is good news." And just the sort of thing to look good on her c.v. later on, when Bridget was job-hunting.

For several years now Bridget's interest in cookery had grown and flourished and she was determined to pursue a career in it. Though reasonably bright, Bridget, unlike Ben, was not academically minded, and like all parents in the current unemployment situation Thanet and Joan were worried about their children's future prospects. Anything which helped was to be wholeheartedly encouraged.

"I'm going to go through the news-sheets tonight, look out the best recipes, then I'll get them off tomorrow."

"How long will it be before you hear? Did they say?"

"Within the next week or two. They want to get this column started quite soon, apparently."

"We'll keep our fingers crossed," said Thanet. "Come on Ben, take your nose out of that book, we're here. I hope that wasn't the only revision you've done for this test."

"Cool it, Dad," said Ben. "I'll do OK."

Thanet shook his head and sighed as he watched them go. If only Ben would realise that it was not enough to be bright, you had to work hard too. And this academic year was crucial for him. Next spring he would learn whether or not he had been selected for the upper schools—the modern-day equivalent of the old grammar and technical schools. If not, his chances of going on to university would be sadly reduced. Whatever the claims for comprehensive schools, the fact was that the standards they achieved frequently fell far short of those required for university entrance. Somehow he and Joan had to get the message across to Ben.

Joan . . . This morning they had been carefully polite and pleasant to each other, but Thanet's apprehension had not diminished. He hated the idea of any note of falsity in a relationship which had always been open and honest on both sides. What could he do about it? Nothing, so far as he could see, but remain aware of what was happening and deal with the situation as best he could, as it unfolded.

On the way up to his office he ran into Detective-Sergeant Bristow. "Heard about the robbery out at Nettleton Grange yesterday afternoon, sir?"

"No. Much taken?"

"A few thousand quid's worth of jewellery, apparently."

"Any leads, yet?"

"Not so far. What about your case?"

"It's early days yet."

They chatted for a few minutes longer before going their separate ways.

In Thanet's office Lineham was already hard at work, sifting through the reports which had come in since yesterday. He gave Thanet a beaming smile.

"Morning, sir."

"Morning. Won the pools?"

Lineham grinned and laid down the folder he was holding. "Heard some good news this morning. My mother rang up, before breakfast."

"Oh?" said Thanet. Lineham's reaction to his mother's early-morning telephone calls was not usually so enthusiastic. Mrs. Lineham senior had never reconciled herself to the fact that her son was a married man with a wife and two children and she could no longer take first place in his life.

"She's getting married again!"

"Mike! That's terrific! Good for her!" Good for Lineham, too. With another focus in her life, the sergeant would at last be free of her undivided attention and the running battle between wife and mother.

They talked for a moment or two about Mrs. Lineham's plans, then turned their attention to work.

"Has Damon Tarrant turned up yet?" said Thanet.

"No. There was one report which mentioned him, though. Someone saw him driving away from Ribbleden at about 5:45 last night. Apparently he was in a tearing hurry and going along those winding lanes much too fast."

"And there's no word from him since?"

"Not so far. Do you think we ought to put out a call for him, sir?"

Thanet strolled across to the window and stood gazing out, absentmindedly admiring the mist of fresh green which now enveloped the silver birches at the far side of the car park. Obviously, if there had been any evidence that Damon had killed his mother, it would have been necessary to track him down without delay, but so far there was nothing to implicate him but the fact that he had been around at the time of the murder and had made a hasty departure just before the body was discovered. Thanet had to allow for the possibility that Damon had been unaware of his mother's death—might still be unaware of it, for that matter. But if so, at some point during the day he should surely hear about it, and if he were innocent he would presumably get in touch. If he didn't, well, that would put a different complexion on matters. Meanwhile, Thanet felt he had to give him that chance.

Suppressing the suspicion that he might also be influenced by Joan's reaction if he didn't, Thanet said, "Not at the moment. We'll give him till this evening, I think."

Lineham shrugged acquiescence.

"All the same, I think his room should be searched for drugs. We'll arrange for that to be done later on today." Thanet nodded at the reports. "Anything else of interest?" He sat down at his desk and began to fill his pipe. He was almost out of tobacco, he noticed. He must remember to get some more.

"They haven't finished the house to house yet, of course, but there are one or two interesting bits and pieces, yes. For one thing, a witness has reported seeing Mr. Speed's car parked in the entrance to a field just around the bend from High Gables at lunchtime yesterday."

"Empty?"

"I assume so, sir. The report doesn't actually say." Lineham was shuffling through the pile. He found and scanned it. "No, it doesn't." He handed it to Thanet.

Thanet skimmed through it. "Benson, I see. Of course, he wasn't to know the significance of this particular car, at that point . . . Get on to him. Tell him to interview the witness again and get a really detailed report. I want to know if Speed was actually seen, where he was going, what he was doing, what time it was, whether the witness saw the car arrive and leave, how far away the witness was, the lot . . ."

Lineham made a note. "You think it's that important, sir? We know she was still alive a couple of hours later."

"I just can't really understand why Speed didn't come clean about this. I noticed we got a reaction, when lunchtime was mentioned . . . But why not own up, if he saw her then? It isn't as if he was denying the affair with her."

"Mrs. Speed claimed he had lunch at home, sir. And she mentioned a neighbour . . ."

"Make sure the neighbour is interviewed this morning."

"Right, sir. I assumed that reaction you mentioned was to do with his son—that there'd been a family row he didn't want aired in public, or something." Lineham shuffled through the pile of papers again. "PC Driver's report seemed to suggest something of the sort. He remembered after talking to us last night. Yes, here we are. Apparently he called in at the garage for some petrol yesterday afternoon, sensed a bit of an atmosphere between Speed and his son."

"What else does he say?"

"Not a lot. He went to the pub last night, as you suggested, but most of what he heard just confirmed what he already knew. Speed's affair with Mrs. Tarrant was common knowledge but opinion was divided as to whether Mrs. Speed knew about it or not. The consensus of opinion was that she didn't. People agreed that although Speed had always enjoyed the odd harmless flirtation, he'd never strayed to this degree before, and there was a general feeling that it was Mrs. Tarrant who was really to blame for initiating the affair and that she had probably now got what she deserved."

"Any suggestion as to who might have done it?"

"I don't suppose they'd have named names with Driver there, even though they do know him. But nods and winks hinted at Tarrant or Speed being strong favourites, apparently."

"Surprise, surprise. No talk of any previous lovers muscling in on the act?"

Lineham shook his head. "No. According to Driver, it was well known that her affairs usually only lasted a few months and the men he knew of who'd been involved with her seemed to take the attitude that they'd take what was on offer, enjoy it while they could and shrug their shoulders when it was over. The last one, a chap called Browning, moved out of the area a couple of months ago."

There was a knock and Doc Mallard put his head around the door. "May I come in?" But he hadn't waited for an invitation, he was in already. "Just to let you know the PM is scheduled for this afternoon. Not that I'm expecting any surprises, but you never know, do you?"

Smiling benignly at them over his gold-rimmed half-moon spectacles, he clasped his hands behind his back then turned to gaze out of the window. He gave a little bounce on the balls of his feet. "Beautiful morning, isn't it?"

Thanet and Lineham still hadn't got used to this benevolent version of the tetchy, irritable little man they had worked with for so many years, and they exchanged indulgent smiles behind his back.

The phone range and Lineham answered it. "Ah, good morning, Mr. Tarrant... You have?"

Lineham's glance and the upward inflexion of his voice alerted Thanet and Mallard to the fact that some interesting information was coming in. Mallard raised his hand in a gesture of farewell and left.

Lineham was listening intently. "Yes... Yes... I see... Hold on a moment, please." He covered the receiver and said to Thanet, "Mr. Tarrant says he's thought of someone with a grudge against his wife. He wants to know if we're coming out to the house this morning."

Thanet nodded.

Lineham brought the conversation to a close and had just replaced the receiver when it rang again.

"DS Lineham... Hullo, Mick. Oh? What's that? Really? What time was that? Yes, thanks, that's very interesting. Cheers." He put the phone down again and said, "Well, well!"

"Mike, stop being infuriating. Well what?"

"Mr. Tarrant's car was seen parked in his drive yesterday, at lunchtime. Around twelve thirty."

"Lunchtime, again. Why didn't he tell us, either? What the hell was going on?"

"Perhaps," said Lineham, his eyes beginning to sparkle with the familiar enthusiasm, "Speed had arranged a lunch-time tryst with Mrs. Tarrant, at her house. Then Mr. Tarrant returns home unexpectedly, catches them at it..."

"Then what? Goes away and thinks about it for four hours, then comes home and pushes her off her balcony?"

"Something like that. Why not?" Lineham was warming to his theme. "He comes home at lunchtime. Speed is already there. Mr. Tarrant hears them together, but doesn't actually show himself. It's not as though it's a complete shock, he's known about the affair all along, his wife had made no attempt to hide it. So he says nothing, does nothing, just goes away, back to the hospital. But during the afternoon he finds he's getting more and more angry. Somehow, hearing them at it had really brought it home to him and he feels he can't put up with it any longer, he must have it out with her. When he gets home he goes straight upstairs to his wife's sitting room. She is out on the balcony. They quarrel, and..." Lineham shrugged. "The scenario as before."

Thanet remembered the crushed, defeated man he had interviewed the previous day. Could Tarrant be guilty? It was quite feasible, he supposed. A moment's anger can bring a lifetime of remorse. And the surgeon had lied to them—or at least, deliberately given the impression that he hadn't been home all day. "I suppose it could have happened like that. And if it did..."

If it had, one way or another he and Lineham would get at the truth.

He began to shuffle the papers on his desk together. "We'll just tidy up a few loose ends here, then we'll be on our way."

SEVEN

"No! I didn't see her yesterday, I swear it!"

They were all crammed into Speed's tiny office at the garage. There was a pungent reek of oil and grease, and a whiff of the expensive hair-oil which Speed used to glue those carefully separated thinning strands of hair to his scalp. There was, too, another smell that Thanet recognised: the smell of fear.

"We have a witness." Thanet, seated on the edge of the littered desk, was implacable. In between questions he had taken in the small, cluttered room: girlie calendar on wall, mess of papers on desk, dirt on floor, grime on windows. If a man's environment said anything about his personality, then Speed was both lazy and disorganised. Was he also, perhaps, a dreamer, oblivious of his surroundings because his mind was busy elsewhere? Was that what Nerine had been to him? Thanet wondered: fantasy made flesh and blood, a taste of the glamour for which his soul had hungered?

In any case, it wasn't surprising that the man's business was foundering. An office like this was scarcely designed to inspire confidence in prospective customers.

Speed was staring at him, eyes bulging slightly as if he were straining to see into Thanet's mind and find out how much the inspector knew. "But that's impossible! I didn't see her yesterday din—lunchtime, I tell you. No one could have seen me because I wasn't there."

"Weren't you?"

"No! I . . ." Speed broke off abruptly, and the lines of his face began to reassemble themselves into a new expression: dismay.

"Yes?" said Thanet, politely.

Lineham, squeezed into a corner behind Speed, shifted slightly and Thanet sensed that the sergeant was hoping to catch his eye, exchange a triumphant glance. But Thanet knew that it was essential to keep his attention focused on Speed. Minute beads of perspiration were beginning to break out on the man's forehead and nose.

"I . . ." The sound was strangled, as if Speed's windpipe had closed up.

Thanet waited.

"I'd forgotten," Speed brought out at last.

"That you'd been to visit her at lunchtime yesterday?"

"No! That I'd stopped . . ." Suddenly the words began to tumble out. "That's why I was so sure I hadn't seen her . . . I mean, because I'd intended seeing her, and then . . . then I couldn't, because her husband was there."

So further corroboration that Tarrant had lied, that he had indeed been home during the day, yesterday. Of course, it was still possible that he hadn't lied about seeing his wife; she might have been out . . .

"You had arranged to see her at lunchtime, then?"

"Oh, no. No." Speed put up a hand and wiped his forehead, leaving a long black horizontal smear. He had been working on a car when they arrived, and had given his hands no more than a token wipe on a rag. "I just happened to have a few minutes to spare din—lunchtime and thought I'd drop in, give her a surprise . . ."

Some surprise, thought Thanet, if Speed had looked as scruffy as this. He thought of Nerine's cool well-groomed beauty, tried—and failed—to visualize Speed in the silken elegance of her bedroom.

Speed glanced at a grubby door in the corner of the room. "I gotta shower here," he said, as if he had read Thanet's thoughts. "I couldn't've gone to see her like this, of course. Anyway, I needn't've bothered. Like I said, I didn't go in because her husband was there."

"How did you know?"

"His car turned into the drive ahead of me."

"So what did you do?"

"Drove on past, of course."

"And then?"

Speed swallowed, his prominent Adam's apple bobbing nervously. "That's what had slipped my mind. I parked for a short while in the usual place, a farm gateway just around the bend from the Tarrants' house. I thought Mr. Tarrant might not be staying long, that he'd just called back at the house to pick up some papers or something. It was most unusual for him to come home dinnertime . . ." He clicked his tongue in exasperation and shook his head. "I suppose that's when someone saw me. You can't blow your nose in this bloody place without someone knowing it."

He seemed much calmer now. He had stopped sweating and had relaxed a little, sitting back in his chair and folding his arms. "Sorry, Inspector. Looks as though I misled you without intending to. It had just slipped my mind . . ."

"You told us you spent lunchtime at home."

"But I did. After going to try to see Ner . . . Mrs. Tarrant."

"How did your wife react?"

"To what?" Unaccountably, Speed was looking nervous again.

"To your appearing at home unexpectedly."

"Oh, yes, well . . ." Speed shrugged, composure recovered. "I'd told her I might be home dinnertime, so she wasn't too surprised."

What other, more alarming area had he brushed against unawares? Thanet wondered. What was the question he should have asked, just then? He had no idea. "Was she surprised that you had showered and changed?"

Speed gave a complacent shrug. "Told her I'd had to see an important customer."

And without more details from the witness who had seen Speed's car, that was about as far as they could go, thought Thanet.

The boy who had been helping Speed when they arrived had now gone out onto the forecourt—too grand a name, really, for the small apron of oil-stained concrete which separated the workshop and office building from the road— and was serving a customer with petrol.

"Is that your son?"

Speed's slightly smug expression was instantly erased. He glanced uneasily out of the window. "Yes."

"I'd like a few words with him. May we have the use of your office?"

Speed rose clumsily to his feet. "Yes, of course."

"What did you say his name was?" said Thanet pleasantly. "Tim?"

Speed cleared his throat. "That's right." At the door he paused. "Er... Will you be wanting me?"

Thanet shook his head. "No, that's all, thank you, Mr. Speed. For the moment."

He watched through the window as Speed approached the boy and spoke to him. Tim glanced over his shoulder at the office and said something. Speed shook his head vigorously.

"What d'you think is going on out there, Mike?"

Lineham shook his head. "I'd give a lot to know."

Despite their attempts to conceal the fact, it was obvious that they were arguing now, the boy with his head down, glowering up at his father from beneath lowered eyelids, Speed with chin thrust forward, hands gesticulating. Both of them kept shooting nervous little glances in the direction of the office. Eventually Tim nodded and, head drooping, began to walk towards the office, reluctance in the sag of his shoulders and dragging feet.

He pushed it open. "Dad says you wanted to see me."

He was a good-looking boy, handsome even, with regular features, firm chin and a tumble of curly brown hair. Well built for his eighteen years, too. A rugger player, perhaps? He looked tired, though, as if he hadn't had much sleep last night.

Thanet gave a reassuring smile. "Just one or two things we thought you might be able to help us out with. May I call you Tim?"

The boy nodded.

"Sit down." Thanet waved a hand at the desk and Tim perched stiffly on one corner. He reminded Thanet of a bird poised for flight as danger approaches.

But Tim was no bird and there was nowhere to fly to. What was he afraid of? In the course of his work Thanet had met countless boys—young men, really—of Tim's age. They came in all shapes and sizes and ranged from the innocent to the depraved. Thanet would have guessed that Tim tipped the scales well down on the innocent side, but his behaviour indicated otherwise. What on earth could he be hiding? The fact that his father was lying? Tim was supposed to verify Speed's alibi. What if he didn't want to, felt it would be better to tell the truth? Was that what the argument had been about, just now?

Thanet introduced himself and Lineham. "Actually, it's the sergeant who wants to have a word with you." Then he turned, folded his arms and leaned casually on the window ledge, apparently dissociating himself from the proceedings. At this stage he wanted the atmosphere to be as unthreatening as possible. As Lineham and the boy started to talk he edged himself imperceptibly around so that he could see the boy's face.

"We understand you're a friend of Damon Tarrant."

Lineham had selected the right opening. Tim relaxed slightly.

"That's right."

"A close friend?"

Tim shrugged. "We know each other quite well, yes."

"Did you know that he had disappeared?"

"What do you mean, 'disappeared'?"

Lineham lifted his shoulders. "Perhaps that's too . . . dramatic a term. Let's say that he left his house yesterday afternoon at about twenty to six, and he hasn't been seen since. Did you know that?"

"I had heard something of the sort, yes."

Naturally, thought Thanet. Every last detail would have been around the village before the last police car had left last night. He was well aware of that strange osmosis whereby news in a village is transmitted without apparent means of communication.

"You didn't see him yourself, last night, then?"

"No. I haven't seen him since Wednesday." Tim gave a sheepish grin. "Several of us finished our A levels that day, and we had a bit of a celebration in the evening. I asked Damon along."

"Do you have any idea where he might have gone?"

Tim shook his head. "Haven't a clue."

"Could you make some suggestions?"

"Not really. He could be anywhere."

"Where, for example?"

But Tim merely shook his head.

"Look," said Lineham, "it really would be to Damon's advantage, if he could be found quickly."

"Why?"

"Has it occurred to you that he might not even know his

mother is dead? How would you like to learn that your mother had been murdered by reading about it in a newspaper, or hearing it on the radio?"

Thanet mentally applauded. That shot had really gone home. Tim's face had darkened and he was gazing down, all his concentration apparently bent upon picking at a piece of loose skin beside his thumbnail.

"Well," demanded Lineham. "Would you?"

Tim sighed and glanced up at the sergeant, eyes narrowing. "You don't suspect him of being... involved, then?"

Lineham shot a little sideways glance at Thanet as if seeking guidance, but Thanet avoided his gaze. Mike was doing very well without any help from him.

"I'll be honest with you," said Lineham "We just don't know. There's no point in my swearing that we've discounted him as a possible suspect because at the moment we just don't know how things will turn out. But... Look, can I trust you not to let this go any further?"

Tim nodded. Lineham really had his attention, now.

"Well," said the sergeant, leaning closer to the boy and lowering his voice in conspiratorial fashion, "it's obvious that there are three possible alternatives. One: when Damon left, his mother was still alive; two: when he left she was dead and he didn't know it; three: when he left she was dead and he did know it. In the first two, he's innocent. It's only in the last that there's any question of his being involved, and I can truthfully say that at the moment we have heard nothing whatsoever to suggest that he might be. Quite apart from the fact that we'd like to find him and break the news gently before he hears it some other way—contrary to popular opinion, we are human, you know—you must see that whichever of these possibilities applies, he just might know something that could be very helpful to us."

There was a pause while Tim considered what Lineham had said.

"Well?" said the sergeant.

A further hesitation, then Tim said, "You really mean that? You honestly have no reason to suspect him?"

"Cross my heart," said Lineham, smiling. "That's right, isn't it, sir?"

Thanet nodded. "It's true, Tim."

"OK. Not that I can help you, really..."

"If you could just make some suggestions," said Lineham, "we would at least have some idea where to begin . . ."

"There are one or two friends he might have gone to," said Tim doubtfully.

"Good. Let's start with them."

Tim managed to come up with four names and, after some thought, two of the four addresses.

"Thanks. Now, if he isn't with any of them, have you any other ideas where he might be?"

"A party?"

"Where?"

Tim lifted his hand in a helpless gesture. "Anywhere. A friend. A friend of a friend. Who knows?"

"OK. Well, if you come up with any other ideas, could you let us know?"

"Right." Obviously under the impression that the interview was over, Tim slid off the desk and stood up.

"Just one other point . . ."

At once the wariness mingled with apprehension was back. "What's that?"

"We understand from your father that you're helping out here at the moment."

"Yes . . ." Tim was obviously on the defensive. "I've finished my A levels, as I said, and we're allowed not to go in if we don't want to, so Dad asked if I'd give him a hand. He's a bit pushed at the moment. It's a waste of time going to school after exams are over, so I agreed. It's all above board."

"I wasn't suggesting otherwise," said Lineham. "It's just that this garage is in a pretty central position in the village and you are very well placed to see all the comings and goings . . . We were wondering if you noticed anything unusual, yesterday, while you were here?"

"Not really, I'm afraid. I have thought about it."

"You were both here all day, you and your father?"

"Most of the time, yes. Dad had a big job on for Mr. Horton. A new gearbox for his Escort. The housing was all cracked, too."

"Ah yes, he told us about that. I understand he took the car for a test drive, at around ten past five."

"Somewhere around then, yes."

"And he was away about twenty minutes."

"Approximately, I suppose."

"What happens at lunchtimes?"

"We stagger it. We both have an hour. I go first, at twelve, then Dad goes at twelve thirty, so the garage is only shut for half an hour or so."

"I see. And this was what you did yesterday?"

"Yes." But Tim was looking uncomfortable.

"I suppose, as you're so close to home, you go there for lunch?"

"Usually."

"And yesterday?"

"We both went home."

Thanet could have sworn the boy was telling the truth, and yet . . .

"I see. Well, I think that's about all I wanted to ask you. Unless the Inspector . . . ?"

Thanet shook his head. "I don't think so, no."

"Right." Lineham smiled. "Thank you, Tim, you've been very helpful."

When they were in the car Lineham said, "I really would like to know why they're so on edge about yesterday lunchtime."

"So would I. The trouble is, it might be completely irrelevant, as far as we're concerned."

"Or it might not."

"Quite." Thanet sighed. "Well, I suppose we'll find out, eventually." Or it might always remain a mystery, he thought, one of those intriguing little puzzles thrown up by an investigation. Most people have secrets which they would prefer other people not to know about. If only they wouldn't get in the way like this . . .

"You did very well with young Tim in there, by the way, Mike."

"Thank you sir."

"Couldn't have handled it better myself."

"Where now, sir? High Gables?"

"Yes."

"I wonder what Mr. Tarrant'll have to say about this character who's supposed to have had a grudge against Mrs. Tarrant."

"Mmm. But apart from that, I think he has some explaining to do, don't you?"

EIGHT

Bridget was longing for a pair of Benetton jeans. Life, Thanet
had been assured, was not worth living without them. *Everyone* was wearing them, and after several excursions in which
Bridget relentlessly drew his attention to everyone who was
wearing them, he was beginning to believe her. All the same,
he was surprised to be confronted by them here, worn by the
girl who answered their knock at the front door of High
Gables. They were topped by a shocking-pink teeshirt, a
round cheerful face liberally spattered with freckles, and a
mop of unruly brown curls anchored by a shocking-pink
bandeau and an assortment of pink hair slides in the shapes
of—Thanet peered while trying not to look as though he was
peering—yes, animals. She was in her late teens or early
twenties.

"Morning. Inspector Thanet?" A wide, uninhibited grin.

Housekeepers these days came in unexpected shapes and
sizes, it seemed. Victoria Cunningham ("Call me Vicky") was
nineteen, had spent a year at the highly respected, long-
established (and expensive) Eastbourne College of Domestic
Enonomy (Cordon Bleu Diploma in the third term) and had
at once landed this very well-paid job at High Gables. She
had worked here for six months, lived in a neighbouring
village, drove to work in a Ford Fiesta Daddy had given her
for an eighteenth birthday present, and was altogether very
pleased with life. All this Thanet learned within a few minutes of being invited into the kitchen (Mr. Tarrant being in

the middle of a lengthy telephone call), where delicious smells filled the air and Vicky tied a white nylon triangle over her hair before resuming her culinary activities.

"You don't mind if I go on with this pud? Oh, sorry, I expect you'd like some coffee. I took some to Roland half an hour ago." The Christian name was another surprise, but Thanet accepted it along with the excellent ground coffee bubbling away in a coffee machine as part of the ambiance of expansive middle-class living which Vicky exuded.

"Thank you. Were you on duty yesterday afternoon?"

Vicky's face grew sombre. "Yes and no. I was on duty, but on Thursday afternoons I go into Sturrenden to do the week's food shopping."

"When did you leave?"

"About twelve. I usually meet a friend who's doing the same sort of job for a quick snack, and we go around Sainsbury's together afterwards. Then I do any other errands they want me to do in the town before coming home—going to the dry cleaners, that sort of thing. I usually get back about three, as I did yesterday."

"Just before Mrs. Tarrant got back from the hairdresser's."

"That's right."

"You heard the ensuing row with old Mrs. Tarrant?"

Vicky grimaced. "Couldn't have missed it. When I'd finished putting the shopping away I went out into the hall. I was going to go up to Mrs. Tarrant's sitting room to ask her something. But I kept well out of it, I assure you, turned around and went straight back to the kitchen."

"Did you go up to see Mrs. Tarrant later?"

"No. It hadn't been anything very important and I decided it could wait until the next day."

"Would Mrs. Tarrant have blamed you at all, for not keeping an eye on the old lady?"

"How could she? She knows I'm always out on Thursdays while she's at the hairdresser's, and anyway that's Marilyn's job."

Vicky finished piping an elaborate pattern of minute cream whorls on what looked like a strawberry mousse, added a few fresh strawberries as a final decoration and put the dish into the refrigerator. Then she sat down at the table, pulled the white triangle off her hair and gave her head a little shake, as if relieved to be free of the restriction.

"And you finished work at four, I understand."

"That's right."

So Vicky had not only been away over the lunch hour yesterday, but had probably left before the murder.

"Look, Vicky, I know it's normally not on, to talk about your employers, but in the circumstances I'd be grateful if you could answer a few questions."

She frowned. "Depends what they are."

She had been willing enough to talk about herself, but now the flow of information became a grudging trickle. She was prepared to supply facts about household routine, but not to discuss the relationships within her employer's family. Reluctantly, Thanet gave up.

"Could you find out if Mr. Tarrant is free, now?"

He was.

"Don't bother to come with us, we know the way." On the way out Thanet paused. "That was a delicious smell, when we came in. What had you been cooking?"

Vicky reverted to her former expansiveness. "Chicken breast with paprika and onions. I don't suppose Roland'll have much appetite, poor man, he didn't touch his breakfast, but I thought I'd make an effort, just in case."

Thanet mentally filed away the ingredients of the dish for Bridget's benefit as he and Lineham pushed through the baize door and walked along the corridor to Tarrant's study.

"Come in."

Tarrant was standing at the window with his back to the room, and swung around as they came in.

"Ah, good morning, Inspector, Sergeant. Sit down, won't you?"

Thanet had expected to find Tarrant crushed, bowed down beneath the burden of sorrow and pain, but here was a man simmering with a barely suppressed excitement. In complete contrast to yesterday's formal attire, he was wearing crumpled cotton trousers and a navy sweatshirt. He had cut himself shaving, Thanet noticed. It was just as well he hadn't gone into work today.

Tarrant plunged straight in. "Sergeant Lineham will have told you why I rang. It came to me while I was shaving." With a rueful grin he pointed to the small red mark on his neck. "I didn't get much sleep last night, as you can imagine. I kept on thinking and thinking about what you'd said . . ."

He began to pace restlessly to and fro in the space between

his desk and the window, pausing occasionally to look directly into Thanet's face while making a telling point.

"At first, of course, I'd assumed it was an accident. Then, when I came to think about it . . . I know that rail isn't very high, and my wife was tall, but even so . . . I just couldn't see how she could have fallen just by overbalancing . . .

"Then, I knew she would never have thrown herself off that balcony deliberately. For one thing, she wasn't the type to commit suicide. She loved life too much. She was . . . greedy for it. Oh yes, Inspector, I was under no illusions about my wife. I loved her for what she was . . . Anyway, if she had wanted to kill herself, she would have had enough common sense to choose another method. After all, how high is that balcony? Fifteen, twenty feet? She would have run the risk of injuring or even paralysing herself, and life in a wheelchair would have been unthinkable to her . . . No, I felt I could rule suicide out, straight away."

Thanet nodded. "I came to much the same conclusions myself."

"So that was when I began to take your suggestion seriously . . . That she might have been . . . murdered."

Tarrant turned his back on them and stood facing the window, though Thanet doubted if the man was seeing anything. Although he was trying hard to conceal it, he was fighting for control of himself. Those deliberately deep, even breaths, and clenched, white-knuckled fists told their own story.

When he continued his throat was hoarse, his voice ragged. "I didn't want to believe it, of course. In fact, even now, I . . . It scarcely bears thinking about. But if it did happen, then the first question to ask is the one I did ask, yesterday."

His voice was gaining in strength and momentum and now he swung around to face them again, his eyes glittering. "Who? Who could possibly want to do such a thing? Nothing had been taken, so far as we could tell, it couldn't have been a burglar. So it must have been someone she knew, or who knew her, someone with a grudge against her. I thought and thought of all the people she knew, and all the possible reasons they could have for wanting to do such a thing . . . And I just couldn't believe it, of any one of them. And then as I said, when I was shaving, it suddenly came to me!"

He sat down abruptly and leaned forward across the desk, lowering his voice. His quiet, even tone and lack of histrionics gave his words credibility and impact. "I thought of someone who wouldn't have hesitated to kill her, if it suited him. Someone, moreover, who had actually sworn to kill her—well, 'get' her was the actual word he used... Have you by any chance ever come across a man called Buzzard, Inspector?"

The unusual name immediately rang a bell with the two policemen and they glanced at each other.

"Halo Buzzard?" said Lineham. "Armed robbery."

"Post office raids," said Thanet. "A spate of them, about ten years ago."

"Right!" said Tarrant, triumphantly. "And I'll bet you anything you like that with the crazy parole system they have nowadays he'll be out by now, for being a good little boy."

"Quite possible," said Thanet.

"Well," said Tarrant, obviously nearing the climax of his revelation, "you may or may not be aware, Inspector, that it was my wife's evidence that put him away."

"Really?" Now that *was* interesting.

"Yes. What happened was this. Buzzard used to wait until the coast was clear and the post office deserted, then he'd pull on one of those stocking masks and go in, armed with a sawn-off shotgun, to carry out the raid. He was a one-man band, if you remember, so he'd leave his engine running and when he came out he'd pull off the mask before driving away.

"In the raid on Nettleton post office, my wife had just pulled up across the road when he emerged. Luckily for her, she dropped her handbag as she was getting out of the car, and she was bending down to pick it up. Buzzard glanced across at her car, couldn't see anyone in it, and assumed the driver was gone. He got into his own car, pulled off the mask, and drove off. But she had seen him quite clearly, wearing the mask, through the windows of her car as she was straightening up. Realising what was happening she sensibly crouched down again, out of sight. Buzzard was naturally in a hurry and having satisfied himself that her car was empty, didn't even glance in her direction again. But she got a clear view of his face when he pulled off his mask, took the number of his car and went straight into the post office and rang the police. Of course, Buzzard claimed he had an alibi, and paraded several of his unsavoury friends to back him up, but my wife's evidence got him convicted. And when he was sentenced, he shouted out, in court, that he'd get her for this, one day. Now..." Suddenly the excitement in Tarrant's eyes faded and his voice trailed away. He shook his head despairingly. "Now it looks as though he has, doesn't it?"

"We'll get onto it right away," said Thanet. "We'll soon be able to find out if he's still inside. And it shouldn't be too difficult to pick him up if he's not."

"I blame myself," said Tarrant. "There were all sorts of things I could have done. I could have made it my business to find out where he was, exactly when he was coming out... I could have made sure she had more protection, more security measures in the house... We could have moved, so that he wouldn't have been able to find us... And above all, I shouldn't have just forgotten about it, let it fade away in my mind so that it wasn't a threat any longer... I should have known, people like that don't forget, and they don't forgive, and they don't care about human life, it has no value for them." He looked pleadingly at Thanet. "But it was so long ago... Ten years..."

"These things are bound to fade, in time. You mustn't blame yourself. Criminals often make threats, in circumstances like that, but very few of them actually carry them out, so many years later. If that is what happened..."

"But if it wasn't him," said Tarrant, "who was it?"

"I'm glad you recognise that we have to look at all the other possibilities, sir."

"Other possibilities?" The dazed look was back in Tarrant's eyes, as if the sustained effort of telling his story had used up his meagre reserves of concentration.

"I'm afraid so. As I said, we will most certainly follow up your theory. But meanwhile, we have to take a closer look at the movements yesterday of all the people connected with your wife."

Unexpectedly, Tarrant gave a harsh bark of laughter. "Beginning, I suppose, with me?"

Thanet's silence gave him his answer.

He shook his head in disbelief. "I don't believe I'm hearing this. I don't believe any of it." His voice rose. "My God, I don't really believe she's dead, even, although I saw her lying there, with my own eyes... And now you're suggesting..."

"No," said Thanet, cutting in. "We are not suggesting anything, sir. Merely asking. As we must, however unpleasant the task may be."

"Unpleasant!"

"Yes," said Thanet, more quietly. "Unpleasant, Mr. Tarrant. There is no pleasure, believe me, in appearing to harass people who are already suffering, as you are... But it has to be done, whether we like it or not. Your wife is dead, and if she was killed we have to try to find out who did it, you must see that."

"What's the point? It won't bring her back."

"Mr. Tarrant. You are a surgeon. Your whole working life is dedicated to saving life, isn't it? You must therefore believe, as I do, that it is of paramount importance. The difference is that whereas your work ends with a patient's death, that's when mine begins. If people were allowed to kill whoever they liked without any attempt being made to bring them to justice, the whole fabric of society would disintegrate."

Tarrant waved a weary hand. "All right, Inspector. Spare me the sermon. I'm well aware of all that. And I also know that in the case of domestic murder it is the husband who is most likely to have committed the crime. It just seems to..." He shook his head again. "Ah well... Go ahead. Let's get it over with, shall we?"

It was Tarrant's very capitulation that made Thanet hesitate. It was true that in the majority of such cases it proved to be the husband who had committed the crime. It was therefore essential to question Tarrant, to treat him not merely as a suspect but as the chief suspect. Thanet knew that he would have to do it, knew that he *would* do it, but part of him hated himself for knowing this, fleetingly despised the man who voluntarily undertook such work. He was convinced that whether or not Tarrant had killed his wife, perhaps in a fit of anger which he now bitterly regretted, he had loved her, was genuinely grieving for her, and it was inhumane to consider treating him like a common criminal.

Thanet could feel the comforting knob which was the bowl of his pipe in his pocket and he longed to take it out and smoke it. Tarrant, however, would no doubt disapprove; there wasn't an ashtray in sight.

No, there was only one possible outcome to his dilemma: he must get on with the job, whether he liked it or not. He became aware that the silence in the room had taken on a puzzled quality. Lineham and Tarrant were both staring at him, waiting for him to speak. Thanet was tempted to signal to Lineham to take over, but the knowledge that it would be a coward's way out prevented him from following what would normally be accepted procedure.

He cleared his throat.

"You may remember, Mr. Tarrant, that just before we left you, yesterday afternoon, I asked you a question to which you took exception, to the degree that you asked us to leave, at once."

Tarrant was nodding his head, wearily. "Stupid of me. I should have known you'd find out about Speed from the first person you asked." He gave a resigned shrug. "My wife never bothered to conceal her little...amusements."

"Is that how you saw them? As amusements?"

"I've just said so, haven't I?" There was an edge in Tarrant's voice now.

"Many men would find it difficult to be so tolerant."

"I am not many men." Tarrant made a *moue* of distaste. "I'm sorry, that sounds very arrogant, and I didn't mean it to be so. I simply meant that it is impossible to generalise in that way. I am myself, my wife was herself, together we were a unique combination, as every couple is a unique combination. And as far as I was concerned, yes, that was precisely how I did see my wife's lovers—and you will notice the plural, Inspector. I have lived with this sort of situation for many years, practically since we were first married, as a matter of fact."

"And it didn't worry you?"

"Of course it worried me! I'm only human, and I loved my wife—hell, I still love her, you don't stop loving a person just because you'll never see them again...But if you mean, did it make me so mad with jealousy that I killed her, then no, it didn't. I've always thought such jealous rage self-defeating. After all, by giving in to it you simply succeed in losing the very person you are trying to keep."

It was all very well to sit there being coolly analytical, thought Thanet, but had Tarrant actually been able to put his theories into practice, maintain an iron self-control in the face of what at times must have been extreme provocation? What if, as Lineham had suggested, the surgeon had come home at lunchtime yesterday and found his wife in bed with the garage owner? Perhaps the long habit of years would have sent him away again, but was it not possible that he had had to endure this particular humiliation once too often? During the afternoon, could he not have stewed and sweated over what he had seen or heard until at last, driven by an impulse which was beyond reasoning away, he had gone home, had one final row with his wife, and pushed her off that balcony at a time when he was simply not in control of his behaviour? It was all too uncomfortably credible. It was and always had been human nature, to make good resolutions dictated by common sense which prove impossible to keep when confronted by the situation which prompted them.

. It was time to put this theory to the test.

"Why didn't you tell us you came home at lunchtime yesterday, sir?"

Tarrant stared at Thanet for a moment. What was he thinking? Was he going to deny it?

Then he shrugged. "For one thing, you didn't ask me. And for another, I didn't think it relevant."

"You certainly gave us the impression you had been away from the house all day."

"I'm sorry if you were misled. But if you remember, you asked me when I had last seen my wife and I told you: at breakfast. That is the truth."

"You didn't see her at lunchtime?"

"No! I told you . . ."

"Strange," said Thanet. "She was here, wasn't she?"

No reply.

"Wasn't she?" Thanet insisted.

Still no reply.

"And if she was, are you really asking us to believe that you didn't look for her and find her? That you simply came home and left without seeing her?"

Again that long, considering stare. Then, once more, the resigned shrug. "All right, Inspector. I can see you're not going to leave me in peace until you're satisfied. I'll tell you what did happen, at lunchtime."

NINE

Tarrant paused for a moment, as if marshalling his thoughts. Then he sat back in his chair, folding his arms.

"When I left home yesterday morning I forgot to take with me some papers I needed for a meeting in the afternoon, so I decided to pop back at lunchtime to fetch them. I got here just after half past twelve. I thought my wife would probably be in, so I naturally went upstairs to her sitting room to look for her. She usually had lunch about that time and she liked to eat it on the balcony, it was her favourite place."

For a moment it looked as though his composure would slip, but he recovered. "She wasn't in the sitting room and I could see through the open french windows that she wasn't out on the balcony, but all the same I went across and put my head out, to check. It was empty. I wondered where she was. Although it was a bit early—I knew that her hairdressing appointment wasn't until two—I thought she might be changing, so I went out into the corridor and along to her bedroom. I put my hand on the doorknob and was about to turn it when... when I heard a voice, from inside. A man's voice. Speed's."

Tarrant gave Thanet an assessing glance and said drily, "Naturally, I decided not to go in. I simply turned away, went downstairs, collected the papers from my study, and left." He lifted his hands. "End of story."

And not surprising, thought Thanet, that Tarrant had been reluctant to tell it. Most men would listen to such a tale with amazement tinged with disbelief, and he himself found it very difficult to swallow.

How would he, Thanet, have reacted in a situation like that? An unwise question, he realised. Slamming a mental door upon the turmoil of violent images which immediately sprang into his mind, he forced himself to concentrate.

Cuckold.

The old term, with all its derogatory overtones, floated into his mind and was hastily suppressed. He wasn't here to make moral judgements, indeed had no right to make them, except insofar as they affected his work. And he did feel genuine sympathy for Tarrant. It must be hell to be forced to admit to a complete stranger that you had found your wife in bed with another man and had done nothing about it.

If that really was what had happened.

Perhaps Tarrant had picked up the overtones of incredulity in Thanet's silence. He said with wry amusement, "I see you find it difficult to believe that I just turned and walked away, Inspector, but I do assure you that that is precisely what I did. For a very good reason."

Tarrant's tone changed, became earnest. "You see, I loved my wife, Inspector. Really loved her. Which means that I knew all her faults and weaknesses and loved her not in spite of them but *because* of them. She couldn't help herself, you see." He leaned forward, as if anxious to convince Thanet of the truth of what he was saying. "That was what nobody else could ever understand, not even Daphne, her own sister. They haven't seen her in tears, as I have, over her infidelities. After every affair she'd say how sorry she was, swear it would never happen again. Of course, we both knew she'd never be able to keep that promise." He shook his head. "She really couldn't help herself," he repeated.

"I know you may find it difficult to understand my attitude, but I always felt that if she had been less insecure, hadn't been—how shall I put it?—so hungry for love, she would never have married me. She would have been... unattainable to me. So you see, I could hardly have rejected her for the very weakness which brought her to me in the first place. In some strange way it forged a bond between us which kept us together all these years where many more apparently stable marriages have long since broken up. She knew, you see, that no one else could have accepted her as I did, that whatever she did, I would never leave her. And I knew that always, every time, she would come back to me. I was prepared to accept her upon any terms, rather than not have her at all."

It was a cry from the heart.

Taken aback at first by Tarrant's unexpected frankness, Thanet had by now realised that the surgeon was seizing what was perhaps the first opportunity he had ever had to attempt to vindicate his wife. Death had released him from the bonds of loyalty and propriety which would have prevented him from openly defending her while she was still alive.

Nevertheless, thinking of the endless humiliations which Tarrant must have had to endure over the years, Thanet wondered if it was possible that the surgeon had truly never felt the need to punish her for all the suffering she must have caused him. Tarrant's sincerity was obvious, but his determined tolerance would have had to falter for only a few moments yesterday afternoon for the damage to be done.

"Have you any idea what gave her this . . . need for love?"

For the last few minutes Tarrant had been gazing down at his clasped hands as he spoke, absentmindedly revolving his thumbs. Now he raised his eyes and gave Thanet a look of gratitude, aware that the Inspector was making a genuine effort to understand. "I've always assumed it was because her mother died when Daphne was born, when Nerine was only three. Her father, of course, was very busy and presumably didn't have much time to spare for the children." He shrugged. "I did try, but I never managed to get her to talk about it, and I honestly don't think she had any idea why she was the way she was. But I always felt that if her mother hadn't died when she did, my wife would have been a very different person. I know she never wanted for anything material, but nothing can compensate for emotional deprivation. I always hoped that one day she would come to realise that she had found what she was looking for in me."

Now, that day will never come.

Thanet responded to the unspoken words. "I'm sorry."

Tarrant stared at him, nodding slowly, as if having come to a decision. "Yes, I believe you really mean that."

"I do." Something now needed to be done to lighten the atmosphere. Thanet thumped his chest and grinned. "Beneath this grey flannel suit bears a heart of gold."

It had been the right response. Tarrant smiled with relief and leaned back in his chair, more relaxed than at any time so

far. He steepled his fingers and said, "Was there anything
else you wanted to ask me, Inspector?"

"Just one or two small points to clear up...To get back to
yesterday lunchtime..."

"Yes?"

"You're sure that it was Mr. Speed, with your wife?"

Tarrant looked surprised. "Yes, of course. Why?"

Thanet shook his head. "No reason." *Except that the
gentleman in question swears he never came near the house.*

"How long were you in the house, would you say?"

"Ten minutes, perhaps. Certainly no longer than a quarter
of an hour."

"I see...Have you by any chance heard from your son
yet?"

Tarrant shook his head.

"You're not worried about him?"

"I told you yesterday, Inspector. Damon is something of a
law unto himself. All the same, I am very worried that he
doesn't yet know about his mother, and I must admit he isn't
usually away as long as this, without contacting us."

"I was going to ask you...I'm sorry, but I'm afraid we shall
have to search his room."

Tarrant suddenly woke up. "What for? He'd absolutely
loathe the idea of anyone poking about in his things...Ah, I
see. Drugs, I suppose...My God, one mistake and you have
the police on your back for the rest of your life, don't you?"

"Not in normal circumstances. But you don't need me to
remind you that these circumstances are not normal. You
must see that this is a routine precaution we must take."

Tarrant's brief flare of anger died away and he slumped
back in his chair and waved his hand. "Oh, very well. Just get
on with it."

"Thank you. But before his room is properly searched, I'd
like to take a look at it myself."

"Why?"

"I just want to reassure myself that there are no signs of
anything other than a normal departure."

"What do you mean?" Tarrant was alert again. "What are
you suggesting?"

"I'm not suggesting anything."

"Oh, but you are, aren't you? You're suggesting he might
have something to do with..." He broke off, clutched his
head as if to control thoughts spinning out of control.

"Mr. Tarrant. I'm not suggesting anything of the sort. I am just being careful, that's all. There could be a very simple, innocent reason for Damon's departure. On the other hand, not knowing as yet the exact circumstances under which your wife met her death, we have to consider the fact that Damon could, quite innocently, have got caught up in it."

"Witnessed it, you mean?" Tarrant was appalled. "My God, you could be right . . . What if this . . . this criminal, Buzzard, was here, and Damon saw something which aroused his suspicions, went after him . . ."

It was a possibility which had not occurred to Thanet, having heard of Buzzard's possible involvement only a short while ago, but he had to admit that it was as likely an explanation as any other.

Tarrant was staring at Thanet, obviously thinking furiously. "That could explain . . ."

"What?"

Tarrant looked a little shamefaced. "I forgot to mention it before, but I saw Damon leave myself. He drove out of the gates just as I drove in. And I must admit he did seem to be in a tearing hurry." He stood up, suddenly infused with energy. "Come on, let's go and take a look."

Thanet despatched Lineham to arrange for the drugs search and to radio in for enquiries to be made in regard to Halo Buzzard, and followed Tarrant to the servants' stairs at the back of the house.

"We converted the attic into what is virtually a self-contained flat for Damon's sixteenth birthday present," said the surgeon as they climbed. "Young people value their independence, don't they? I know I did."

Thanet murmured assent. He certainly agreed that independence was the aim of parents and children alike, but he thought that, special cases apart, sixteen was much too young for such a degree of autonomy. He was beginning to wonder if this family had ever lived together, in the accepted sense of the word. They seemed so . . . fragmented. Nerine Tarrant had her own sitting room, bedroom and bathroom and so, apparently, had her son. What about Tarrant? Had he, too, had his own quarters? Then there was old Mrs. Tarrant and her companion, again in a separate wing. Had they ever congregated, as families do (or should, in Thanet's opinion), in the kitchen, dining room or sitting room? Or had they all pursued their own separate existences, divided from each other by physical as well as emotional barriers? It wasn't surprising, he thought, that Damon had problems.

"How did he get on with his mother?" he asked.

Tarrant shrugged. "You know what adolescents are."

"There were arguments?"

"My wife wasn't a very maternal person."

No, thought Thanet, if all Tarrant had told him were true, Nerine had been too engrossed in her own search for love to have any to spare for anyone else.

Perhaps he was being unfair, and Nerine had been more to be pitied than condemned, but he couldn't help feeling anger on behalf of this boy he had never seen. What was it that Tarrant had said, just now, about his wife? "She never wanted for anything material, but nothing can compensate for emotional deprivation." Couldn't the man see that the very same pattern was being repeated in the life of his son? Perhaps he could, but had felt helpless to do anything about it, at least as far as his wife was concerned.

"Here we are."

They were at the foot of a white-painted wrought-iron spiral staircase, its intricate design stark against the slate-blue walls of the landing.

"More interesting than simply putting in another flight of stairs, we thought," said Tarrant proudly.

"It's beautiful." Thanet paused on the way up to admire the clusters of iron grapes, the delicate entwined tracery of vine leaves and tendrils. Nerine Tarrant might have been unable to give or receive human love, but she had obviously had a love of beauty for its own sake, and an unerring eye for visual effect.

A moment later this impression was heavily reinforced.

They stepped from the circular opening at the top of the staircase into a dazzle of light and space. Thanet drew in his breath sharply and stood quite still, taking it all in. It was one vast room, perhaps sixty feet by forty, taking up perhaps two thirds of the entire attic space of the house and visually divided by the timbers which supported the roof. Sunshine was pouring in through some of the huge skylights, spilling over the grass-green of the fitted carpet which covered the entire room and creating the illusion that the profusion of tall plants was actually growing outside in some enchanted garden, where the geometric shapes of the furniture were really futuristic sculptures, carefully sited for maximum impact.

"Everything looks pretty normal to me," said Tarrant. He glanced at Thanet, saw his expression. "My wife designed it," he said sadly. "She had an eye for that sort of thing."

"It's amazing," said Thanet. "I've never seen anything quite like it, outside magazines. She should have taken it up as a career."

Tarrant looked at him, startled. "You think so?"

"She must have considered it, surely?"

The surgeon didn't answer, just shook his head and then stood gazing around as if, for the first time, he were seeing the place as revealing a dimension of his wife's character.

Thanet began to wander about, careful not to touch or to disarrange anything. A closer look told him that although Damon may have valued (or hated) the privacy (or isolation) that this flat give him, he certainly hadn't appreciated it in any other way. The grease-stained cooker, the scarred wooden work surfaces in the tiny kitchen area, the numerous stains on the carpet where liquid of one kind or another had been spilt, the drooping leaves of some of the taller shrubs and plants, the scatter of dirty clothes in the sleeping area, the general litter of books, records, unwashed mugs and plates and overflowing ashtrays all told their own story of indifference and neglect.

Tarrant was now keeping pace with Thanet.

"It's only cleaned once a month," he murmured apologetically. "Damon hates anyone else coming up here. But as I say, it all looks pretty normal to me . . . Have you seen all you wanted to see, Inspector?"

Thanet took the hint. He turned back towards the spiral staircase. "Yes, thank you."

"And you're satisfied?"

Thanet nodded. Though after such a cursory examination it was impossible, given the general untidiness, to detect signs of a hasty departure.

"We'll just have to hope he turns up soon, sir. If he's not back by this evening we may have to put out an appeal."

"Oh. Oh, dear. But if he hasn't heard about his mother's death . . ."

"That's what's worrying us. But against that, you have to consider his safety. It would be good to know that he's all right. Also, of course, we're very anxious to hear what he can tell us."

Lineham was waiting for them at the foot of the spiral and

she have felt about Nerine, in view of the constant humiliations inflicted upon Tarrant by his wife?

Thanet put out his hand and touched her gently on the arm. "I wonder if we could have a brief word together first, before I see Mrs. Tarrant senior?"

She hesitated. "All right. But I don't like to leave her alone for too long..."

"Just a few minutes," said Thanet.

She pushed open a door. "In here, then," she said.

TEN

The bare dressing table and general air of emptiness indicated that this was an unused guest room. Nerine Tarrant's flair for interior decoration was evident in the combination of ivory carpet, jade-green silk curtains and ivory-and-green wallpaper with a delicate, almost Oriental design of herons.

Marilyn closed the door and stood awaiting Thanet's questions with an air of slightly impatient resignation. Her eyelids drooped, and the flesh beneath her eyes looked slack and bruised, as if she had slept badly. The strain of yesterday was clearly taking its toll.

"Before I speak to old Mrs. Tarrant," said Thanet, "I just wanted to ask you . . . You remember you told us that when you went back upstairs at half past five yesterday afternoon, to get her up after her delayed rest, she seemed frightened. It took you five or ten minutes to coax her out of her room, you said . . ."

Marilyn nodded. "That's right."

"Have you by any chance talked to her about this, asked her just what she was afraid of?"

"No. I told you, at the time I simply assumed she was frightened of another scene with Mrs. Tarrant. And it's usually pretty pointless to try to discuss any recent event with Lavinia. She often can't remember things from one moment to the next."

Not very promising, thought Thanet, though scarcely unexpected.

"You said, 'often.' Sometimes she does remember?"

"Sometimes, yes."

"So it might be worth a try?"

Marilyn gave a little shrug. "Try, by all means. Her memory is so unpredictable that you can never tell... Her long-term memory is quite good, of course. But her short-term memory is hopeless. You can have virtually the same conversation with her over and over again within the space of minutes. And then sometimes you think to yourself, 'She'll never remember that,' and she astonishes you by having total recall. You'll see what I mean, when you talk to her."

"How do you think she would react, if I tried to discuss it with her?"

"It really is impossible to tell, in advance."

"I was wondering... Would it be kinder, d'you think, if you were to question her about it?"

"Perhaps. I could try, if you like."

"Thank you. It might not be necessary, of course. Perhaps I'll be able to do it. I'll have to play it by ear. In any case, I'd like to have a general chat with her first, and I'd like you to be present."

"Of course." She turned away, evidently under the impression that the interview was over.

"Er... There are just one or two other small points, Miss Barnes..."

She turned back with a little sigh. "Yes?"

"I wanted to ask you... You were here at lunchtime, yesterday?"

"Yes, I was."

Had he imagined the wariness in her tone? "Did you happen to see Mr. Tarrant? He tells us he came home briefly at lunchtime, to fetch some papers he'd forgotten..."

This time there was a definite hesitation. "Yes... Yes, I did see him. I didn't speak to him, though."

"This was at what time?"

"Soon after half past twelve, I think. Yes, it must have been."

"And where was this?"

"Where...?"

Was she prevaricating in order to give herself time to think? Thanet wondered.

"Where was he, when you saw him?"

"In . . . In the corridor, outside Mrs. Tarrant's bedroom." A faint flush was creeping up her neck and into her cheeks.

Could her reluctance be simply due to embarrassment, that she had caught Tarrant listening outside his wife's door when she, Marilyn, knew that Nerine had been entertaining her lover?

"Did he go in?"

She shook her head. "I saw him try the door handle, then he hurried away downstairs." She avoided Thanet's eye. "I assumed the door was locked and he decided she wasn't in there," she murmured.

Marilyn Barnes was a very poor liar, thought Thanet.

"Miss Barnes, I do understand your commendable sense of loyalty to your employer, but I assure you that there's no point in trying to cover up Mrs. Tarrant's . . . unfortunate behaviour. We know that Mr. Speed was her lover, Mr. Tarrant himself told us so, and he also told us that he didn't enter his wife's room at that point because he realised that Mr. Speed was in there with her."

She was nodding slowly, as if relieved that the burden of decision had been taken from her.

"So I wanted to ask you: Did you, yourself, see Mr. Speed in the house at lunchtime yesterday?"

"No."

In that case, why the hesitation, earlier? And had he imagined the gleam of relief in her eyes, just then? Yet the monosyllable had been unequivocal and to Thanet's ear had the ring of truth about it. He decided to leave it, for the moment.

"I also wanted to ask you . . . Having thought over the events of yesterday, as I'm sure you have, can you recall anything else that you think might be of the slightest interest to us?"

She gave a quick, tight shake of the head and avoided his eyes again.

Yes, there definitely was something . . . Something to do with Roland Tarrant?

But the stubborn set of her lips told him that, whatever it was, she wasn't going to tell, at the moment anyway.

It was time to move on to old Mrs. Tarrant.

Marilyn led them along the corridor to the next room and entered without knocking.

"I've brought you some visitors, Lavinia. Some gentlemen. You met them yesterday, remember?"

The room was cluttered with furniture, pictures and ornaments and there were photographs scattered about on every available surface. Thanet guessed that when Nerine moved in as mistress of the house and began to redecorate to her own taste, old Mrs. Tarrant had gradually accumulated in her own quarters those things which were of special sentimental value to her. She was sitting in a wing chair in the sunshine, gazing out of the window.

"Hullo, dear. Visitors, how nice." She smiled without recognition at Thanet and Lineham, put her hands on the arms of the chair and began to lever herself up.

Thanet smiled back. "Please, don't get up."

He would scarcely have recognised her as the extraordinary vision he and Lineham had seen on the stairs yesterday. She was still wearing make-up but it was discreet and carefully applied, probably by Marilyn, Thanet thought. Her clothes were sober, a navy linen dress and thick while cardigan, sensible flat-heeled navy sandals. Her faded blue eyes betrayed uncertainty. "I'm sorry, I don't remember . . ."

Thanet shook his head. "It doesn't matter."

She waved a gracious hand. "Do sit down."

They complied, Marilyn perching on a low stool beside her employer, Thanet choosing an armchair and Lineham a more upright one a little further away.

Marilyn put an affectionate hand on Mrs. Tarrant's arm. "Inspector Thanet is a policeman, Lavinia. He is trying to find out about the . . . accident."

"Accident?"

"To Nerine."

"Has Nerine had an accident?"

Marilyn glanced at Thanet. *You see what I mean?*

"Lavinia," said Marilyn patiently. "I told you. Yesterday. She fell from her balcony and . . . and died."

"Died?" The old lady stared at Marilyn. "Nerine is dead?"

Marilyn nodded.

How many more times, Thanet wondered, would she have to break the news to the old lady? Senility was a terrible disease. In this particular case it didn't matter so much. By all accounts there had been no love lost between old Mrs. Tarrant and her daughter-in-law. But what must it be like when it is the news of the death of a much-loved husband, wife, son or daughter that has to be broken over and over again, when the shock of hearing it must be suffered not once but many times by someone already enfeebled by age and illness?

"I did tell you," said Marilyn.

Mrs. Tarrant shook her head. "I don't remember." She sighed, and glanced at Thanet. "My memory isn't very good these days, I'm afraid..."

She was silent for a few moments and then she said, "But I can't pretend I'm sorry—that's she's dead, I mean." She leaned forward and said conspiratorially, "She was trying to get rid of me, you know." She glanced at Marilyn for confirmation. "Wasn't she, dear?" One claw-like hand clutched at Marilyn's for reassurance. "She wanted me to sign some papers, so she could put me in a home. But Roland wouldn't let her. My son."

Automatically she reached for a photograph which stood to hand on a small table beside her chair. She glanced at it before handing it to Thanet. "That's him," she said proudly, "with Damon, my grandson, on his first birthday."

The snapshot had been taken in the garden. Tarrant was squatting in a patch of sunshine under the trees on a carpet of autumn leaves, both hands supporting the baby standing with splayed legs in front of him.

"Damon took his first step that day," said the old lady reminiscently. "Roland was so proud." Her face darkened. "He's a good boy and deserves better than that wife of his." She glanced at Marilyn, a curiously arch, knowing smile. "Doesn't he, dear?"

So the old lady either knew of Marilyn's feelings for Tarrant or at least suspected them, thought Thanet.

Marilyn was attempting to cover up. She patted the old lady's hand and said quickly, "The Inspector is trying to find out how the accident happened, Lavinia."

"Accident?"

"To Nerine." Marilyn glanced at Thanet again. *Now you really must see what I mean*. With commendable patience she explained it all again. Mrs. Tarrant listened with an almost child-like air of trust, then sighed. "It's so frustrating, when you can't remember things... So Nerine is dead..."

Again she was silent for a few moments and Thanet was waiting for the conversation to follow the same track as before when she nonplussed him by impaling him with a sharp, knowing look and saying, "Are you sure it was an accident, Inspector? Knowing Nerine, it wouldn't surprise me in the least if someone helped her on her way."

Marilyn was looking amused and rather proud, like a parent whose offspring unexpectedly walks off with a prize at speechday.

"That's what we're trying to find out," said Thanet. "And we wanted to ask you. Did you by any chance see anyone in the house, yesterday afternoon?"

Mrs. Tarrant stared at him, her eyes opaque with—what? Thanet wondered. Concentration? Indecision? Briefly, so briefly that Thanet wondered if he had imagined it, they darkened as if a shadow had passed across them. She shook her head. "I'm sorry, I can't recall . . ."

"What about your daughter-in-law? Did you see her at all, yesterday afternoon?"

The old lady shook her head. "No, I don't think so." She turned to Marilyn. "Did I, dear?"

Thanet and Lineham exchanged glances. *She doesn't even remember the row in the bedroom.*

Marilyn gave Thanet a questioning look.

He nodded. *Go ahead.*

"You don't remember the . . . argument with Nerine, early in the afternoon, Lavinia?"

"No. No, I don't." Mrs. Tarrant cast at Thanet a look composed of a curious mixture of guilt, embarrassment and glee. Then she leaned towards Marilyn and said a near-whisper, "Was it because . . . ?"

Marilyn nodded. "I'm afraid so."

Mrs. Tarrant's hand went to her mouth, the gesture of a naughty child caught in some trivial misdemeanour. "Oh dear. Was she cross?" It was obvious that she was hoping the answer would be "Yes".

Marilyn's nod was emphatic, her tone full of reproof. "Very cross, Lavinia." She hesitated, then said, "That's why I wondered if you'd seen her again, later. When I went to get you up after your rest you seemed rather . . . upset."

"Did I?" Mrs. Tarrant stared at Marilyn as if she held the key to her locked-up memories. She shook her head helplessly. "I don't remember."

This was pointless, Thanet decided, a waste of time.

"Never mind," he said gently. "It really doesn't matter."

Not true, but still... "Perhaps, if you do remember something, Miss Barnes would be kind enough to let me know?"

Marilyn nodded. "Of course."

Mrs. Tarrant seemed to have lost interest in the conversation. She was leaning forward, gazing down out of the window. Something had obviously attracted her attention.

Curiosity brought Thanet to his feet. This room must be at the back of the house. It overlooked the converted coach house and the garages. A woman wearing a blue skirt and white sweater was walking aimlessly away across the drive towards the left-hand corner of the house, head down, hands clasped behind her back.

"Is that Miss Linacre?" he said to Marilyn.

"Yes. It looks as though she's feeling a bit better today."

Well enough to be interviewed, Thanet hoped.

He turned back to the old lady. "Well, thank you, Mrs. Tarrant. You've been very helpful."

She gave a gratified smile. "Have I? Good. Do call again, won't you? It's lovely to have visitors. Oh..." She glanced at Marilyn. "What am I thinking of? We haven't offered our guests any refreshment, dear. Could you arrange some coffee for us?"

"I'm afraid we have to go now, Mrs. Tarrant," said Thanet. "Next time, perhaps?"

She beamed. "Next time, yes. I shall look forward to that. Marilyn, see the gentlemen out, would you?"

"No, it's all right, thank you, we know the way."

Outside Lineham said, "Whew, stuffy in there, wasn't it!"

Thanet agreed. "Let's go and get a breath of fresh air."

At the front door he paused to light his pipe and exchange a few words with the constable on duty before making for the terrace where Nerine's body had been found.

"Is that the path you were talking about yesterday?"

Beyond the terrace was a rectangular lawn, enclosed on three sides by tall, well-clipped yew hedges. The path, which was of crazy paving, ran along the base of the left-hand hedge and disappeared through a gap at the corner.

"Yes. That report said that Speed's car was parked at the entrance to a field just around the bend from High Gables, didn't it? He could easily have got into the house through the garden and no one would have been any the wiser."

"Is there a gardener?"

Lineham grimaced. "Yes, but unfortunately he wasn't here yesterday. He doesn't come in on Thursdays."

"Pity. Let's take a look, shall we?"

They set off along the path. After a few paces Lineham said, "I think I'd rather be dead than senile."

"Wouldn't we all."

"I still think it's possible that the old lady might have shoved her daughter-in-law off that balcony, even if she has forgotten all about it. You must admit it's obvious there was no love lost between them. I got the impression she enjoyed messing up Mrs. Tarrant's bedroom, just to spite her. If so, Mrs. Tarrant could have sensed that it was deliberate, and that would have made her even more mad. Though the old lady certainly hasn't lost all her marbles, has she, sir? Once or twice she seemed pretty sharp. I was wondering... Did you notice that look she gave Miss Barnes, when she was talking about Mrs. Tarrant being an unsuitable wife for her son?"

"Ah, you spotted that too. Yes, I did."

"Well, it's obvious that she's fond of Marilyn Barnes. Apart from being afraid that her daughter-in-law might persuade Mr. Tarrant to get rid of Marilyn, don't you think it's possible she might also have thought that with Mrs. Tarrant out of the way Mr. Tarrant might marry Marilyn? I should think she'd be delighted at the prospect. And if so, it would certainly strengthen her motive for getting rid of Mrs. Tarrant, wouldn't it?"

"True." Much as he disliked the idea, Thanet was forced to acknowledge its plausibility.

"D'you think there might be something going on between Mr. Tarrant and Miss Barnes, sir?"

Thanet shrugged. "Who knows?"

"If he is in love with her, it would give him an even stronger motive, wouldn't it? Because he can swear black and blue that he didn't care about his wife's lovers, but I find it impossible to believe he could go on year after year and never want to do anything about it."

"I'm not sure I agree with you there, Mike. I think I'm prepared to give him the benefit of the doubt, for the moment, anyway."

Lineham looked sceptical, but didn't argue. "But as far as Miss Barnes is concerned... If she is in love with him, it gives her an additional motive too, doesn't it? If she was in danger of losing her job, I mean..." Lineham caught Thanet's

eye and, obviously recalling his own attitude the last time
they had discussed this particular possibility, gave a slightly
embarrassed grin. "I still don't like the idea that she could
have done it, I must admit. I'm just trying to keep the open
mind you're always on about."

"Just as well at this stage. There's certainly no shortage of
suspects."

Thanet stopped walking. They had reached the corner of
the yew hedge and he stood gazing about. Here the crazy
paving gave way to gravel and the path divided. To the left it
started to curve away between densely packed beds of tall
shrubs towards the edge of the garden; to the right it ran
along the back of the hedge and disappeared in the direction
of the front gate. Thanet supposed that in a garden of this size
it was necessary to have a whole network of paths; there
would be a great deal of wheeling about of rubbish, tools,
fertilisers and so on.

They took the left fork, ducking and side-stepping occasionally to avoid stray branches of philadelphus and shrub
rose, viburnum and holly. Fifty yards or so further on the
gravel became beaten earth, the shrub borders ended and a
narrow belt of silver birch and Scots Pine began, stretching
away to right and left and creating, Thanet imagined, a
windbreak around the entire garden. Beyond the trees was a
tall, close-boarded boundary fence and here again the path
divided, running along the base of the fence in both direc-
tions and presumably providing, at intervals, access to different areas of the garden.

They paused.

"I imagine that the field where Speed parked his car is on
the other side of this fence," said Lineham. "There must be a
gate somewhere."

They followed the path to the right first, but the fence
continued in an unbroken line as far as the hedge which
bordered the road. Retracing their steps to the point at which
they had emerged they walked on in the opposite direction.

"There it is!" said Lineham triumphantly.

The gate was almost invisible until they were upon it,
being constructed of the same close-boarding as the fence.
There was no lock, only a latch.

"You'd think they'd take a bit more care over security,"
grumbled Lineham as he opened it.

Thanet was not surprised to find a footpath on the other

side. It was obvious that long before High Gables had been built on its little projecting spit of land, people from the village would have established a right-of-way across this short cut behind it. A couple of minutes' walk confirmed that after leaving the boundary fence the footpath cut across a field to the gateway in which Speed must have parked his car. Over to the right a country hedge of hawthorn, dogwood, field maple and wild rose delineated the sharp bend in the road.

"No problem, then," said Lineham. "He had a nice little private route to the house, whenever he wanted to visit her. When are we going to talk to him again?"

"All in good time," said Thanet. "I want to read a full report from the witness who saw him park, first." He turned and began to walk back in the direction of the gate, hands in pockets, head down, shoulders hunched. Lineham, recognising the signs, followed in silence.

Just before they reached the gate Lineham hesitated, then reached out to pluck at Thanet's sleeve.

"Sir," he whispered.

Thanet turned, still abstracted. "What?"

Lineham nodded in the direction of the village.

Approaching them along the footpath was the woman they had seen earlier from old Mrs. Tarrant's window.

They were at last about to meet the elusive Daphne.

ELEVEN

At the sight of the two men Daphne Linacre's step had faltered.

Scarcely surprising, thought Thanet. The soaring statistics of rape, muggings and crime in general had resulted in fifty per cent of the female population being afraid to go out alone at night. And here, on a deserted country footpath...

He stepped forward boldly and raised a hand in greeting.

"Good morning, Miss Linacre," he called. "Detective-Inspector Thanet, Sturrenden CID. I hope we didn't startle you."

She had stopped when he first spoke. Now she started walking again. Thanet had already noticed that despite the dense shade along the footpath she was wearing sunglasses, and he cursed the migraine which had presumably made them necessary. He hated talking to people without being able to see their eyes. More than any other feature, eyes reveal what their owner is feeling.

Close to, he could see that Daphne Linacre's clothes were expensive, the blue linen skirt elegantly cut, the white cotton sweater handknitted in an intricate design. Unfortunately their owner's body did not match up to them. It was as if nature had used up all her skill, all her art, in creating the physical perfection that had been Nerine. Daphne was too stocky, her waist too thick, her breasts too flat, her hips too lumpy. But there was plenty of character in her face: determined jaw, firm mouth, and a resolute tilt to the head which went some way towards explaining why she had become such a successful businesswoman.

"Not at all." She patted a bulge in her skirt pocket. "I was out of cigarettes. And, to be honest, I wanted an excuse to get out of the house for a while. I loathe being cooped up with nothing to do."

Thanet admired her honesty. He knew that death imposes a strait-jacket of conventions and inactivity on those who are left behind. An unspoken conspiracy, born of love and desire to alleviate the burden of grief, frequently exists to prevent the bereaved from performing even the simplest task, like making a cup of tea. Many people, of course, both enjoy and appreciate such attention, but some find the strain well-nigh intolerable. Few, however, can bring themselves openly to admit it.

"I'm glad to see that you're feeling better today. Mrs. Haywood told us about your migraine attack. Oh, sorry. This is Detective-Sergeant Lineham."

She nodded a greeting at Lineham and said, "Much better, thank God. Sometimes I'm laid up for days."

"We were on our way back to the house . . . Do you feel up to answering a few questions?"

"Yes, of course."

Thanet opened the gate and stood back for her to precede him. She turned right, followed the path along the fence for a short distance and then cut off to the left. Thanet and Lineham walked behind her in single file and they all emerged eventually onto the drive, opposite the north side of the main house and about seventy-five yards from the coach house.

Beatrix Haywood was crossing the open space between the two houses, carrying a large cardboard box overflowing with clothes. They all converged at the coach-house door.

Lineham took the box from her.

"Thanks," she said, puffing slightly. Her cheeks were pink and there was a sheen of perspiration on her forehead. Today she was wearing a shapeless dress made out of what looked like sacking, several strings of multicoloured beads and long, dangling earrings. "It's surprisingly heavy. More jumble," she added as she let them in. "Just put it with the rest of the stuff, will you? The vicar's supposed to be picking it up before lunch."

There were three more boxes lined up in the hallway.

"You'll take some coffee, Inspector?" said Daphne. "I could do with a cup myself."

"That would be very welcome, thank you."

Without a word Mrs. Haywood disappeared into the kitchen. Mr. Tarrant may have thought that it was rash of Daphne to offer a home to her dead fiancé's mother, thought Thanet, but he suspected that Daphne had known what she was doing. Good domestic help is like gold dust these days: expensive and difficult to find. A devoted, unpaid housekeeper is a prize indeed.

Daphne led the two men into the sitting room and they all sat down. The paintings on the walls appealed to Thanet even less this morning, their only distinction being that so many of them hung in one room. He wondered how Jocelyn Haywood had managed to secure the commission for the Linacre Nursery catalogue in the first place.

"Now, how can I help you?" she said.

"It's fairly simple, really," said Thanet. "We're trying to build up a picture of everyone's movements yesterday afternoon. There are just a few routine questions we'd like to put to you." He glanced at Lineham. *Take over.*

It didn't take long for Daphne to confirm what Mrs. Haywood had told them. She had gone to work in the morning as usual and during the afternoon had begun to feel unwell. By four o'clock she knew she was starting a migraine attack and had decided to go home. She had finished up one or two urgent tasks before leaving the nursery at around twenty past four, and had arrived home at about twenty to five.

"When I got here I went straight to bed."

Mrs. Haywood came in with a tray. Only three cups, Thanet noticed.

Daphne smiled up at her as Mrs. Haywood handed her the coffee. "Thank you, Beatrix." She patted Mrs. Haywood's hand and said, "Of course, Beatrix is wonderful when I have one of my attacks. I don't know what I'd do without her."

Mrs. Haywood gave a gratified smile.

"Beatrix, you've only brought three cups," said Daphne. "Aren't you having any?"

"I . . ."

"I know, you've already had one," said Daphne with a little smile. "But I'm sure you could do with another."

"I won't be long," said Beatrix in a stifled voice. She hurried out.

Thanet had watched this little exchange with interest. What, exactly, did it signify? Was Daphne perhaps ashamed to see Mrs. Haywood behaving like a servant and apparently expecting to be treated as one, in front of outsiders? Or was this self-confident, capable woman more vulnerable than she looked, and in need of moral support?

"Did you see anyone about, when you arrived home?" asked Lineham.

Daphne frowned, then shook her head. "No. And even if I had, I don't suppose it would have registered. At that stage all I could think of was lying down in a cool, dark room."

"What about later on?"

She shook her head. "Sorry, no. I can see you're not a migraine sufferer, Sergeant. If you were you'd know that during an attack you're pretty well deaf and blind to anything else."

"So when did you hear of your sister's death?" said Thanet.

Mrs. Haywood came back into the room with a cup of coffee and sat down on an upright chair near Lineham, glancing apprehensively at his notebook.

Daphne grimaced. "Some time during the evening. I've no idea when, exactly. I think Beatrix would have preferred to wait to tell me until the worst of the attack was over, wouldn't you, Bea? But during one of my sorties to the bathroom I happened to glance out of the window and see that the place was crawling with police, so..."

"Sorry to interrupt," said Lineham, "but I thought you said that at that stage you were virtually deaf and blind..."

"Aha," said Daphne theatrically. "Ze vitness contradicts herself." Then, in her normal voice, "Sorry to disappoint you, Sergeant, but I think you will have to agree that it's one thing to register that your garden is overrun with police, another to notice a given individual at a given time..." She waited for Lineham's nod before saying, "Anyway, at that point I naturally asked her what was going on. So... so she told me."

Suddenly there was a tremor in her voice, a huskiness in her throat. It was the first hint of grief she had displayed.

If only he could see her eyes, thought Thanet.

"You were fond of your sister, Miss Linacre?" he said. He could see himself reflected in her dark glasses, a distorted little mannikin with bulging eyes in an elongated pale oval of a face.

Daphne shrugged. "She was my sister, the only blood relation I had left." The moment of weakness had passed and she was in control of herself again. She glanced at Mrs. Haywood. "Beatrix told me of your suspicion that Nerine's death was no accident, and frankly, the idea wasn't too much of a shock. To put it bluntly, the way she carried on, she was asking for it."

"You think one of her lovers, past or present, was responsible?"

Daphne shrugged. "It would seem to be the obvious answer, wouldn't you agree? *Crime passionnel* and all that."

"Did you have anyone special in mind?"

"Not really, no. But I'm sure you won't have to look far."

"Perhaps you could help us out with some names?"

"Sorry, no. I'm afraid my sister's grubby little affairs had no interest for me." She brushed an imaginary piece of fluff off her skirt, as if trying to erase the memory of Nerine's never-ending string of lovers.

"You do realise, Miss Linacre, that most crimes of this nature are carried out by a member of the family?"

"I have a great respect for statistics, Inspector, but they can be misleading. If that is an indirect way of asking if I suspect Roland of having done it, or Damon, even, then you're barking up the wrong tree. And as for myself..." Daphne shrugged. "Well, I can't pretend Nerine and I were bosom pals, because we weren't, but all I can say is, I really cannot see why I should suddenly decide to shove her off her balcony for no apparent reason. After all, if there had been bad blood between us I'd never have come to live here in the first place. It wasn't as though I was hard up; I could have bought a house anywhere I liked."

This was unanswerable.

"You'll make up your own minds, of course, but let me tell you this..." Daphne leaned forward, the huskiness back in her voice. "My mother died when I was born. Nerine was only three, but I can still remember... She was mother and sister to me, all through my childhood. She looked after me, watched over me, and I adored her. I'd have done anything for her. Anything." She glanced away, out of the window, as if looking into the past and seeking to recapture the intensity of that passionate childhood devotion. Then she sighed, shrugged.

"Things changed, of course, as we grew up. Our interests, our tastes were so different...And I can't pretend to have approved of the way she played around with men..."

Briefly, there was an ugly, bitter twist to Daphne's mouth. Inspired, perhaps, by jealousy, thought Thanet, the jealousy of a plain spinster unfortunate enough to have lost her one and only suitor by a cruel twist of fate, for a beautiful older sister who all her life had had only to crook her little finger for men to come running after her?

Daphne shrugged again. "But there we are. That was her affair and didn't affect me in the slightest. I had my own life to live. I enjoy my work, get a lot of satisfaction out of it, and Bea and I get along like a house on fire, don't we, Bea?"

Mrs. Haywood gave a quick, nervous smile and cleared her throat. "Oh, yes, we *do*," she said.

"So I'm sorry, Inspector," said Daphne. "I'm afraid you'll have to look elsewhere for your murderer—if there is one."

"You have no further suggestions to make?"

"Only the advice I gave you earlier. *Cherchez l'homme.*"

At the door Thanet hesitated. "You mentioned Damon just now... He hasn't turned up yet and I was wondering... Have you any idea where he's gone?"

Daphne shook her head. "Sorry, no... You mean, he hasn't even rung Roland, to say when he'll be back?"

"Not so far."

"Oh. Oh, dear." For the first time her composure was shaken, and she glanced at Beatrix Haywood, who had moved up to stand close behind her. "That's not like him. I hope he's all right... My God, it's only just occurred to me... You mean, he doesn't even know his mother's dead yet?"

"It looks that way," said Thanet.

"Poor boy," said Beatrix. Her lips were trembling and she put her hand up to her mouth.

"With any luck he'll turn up soon," said Thanet, hating the note of false reassurance in his voice. "But I thought I ought to warn you—if he's not back by late afternoon, we might have to put out an appeal, on TVS. Anyway, if either of you comes up with an idea as to where he might be, let me know, will you?"

"Of course."

Outside, Lineham said, "Not much sisterly devotion there now, is there, whatever she says about the past."

"True. But lack of love is different from positive hatred.

She made a good point, I thought, when she said she wouldn't have come to live in the coach house if there'd been ill feeling between them. And it's difficult to see why, after all these years, she should suddenly decide to come home from work in the middle of the afternoon and shove her sister off a balcony."

"She'd be capable of it, though, don't you think?"

"If she had a strong enough motive, yes. But there's been no hint of any quarrels between them. They seemed to lead such separate lives, I can't really see what could have been such a burning issue between them."

"What now, sir?"

"Mmm?" Thanet was abstracted. He had just thought of someone else he would like to interview, but he wasn't going to mention it to Lineham yet, not until he'd mulled the idea over for a little while longer. But it could prove very interesting.

He smiled with satisfaction. Yes, very interesting indeed.

ahead, just as a woman, tired after an exhausting day, savours the prospect of a leisurely hot bath. It was, quite simply, his reward for duty done, a self-indulgence justified only by the merest thread of necessity.

Lineham had thought it a waste of time.

"What's the point of going to see her? It's years since she set eyes on any of them."

But Thanet couldn't resist the idea. Who could give him a better insight into the dead woman than the housekeeper who had virtually brought her up?

And here he was. He pulled into the parking area and switched off the engine.

Thanet was aware that sheltered housing for the elderly, both private and council-funded, is the biggest "growth area" in new building these days. By the end of the century the population of Great Britain will be heavily weighted in favour of the over-sixties, and Thanet sometimes wondered if the younger generation would be able to carry the crippling burden ahead. The Government was doing its best. Traditional nursing homes were out, community care and other schemes which enable pensioners to maintain their independence to the last were in.

Rainbow Court was typical of the latter.

Only a few minutes' walk from the centre of Sturrenden with all its amenities, old people could continue to shop, enjoy their chosen entertainment and generally live a full and independent life (health allowing) long after they could no longer afford expensive public transport or bear the expense of running a car. Four blocks of clearly numbered low-rise flats, one no doubt occupied by a warden, were grouped around a paved courtyard attractively furnished with wooden benches, tubs of bedding plants and a central, raised rose-bed full of pink floribundas in bloom.

Ignoring the lift, Thanet climbed the stairs to Flat 15 on the third floor.

The door was wide open.

"Is that you, Ellie?" called a cheerful voice as he approached. "I've just finished it. Come and see. Oh," a different inflection as the woman realised her mistake. "Sorry, I was expecting someone else."

Thanet had recognised her at once. The transition from middle-age to old-age does not bring about nearly such a radical transformation as youth to middle-age. She must,

Thanet had worked out, be in her eighties by now but the years had treated her well. She was neither shrunken nor obese, and although the wrinkles on her face had multiplied and the brown hair gone grey, her carriage was still upright, her eyes alert and intelligent. She was wearing a long-sleeved floral cotton shirt-dress and a white apron. A vivid memory of the pathetic, confused figure of Lavinia Tarrant flashed through Thanet's mind and he understood why Beatrix Haywood found the thought of this woman so reassuring.

"Mrs. Glass?" He paused on the threshold, took out his ID card and introduced himself.

Her welcoming smile faded. "Oh."

She took the card and compared the photograph with the reality before taking off her apron and saying, "You'd better come in. It's about Nerine, I suppose."

"I'm afraid so."

"I heard about it on the wireless."

She moved aside and he stepped into the small, comfortably furnished room, his attention at once drawn to a round table near the window. On it were displayed all three tiers of a beautifully decorated wedding cake, the smallest tier still on a revolving icing stand, familiar to Thanet from Bridget's attempt at decorative icing. The sheet carefully spread beneath the table to protect the carpet, the bowls with their tell-tale traces of icing, the clutter of icing nozzles and piping bags all told the same story.

Thanet pursed his lips in admiration and moved to take a closer look. The top tier was edged with alternating miniature footballs and bunches of flowers.

"You did this?"

Mrs. Glass nodded, with justifiable pride. "I like to keep my hand in."

"It's magnificent! A work of art."

"It's for the granddaughter of a friend of mine. She's getting married on Saturday." She grinned. "As you may have gathered, she's a florist and he's a footballer. I work in here because I like to have a bit of elbow room when I'm icing, and my kitchen's so tiny I fall over my own feet if I'm not careful. Though I mustn't grumble. This place suits me perfectly."

"I've never been in one of these sheltered housing flats before."

Clearly anxious to delay discussion of Nerine's death, Mrs.

Glass seized on this as an excuse to show him around, and Thanet was given a guided tour of the only bedroom, the minute kitchen and even smaller bathroom. Every room had an alarm cord which would summon help in case of emergency, and the warden apparently did a quick round of her protégés night and morning to check that they were all right.

"At my age, you can't imagine the sense of security that gives you."

By now they were sitting down, the atmosphere was relaxed and Mrs. Glass was chatting freely.

"Have you always lived in this area?"

Gently, Thanet led the old lady through the years, from her impoverished childhood ("I always longed to be educated, these days I'd have gone to university") and her entry into domestic service at the age of fourteen, past early marriage and widowhood in the 1914–18 war to her eventual appointment in 1944 as housekeeper to the Linacres.

At this point her eyes grew troubled, her manner hesitant. I only he could help her to keep up the flow of reminiscence, thought Thanet . . .

"You never remarried?" he asked, striking off obliquely.

"No. I got used to being independent . . . Look, Inspector, I've enjoyed our chat and it's helped me to relax. I appreciate your taking the trouble, a lot of men wouldn't have bothered, I'm sure, they'd just have barged in, asked their questions and been off . . . I'm just trying to say that if you want me to talk about Nerine, I'm ready now." And she gave an apprehensive smile.

Thanet was touched. It was a declaration of faith, after all. *I trust you not to upset me too much*.

"Thank you," he said gently. "I appreciate your frankness."

Her smile was a little bolder now. "To be honest, I can't really see why you want to talk to me at all. It's so many years since I saw Nerine. Daphne visits me once a month, though, regular as clockwork."

"Does she?" Thanet was surprised, he wasn't sure why. Mrs. Glass, after all, would have been Daphne's mother-substitute.

"I understand they were very close, as children."

Mrs. Glass's eyes glazed reminiscently. "They certainly were. Inseparable. Nerine had adored her mother, you see, and Mrs. Linacre used to make such a fuss of her . . . So did her father, for that matter, but then he would have done anything to please Mrs. Linacre and later on, after Mrs. Linacre died, I did wonder whether he'd only been pretending affection for Nerine to please his wife."

"You mean, after his wife's death he took no interest in Nerine?"

"That's right. No interest in either of them, for that matter. In fact, he couldn't bear the sight of Daphne, blamed her for her mother's death, I think. He'd worshipped Mrs. Linacre and it hit him hard."

"How did Nerine react?"

Mrs. Glass grimaced. "It was pathetic, really. To begin with, she used to follow him around like a little dog, but he just couldn't be bothered with her and eventually she got the message. She went through a very bad time—well, you can imagine how she must have felt, losing her mother and, to all intents and purposes, her father, both at once. Poor little scrap, I was really worried about her for some time. I could scarcely get her to eat anything, or take any interest in anything—she just used to lie around on the floor, sucking her thumb and gazing into space . . ."

"She was lucky to have you. At least there was some continuity in her life."

"I suppose so. The trouble was, I had that big house to run and I couldn't really give her the time and attention she needed . . . Mr. Linacre got a nanny for the baby, of course, but babies need a lot of care and Nerine tended to miss out there, too. And I don't think the girl really understood what the child was going through. She was good-hearted but not very bright . . . Anyway, after a while Nerine turned her attention to Daphne, and soon you couldn't have prised them apart with a shoe-horn. Nerine used to spend all her time with her, played with her, pushed her about in her pram, created a terrible fuss if ever they were separated . . .

"I remember when she started school. When the day came, she couldn't believe that Daphne wasn't to be allowed to go with her. The scene she created! I honestly thought she was going to scream herself into some kind of fit! We had to call the doctor, to give her a sedative. And every morning it was the same, until in the end her father got really fed up and said it was nothing short of emotional blackmail and if she carried on like this he'd jolly well send her away to boarding school and she wouldn't see Daphne at all . . . Well, that did the trick and she gave in. But I'll never forget her little face looking back over her shoulder at Daphne as she left for school each morning. She looked so lost and bewildered, as if she simply couldn't understand why she had to be sent away. I honestly think she thought she was being punished for something, and couldn't understand what."

"Didn't the situation improve when Daphne started school?"

"Well, to some extent, of course. But Nerine always hated school, never did a stroke of work. Daphne was a very different matter. She absolutely loved it, took to it like a duck to water—well, I think she was bored and lonely after Nerine started, and couldn't wait to get there."

"So how do you think this experience affected Nerine, in the long term?"

Mrs. Glass paused, eyes narrowed, thinking. Then she sighed. "I think it made her very self-centred. As if the only thing that mattered was to look after number one. And yet, it wasn't her fault, you see. She didn't start out like that. Before Daphne was born she was the sweetest, sunniest little girl you could imagine. It was such a shame. Oh dear. I hate talking about her like this, when . . . I mean, she's not here to defend herself any more, is she?"

"I know. Will it make you feel any better if I say that all this is invaluable to me? In order to find out why she died I really need to understand her, as a person . . ."

"Is it true, what they're saying? That she might have . . . That it was . . ."

"That someone might have killed her, you mean? I'm afraid it's all too likely. Everyone seems to agree that she was the last person to commit suicide, and from what you've just been saying . . ."

"Oh, I agree," Mrs. Glass broke in vehemently. "Nerine would never have killed herself. Never."

"And it's very difficult to see how it could have been an accident. She fell from a balcony, you see, and the rail was too high . . . We haven't entirely ruled out the possibility, but . . ."

Mrs. Glass was nodding. "I see. Oh dear. But I suppose . . ."

"What?"

"Well . . ." She was speaking slowly, working it out. "I was just thinking that Nerine's problem was that she was so . . . engrossed with herself that she was incapable of taking thought for anyone else's feelings, or even beginning to understand them. She didn't want to understand them. She

was so... insensitive, that way. I remember when she and
Daphne were in their teens... Nerine was a beautiful girl,
quite exceptionally so, whereas Daphne... Well, I suppose
you've seen her, haven't you? I'm fond of Daphne, but she's
no oil painting, is she? Nerine used to have hordes of
boyfriends, they used to fall over each other trying to get her
to go out with them, whereas Daphne was always ignored,
passed over, as if she was invisible or something. And Nerine
never seemed to realise how Daphne must have felt about it.
I honestly don't think it ever entered her head to wonder."

"How did Daphne react?"

Mrs. Glass shrugged. "She just seemed to accept it. But I
couldn't help feeling sorry for her, especially when her fiancé
was killed in that car crash. A real tragedy that was. He was
the first man ever to take an interest in her, and she was on
cloud nine from the day they started going out together."

"What happened?"

"Oh, it was awful. Terrible. Even now, after all these years,
it upsets me to think about it."

She wasn't exaggerating. The memory had clouded her
eyes, sharpened the lines in her face. Absentmindedly, she
took a handkerchief from the pocket of her dress and began to
pick at one corner, tiny, suppressed, agitated movements
which mirrored only too clearly both her distress and the
struggle to control it.

Thanet said nothing, waited.

"Daphne met him at work. He'd been commissioned to do
a cover for the Spring Catalogue. He was an artist... She
kept very quiet about him, but I knew something was up.
She was... transformed. Radiant." Her eyes flickered towards
the wedding cake. "Like a bride." She pulled a face. "I don't
think either Nerine or her father ever even noticed. Anyway,
a couple of months later they got engaged. There was a
terrible row, when she told her father. I was there. She
guessed there'd be trouble and she asked me to be with her,
for moral support. I'd been with them twenty-five years by
then, and I suppose she thought of me as family. He was
furious. Called Jocelyn a jumped-up little fortune hunter.
Daphne was so angry... I'd never seen her really stand up to
her father before, but she certainly did then. I think, by that
stage, they'd both forgotten I was there.

*To be honest with you, Father, I don't care what you think.
You've never taken the slightest interest in my welfare, and I*

have no intention of allowing you to influence such an important decision.'

'Never taken the slightest interest in your welfare! I've fed you, haven't I? Clothed you, educated you . . .'

'Loved me? Ah, I see you can't answer that one. Oh, I grant that you have maintained me, materially speaking, because it was the done thing to do. But Jocelyn is the first person in my life ever to love me for myself, and nothing, I repeat nothing, will make me give him up.'

'Love you for yourself? Daphne, I don't want to be unkind, but didn't you say he was an artist? And therefore a lover of beauty? I hate to say this, but I think you only have to look in the mirror to see that you must be deluding yourself.'

'I won't listen to this! I told you, Father, I don't care what you think and I don't care what you say. I'm going to marry him and that's that.'

'He can smell money, that's the trouble. Perhaps he wouldn't be so interested if he didn't think you'd get the business when I'm gone.'

'Father, you are fifty-two years old and in perfect health . . .'

'Now, maybe. But looking to the future . . .'

'Who's interested in the future, at our age?'

'I'll tell you who. Artists. Artists are interested in only one thing, the freedom to paint. And if the future can be manipulated to provide that freedom then believe me, they are very interested indeed.'

'The trouble with you, Father, is that the nursery has been your life for so long you've forgotten what it's like to love someone.'

'Oh, no, Daphne. You're the one who's forgotten. I lost the person I loved and got you, instead.'"

Mrs. Glass shook her head. "As soon as the words were out, he knew he'd gone too far. I'll never forget her face, when he said that. She just stared at him for what seemed like ages. Then she said, 'I rather think you've just proved my point, Father, don't you?' And she turned and walked out."

"But if they didn't get on, why did she go to work for him in the first place? She's obviously a very capable woman, she could easily have found a job elsewhere."

"Oh, don't misunderstand me. Until this row blew up they'd got on well enough. They lived together in the same house, worked in the same place, and they were always perfectly polite to each other. Unnaturally so, I always thought. The thing is, the nursery was Mr. Linacre's life. After his wife died he spent all his time there, and he built it up into a really successful business. They've got an international reputation, you know... And I'm sure the reason why he encouraged Daphne to take that Business Studies course and then to work for him was because he wanted her to take over the nursery after he died. There was no one else, you see. It was obvious that Nerine wouldn't make a businesswoman in a million years. I suppose he'd always hoped Daphne would marry someone who'd be able to help her run the place."

"How did Nerine react to the news of Daphne's engagement?"

"She just grinned and said, 'Well done, little sister. Looks as though you'll beat me to the altar after all.' She'd been going out with Mr. Roland for several months, by then, and I know he was keen to get her to agree to marry him. But at that point there'd been no news of an engagement. I think she was just enjoying having a good time."

"So what happened, after the row when she told her father she was going to get married?" Thanet found himself as eager to hear the next instalment as a soap-opera fan waiting for his daily fix. Except that this, he reminded himself, was real life, these the people with whom Nerine had spent her days.

Mrs. Glass shrugged. "Things seemed to settle down, after a while. Mr. Linacre raised no more objections, to my knowledge—I suppose he could see it was pointless. A couple of months later, Daphne had a perforated appendix. She was desperately ill—nearly died, as a matter of fact—and she was away in hospital for six weeks. Then, the night before she was due to come home..."

She hesitated, fingers once more picking away at the corner of the handkerchief. It was starting to fray, Thanet noticed.

"Yes?"

"It was March, I remember, and a wild night, with a strong wind blowing and gusty rain. The coroner thought the weather conditions may have contributed to the accident... Mr. Roland was at the house. He'd only come back from Australia a few days before, he'd been out there since just after Christmas. An aunt had died and left him all her money, and he'd had to go out to sort out the estate with her lawyers. When he arrived I let him in and half and hour later Nerine brought him into the kitchen, where I was preparing dinner.

There was a... glitter about her that I'd never seen before.
'Ah, there you are, Mrs. G,' she said. 'We've got some news
for you.' And she held out her left hand. 'How d'you like my
ring?' she said. It was the biggest diamond I'd ever seen in
my life. Mr. Roland was smiling all over his face and looking
so happy. 'It was my grandmother's,' he said. I couldn't help
feeling glad for him, though I must admit I thought he'd have
a difficult time of it, with Nerine for a wife. 'So come on, Mrs.
G,' says Nerine. 'Dig a bottle of champagne out of the cellar,
and bring it into the drawing room. This is a celebration.
Daddy's like a dog with two tails.'

"Well, I couldn't help remembering how poor Daphne's
news had been received, and feeling glad she wasn't there to
see the contrast, but I did as she said and we were all
drinking a toast when there was a knock at the door. It was
Jocelyn, carrying a huge bunch of red roses for Daphne's
homecoming. My first thought was, oh dear, how awkward,
but I couldn't shut the door in his face and it was far too
windy to leave it open, so I invited him in and was just about
to ask if he'd like to put the flowers in water when Nerine
came into the hall. 'Who is it, Mrs. G?' she says. 'Oh,
Jocelyn. Come along in and have a glass of champagne.
Roland and I are celebrating our engagement.' And she held
out her hand, to show the ring.

"Just then Mr. Linacre and Mr. Roland burst out laughing,
in the drawing room, and Jocelyn... Well, I suppose he
couldn't help remembering how Daphne and he had been
treated when they got engaged... He went white, and said,
'No thanks. I wouldn't want to intrude.' And he pushed the
flowers into my hands and was gone. Nerine just raised her
eyebrows at me, shrugged, and went back into the drawing
room. A couple of hundred yards down the road Jocelyn's car
skidded, went out of control and hit a tree. He was killed
instantly."

"And Daphne?"

Mrs. Glass shook her head. "She never got over it. Oh, she
pulled herself together after a while, but it was a bad time for
her. She was only just getting over her illness, and then, on
top of Jocelyn's death, to have to put up not only with the
news of Nerine's engagement and their father's obvious pleasure at the prospect of having Roland as a son-in-law, but all
the preparations for the wedding... It was just too much."

"Nerine didn't think of postponing the wedding?"

"I don't think the idea would have entered her head. I told you, she was completely insensitive to other people's feelings."

"When you said that before . . . Were you trying to say that you think this insensitivity might have caused her death—that she had hurt someone so badly that he—or she—was driven to kill her?"

Mrs. Glass shrugged. "How can I tell? As I said, I haven't seen Nerine for years. But I shouldn't think she's changed much."

"D'you think Daphne ever forgave her sister, for going ahead with the wedding so soon after Jocelyn's death?"

Mrs. Glass sighed. "Oh yes. You see, I don't think Daphne ever forgot those early years, when Nerine made so much of her. I suppose you'd find that difficult to understand, but to have Nerine's exclusive attention was like . . . like . . . well, it was as if the sun was shining especially for you. It's a feeling that's difficult to describe, and I've never experienced it with anyone else. She could make you feel you were the most important person in the world, at that particular moment, and even though you were aware of all her faults, that feeling would keep you . . . bound, to her, somehow." Mrs. Glass shook her head. "I'm not putting this very well, I'm afraid. But the point is, Daphne never forgot how much she'd meant to Nerine, when they were little. And after Mr. Linacre died, of course, Nerine was the only family Daphne had. That was why, when the opportunity of living in the coach house came up, Daphne jumped at the chance to buy it."

"She didn't give me the impression that she was deeply distressed over Nerine's death."

"No, I don't suppose she would. She and Nerine haven't been particularly close for years now. But don't be misled. She'll be upset in her own way, it's just that she's always been good at hiding her feelings."

There was a clatter of feet on the staircase, a knock at the door.

"Yoo-hoo, Barbara. It's me."

Mrs. Glass rose stiffly to her feet, betraying her age for the first time. "That'll be the friend I was expecting. The one whose granddaughter is getting married."

Ellie was a tiny, bird-like woman, with a restless, eager air. She came in with a rush, apologising for her lateness, widening her eyes at Thanet's presence and finally twittering over the cake, dragging him into further admiration of its beauties.

Eventually Thanet managed to make his excuses, thank Mrs. Glass and leave. He walked slowly down the stairs, thinking over all that she had told him. He was glad he had come. For the first time he was beginning to feel genuine sympathy for Nerine, the "sweetest, sunniest litle girl you could imagine," whose life had overnight become transformed from a joyous, secure existence to a wasteland devoid of warmth and love. Small wonder that she had spent the rest of her life searching for those dimly remembered joys, flitting from lover to lover, restless and dissatisfied. And too blind to see that they had been right there beside her, all the time.

THIRTEEN

As Thanet drove home that evening he couldn't help remembering how he had felt the night before: at peace with the world.

Tonight it was very different.

For one thing, he was tired. It had been a hectic day; stimulating of course, but requiring intense and unremitting concentration, crowded with new people, new impressions, and filled with that sense of urgency unique to the start of a murder case. True, things had gone reasonably well, but at the moment he had no inkling of who the murderer might be. As he'd said, there was certainly no shortage of suspects.

Secondly, his back was aching. In the privacy of his car he allowed himself the luxury of a little groan as he tried to ease himself into a more comfortable position. Twice in the past he had managed to injure his back. On the first occasion he had foolishly tried to heave a lawnmower into the boot of his car and on the second—well, he preferred not to think about the second, if he could help it. About to escort a newly arrested murder suspect back to the police station, he had stooped to open the car door and found he couldn't straighten up again. The suspect and Lineham had actually had to help him into the back seat. And as for his arrival back at the station... It had been one of the most humiliating experiences of his life.

Thirdly... well, of course, this was where the root of his depression lay. Thirdly, there was Joan, and this clash of interests and loyalties which was threatening to undermine his marriage. It was pointless to remember that he had never really wanted Joan to go back to work in the first place, or to remind himself that he had foreseen precisely this sort of difficulty from the moment when Joan had first told him she wanted to train as a probation officer. The fact remained that for one reason and another (primarily the fear of losing her if he continued to oppose her wishes) Thanet had given in and until last night, he had to admit it, things had gone reasonably smoothly. There had been difficulties, true, but sensible discussion and a determination to overcome them had always won the day. But now...

He could see Joan's point of view, of course. Here she was, with a first offender whom she had every hope of putting permanently on the straight and narrow. Then along comes something like this, a disaster perhaps not of the client's making, and the whole fragile edifice comes tumbling down, negating months of careful, sustained effort.

She's bound to be angry over the television appeal, Thanet told himself, forgetting his earlier optimism. It's perfectly natural. I must just be prepared for it. It'll blow over, in time.

Anyway, what choice did I have? he asked himself.

You could have left it another twenty-four hours.

"No!" he said aloud, glad that there was no one in the car with him to look at him askance.

Look at the circumstances, he argued. A woman is dead. Her son is on probation. He is missing from the moment of the murder, and despite all attempts by the police to trace him, he still hasn't turned up a day later...

No, he had had no choice.

Ben was mending a puncture, his bicycle upturned on the drive. Thanet edged the car carefully in alongside it and chatted with his son for a few minutes. Delaying tactics, he thought sadly as he let himself into the house. Who would ever have believed the day would come when he was reluctant to meet his wife?

The kitchen was empty and in the living room Bridget was sitting on the floor, school magazines spread out all around her. She was snipping away at one, tongue between her teeth.

"Hi," she said, greeting him with a smile. "I'm cutting out some recipes for the *KM*. And I've written them a letter. D'you think you could have a look at it after supper, see if you think it's OK?"

"Yes, sure. Er. . . where's your mother?"

"Upstairs, in the study."

This was the grandiose title given as a joke to the shoe-box of a fourth bedroom where both Thanet and Joan worked in the evenings, when necessary.

"She's finishing a report for tomorrow." Bridget hesitated, scissors stilled. "I don't know what's up, but she's in a pretty grim mood."

Thanet pulled a face. "I'd better go and see."

"Your supper's in the oven," Bridget called after him as he left the room.

"Thanks."

But the thought of food made his stomach churn as he climbed the stairs, feet dragging. At the top he paused for a moment and then, without allowing himself to hesitate further, flung open the "study" door, said "Hullo, darling," took the two necessary paces to arrive at the desk and stooped to kiss her.

Instead of turning her head to kiss him on the mouth as usual she remained quite still, staring at the papers spread out on the desk, and the kiss landed on her temple.

"What's the matter?" he said, and was immediately angry with himself. What was the point in pretending?

Slowly, now, she turned to look up at him. "Need you ask?"

He perched on the edge of the desk. "The television appeal, I suppose."

She nodded. "The television appeal. Oh, Luke, couldn't you have waited just another twenty-four hours?"

"No, I couldn't. I'm sorry." Then, as she remained silent, he said with quiet intensity, "Look, I did everything that could be done. We've consulted you, as his probation officer, tracked down his friends, followed up every lead we've been given, and there's been nothing. Not a trace of him, anywhere. He's just disappeared off the face of the earth. And there's been plenty of publicity over the murder. I imagine he has a radio in his car, most young people seem to, these days. . . So why hasn't he come forward? He really should have heard by now."

"And if he hasn't? It'll be enough of a shock for him to find out his mother's dead, without hearing that he's wanted by the police."

"He's not wanted by the police—not in the way you mean at least! Didn't you notice how carefully worded the appeal was, to avoid giving that impression? We just want to talk to him, that's all." Thanet shook his head. "Look, love, I can see your point of view. I was thinking about it on the way home in the car, and I can understand how concerned for him you must be, and how disappointed you must feel that all the work you've done with him might be wasted, if he reacts badly to all this. But you must try and look at it from my point of view, too. And the one thing I cannot allow myself to do is behave any differently towards him just because he happens to be your client. You must see that. So this afternoon, when I was debating whether or not to put out that appeal I had to ask myself why I was debating it at all. And I realised that if he hadn't been your client I wouldn't even have hestitated. The fact is that he disappeared around the time of the murder, and even if he is not implicated himself, he could have vital evidence..."

"If he had, I'm sure he would have come forward with it."

Thanet shrugged. "Perhaps."

Joan shook her head stubbornly. "I still think you could have given him another twenty-four hours. I'm sorry, Luke, I'm afraid we have to accept that we just aren't going to agree over this, however much we talk about it."

I knew it, Thanet wanted to say. *I knew this would happen one day, if you went into the probation service. Don't you remember my saying so, right at the start?*

But nothing was to be gained by an I-told-you-so attitude and he left it at that. Over supper he brooded, his mind ranging to and fro between the various interviews he had conducted today, but always returning at intervals, obsessively, to Joan. At the moment he could see no way out of their predicament. He could recall that conversation seven years ago as though it were yesterday.

'It would be ideal, Luke, don't you see?'

'Ideal for whom?'

'Well for me, of course. What do you mean?'

'Have you thought how it could affect us?'

'Us? In what way?'

'You haven't thought that there could be a certain, well, clash of interests?'

'No. Why should there be?'

'Look, the probation service and the police, they're often poles apart in their attitudes to criminals.'

'But they're both on the same side really, surely? They're both concerned to maintain peace and order in society?'

'Maybe. But that doesn't stop them frequently being in conflict. I don't suppose you've had much to do with probation officers, but I have. And I grant you they do very fine work, many of them. But that's not the point. The point is, as I say, that their attitudes to criminals are different. Don't you see that it's impossible to shed one's working attitudes in one's private life? They become an integral part of one, as basic as breathing. I can see all sorts of situations in which this thing could become a barrier between us.'

'How, for example?'

'Well, for one thing, I've always shared my work with you, haven't I? Told you everything, without reserve, knowing that I could trust you not to talk about it.'

'But I still wouldn't. You know that, surely?'

'Maybe you wouldn't talk about it, but your attitude to what I tell you would be bound to be different, don't you see? It's inevitable that you'd be looking at the whole question of crime from a different point of view, from the side of the criminal, his guilt, his rehabilitation, whatever...Darling, don't you see that? You must, surely.'

'Not necessarily. Probation officers have to be detached, they can't afford to identify with their clients or they couldn't work properly.'

'And what if it turned out that we were both working on the same case ...?'

'I would think that the chances of that happening would be very slight. And if it did happen, couldn't one or the other of us request that we should be taken off the case?'

'And that would create a barrier between us, too. Joan, you must see that. It would limit us, put restrictions on our work. We'd be bound to resent it. And there would be other barriers—just in ordinary life, in casual conversation, we'd have to be guarding our tongues, watching what we say to each other...'

And now it's happening, thought Thanet. All my worst fears are being realised.

"Did you enjoy that?" Bridget had come in, gesturing at his plate and clutching a piece of paper.

The plate was empty, so presumably he had eaten his supper, though he had no memory of doing so.

Bridget was laughing. "Oh Dad, your face... Did you even notice what you were eating?"

"Well..."

"I knew it! I work my fingers to the bone and look what happens! I might just as well have made you a cardboard sandwich."

"Ah, well, now that I might have noticed. By the way, I came across an interesting dish today—at least, it smelt delicious. Now let me see, what was it..."

They chatted for a while, and Thanet looked over the letter she had written to the *Kent Messenger.* He was impressed, and said so. "If that doesn't make them take you on, I don't know what will."

"D'you think so? Oh, Dad, I do hope so."

"Well don't get too excited about it, just in case."

Ben came in to wash his hands.

"Finished?" said Thanet.

Ben nodded. "Took me ages."

"How was the History test?"

Ben shrugged. "OK. Seven out of ten."

"Good."

And so the evening passed. Joan did not come down to join him later on as she usually did. Instead she took a leisurely bath and went straight to bed. When he went upstairs she was either asleep or pretending to be so.

It took him a long time to get to sleep himself.

Next morning they again kept up a pretence of normality for the sake of the children, a simple matter in the fragmented bustle of bathroom, breakfast and departure. Joan kissed him goodbye as usual, but there was no warmth in it, merely a brief contact of flesh against flesh, as impersonal as a social kiss at a party.

It was another glorious summer morning, but today Thanet was not in the mood to appreciate the beauties of nature. He arrived at the office early, determined to drown his private sorrows in work. Lineham was late, and by the time he bounded into the room whistling the Wedding March Thanet had already skimmed through the reports which had come in overnight. His heart sank as he noted the sergeant's bright and smiling face. He hoped Lineham wasn't going to be overpoweringly cheerful this morning, he didn't think he could stand it.

"Any news of the boy, sir?"

"Quite a number of possible sightings, but none of them has come to anything, as yet."

"But not a word from the lad himself?"

"Not so far."

Thanet slapped the report he had been reading down on his desk. "Why on earth can't people tell the truth?"

He knew the answer, of course: because they were afraid. But it was a time-wasting business trying to get people to be frank. There was something about a murder investigation which made them clam up, innocent and guilty alike. The lengths to which people would go to conceal some very minor peccadillo never ceased to amaze Thanet. The problem for the police was trying to sift the wheat from the chaff.

"Why, who's been putting up smoke screens now?" Lineham perched on the edge of Thanet's desk, looking as keen and alert as a labrador awaiting the word of command.

Thanet flapped an irritated hand. "Do go and sit down, Mike. I can't think with you looming over me like that."

At once he was angry with himself, the look on Lineham's face a silent reproach as without a word the sergeant slid off the desk and retreated to his own.

The phone rang and Thanet answered it: Beatrix Haywood, enquiring after Damon. Thanet assured her that he'd let her and Miss Linacre know the moment there was anything definite, and rang off.

"Sorry, Mike, I didn't mean to snap at you. I seem to be in a bit of a mood this morning, I can't think why." *Liar.* "You'll just have to try and ignore it if I let fly from time to time."

Lineham was looking mollified. "Nothing wrong, sir, is there?"

The negative question provided Thanet with his escape route. "Oh no . . ." He managed to grin. "I expect I just got out of bed on the wrong side." He glanced at the reports scattered on his desk. "And now I find that not one but three of our main suspects have been either lying to us or misleading us."

Lineham leaned forward, the eagerness back in his face. "Which?"

"The oh-so-innocent, butter-wouldn't-melt-in-my-mouth Mrs. Speed, for one. You remember she went sick-visiting after her meeting, in the afternoon? That's been confirmed. What she didn't tell us was that she also paid a call on Nerine Tarrant."

"Really? At what time?"

"Well, that's the interesting thing. It sounds as though she was in two minds about it. First of all she was spotted just after four o'clock, when the meeting in the village hall ended, standing by the gates of High Gables, staring up the drive towards the house. Then later on, about ten past five, presumably after she'd finished her sick visit, she was seen actually walking up the drive."

"Two different witnesses?"

"Yes."

Lineham pursed his lips in a silent whistle. "Interesting."

"Also," said Thanet, shuffling through the papers for the appropriate report, "there's confirmation that Speed was lying about his movements at lunchtime on the day of the murder. Remember he gave us the impression he hadn't put a toe outside his car while he was parked in that field? Well we guessed that couldn't be right for a start. If he'd been watching for Mr. Tarrant to leave he wouldn't have been able to see a thing from there. As you know, the witness who reported seeing the car lives in that little cottage further on around the bend from High Gables. She was away most of yesterday and couldn't be contacted until evening, but she says that the car was parked from about twenty-five to one to around ten to one that day. About a quarter of an hour, in fact. The reason why she's so sure is because Speed always parked in that farm gateway when he went to visit Nerine Tarrant, and he usually stayed much longer—forty to forty-five minutes, on average. And she swears that on Thursday he got out, locked the car and walked along the footpath towards High Gables as he always did."

"A quarter of an hour," said Lineham thoughtfully. "Not long, even for a quickie."

"Quite. And by then, Mr. Tarrant was already in the house."

"And if *he's* telling the truth, and went straight up to his wife's rooms..."

"... who was it he heard in the bedroom with his wife?"

"Exactly."

The phone rang again: Tarrant, this time, also enquiring about Damon. After a brief conversation Thanet replaced the receiver and said, "He's really getting worried about the boy now."

The two men stared at each other in silence, thinking.

"If Mrs. Tarrant had taken a new lover," said Lineham at

last, "and Speed knew about it, it would certainly give him a motive, wouldn't it?"

"I would have thought so, yes. Though if you remember, according to PC Driver it was extraordinary what a knack she had for discarding her lovers without turning them against her." Thanet remembered what old Mrs. Glass had said. *To have Nerine's exclusive attention was as if the sun was shining especially for you.* "Despite her reputation it was almost as though they regarded it as a privilege to have been admitted to her bed at all, and went into the affair accepting from the beginning that it was too good to last. Though, come to think of it, I know for a fact that that certainly didn't always apply." And he told Lineham about Doc Mallard's friend.

"But it's surely unlikely that she should have been killed by a past lover. I mean, the time when that sort of violence erupts is when feelings of jealousy and rejection are still running high, not months afterwards. And Speed has been the current favourite for some time."

"I remember Beatrix Haywood saying that a few months was par for the course and any minute now he would be finding himself supplanted. It looks as though it might already have happened."

"And he suspected it!" said Lineham. "He probably sensed she was going off him and got suspicious when she started trying to put him off. I expect he was desperate to find out who the new man was, and thought he'd do a bit of spying."

"Maybe."

"So then, later on in the afternoon, he goes back to have it out with her."

"Could be . . . If we're right about all this, Mike, I wonder if Tarrant knew about this new lover."

"I doubt it. If he realised the voice wasn't Speed's, why should he lie about it?"

"I'm not so sure. It can't be much fun admitting that your wife was having an affair and that you actually walked away from her bedroom door knowing she was with her lover. But to put her in an even worse light by informing us that, well, as a matter of fact it wasn't the lover we knew about but yet another one . . . It would have made her look a bit of a whore, wouldn't it?"

"Well, let's face it, sir, that's what she was, practically. High-class, perhaps, choosy—well, yes, to the extent that she only had one man at a time, but . . ."

"Perhaps. But it's one thing for her husband to have to admit that to himself, another to have to acknowledge it to the police."

"Possibly . . . I suppose that if Mr. Tarrant realised that the voice he heard wasn't Speed's that could have been the straw which finally broke the camel's back. He could have gone away, brooded over it all afternoon and finally decided he'd had enough."

"On the other hand we have to accept that he might just have assumed the man with his wife was Speed, and still genuinely believe it. Well, there's not much point in wasting time speculating. We'll have to see them both again, obviously. Mrs. Speed, too. What was she up to, I wonder?"

"Anything else of interest come in, sir?"

"Yes." Thanet grinned. He had kept the most dramatic bit of news until last. "There's a possibility that our outsider might be coming up fast on the rails."

"Buzzard?"

"Yes. There's been a sighting in the area, on the afternoon of the murder. He was driving an old green van. An alert PC who happened to be involved in Buzzard's trial recognised him waiting at the traffic lights by those major road works on the Ashford Road just outside Sturrenden, at around five o'clock."

"Really? But that's only a few miles away from Ribbleden!"

"Exactly. I want him picked up and brought in, Mike. Who knows? We might have to look no further, and we can leave all these people in peace."

"I'll get on to it right away, sir."

"But meanwhile we can't sit about twiddling our thumbs. As soon as you're ready we'll go and see Mr. Tarrant again."

FOURTEEN

The lawns of High Gables had just been cut and the scent of new-mown grass hung on the air. Thanet inhaled appreciatively as he and Lineham crossed the gravel to the front door.

Vicky Cunningham answered their knock. Today she was wearing red-and-white striped trousers, a white teeshirt decorated with red hearts and red butterfly clips in her hair. The gravity of her expression belied the gaiety of her attire. "He's in the garden. He's . . ."

"What?" prompted Thanet.

She pulled a face, shrugged. "You'll see for yourself."

"Where is he, exactly?"

"Around the back. He said he was going to have a bonfire."

"Not exactly bonfire weather," said Lineham as they walked along the front of the house and turned the corner onto the terrace where Nerine Tarrant's body had been found. "It must be in the seventies by now."

Thanet stopped. "I wonder . . ."

"What's the matter?"

"I was just thinking . . . If we're right, and Speed came here on Thursday not to meet Nerine, but to spy on her, he must have found himself a vantage point . . ."

Thanet set off purposefully along the path they had followed the previous day. When he reached the gap in the yew hedge he turned right instead of left, walked as far as the corner, then paused. Here there was no gap; the hedge was a dense, impenetrable right-angle. Ahead, the path continued, curving past a border of tall shrubs which backed onto the third side of the hedge, and skirting a huge clump of rhododendrons.

The rhododendrons were the answer, Thanet decided. He approached them, then turned to look back at the house. Yes, from here there was a clear view of both the front door and the gap in the yew hedge through which any clandestine visitor would have to emerge in order to get out of the garden via the gate in the back fence.

Thanet turned to study them. At their tallest they were perhaps fifteen feet high. Here and there late flowers still bloomed, the spectacular purity of their candy-floss pink enhanced by the glossy dark greens of the dense foliage and the withered bracts of dead blossoms. Stooping, Thanet thrust his way into the heart of the bushes. It was like stepping into a low cave. Green filtered light penetrated the canopy of leaves, imparting to the thick gnarled branches a mysterious, almost sinister air. Despite the oppressive warmth of the enclosed space, Thanet shivered.

"Find anything, sir?"

Lineham's face, suspended like that of the Cheshire Cat, appeared in a gap in the foliage.

"Just a minute. Ah..."

Thanet took some tweezers and a plastic bag from his pocket and bent to retrieve a small object from the ground. Then he thrust his way back through the embrace of the branches onto the path and handed the bag to Lineham.

The sergeant's nose wrinkled in distaste. "Fag end. Pretty stupid if you ask me, smoking while he waited. I mean, anyone could have seen the smoke and come to investigate."

"Still, potentially useful evidence. If it's his. It could have been thrown there by anyone. We'll get a saliva test done."

"Talking of smoke, sir..." Lineham nodded in the direction of the back boundary, where a murky, dun-coloured cloud was swirling up between the tops of the trees. "Mr. Tarrant's bonfire, presumably."

As they drew nearer the crackling of the fire grew louder, punctuated by the irregular thud of an axe and a sharp crack of snapped branches. At the edge of a small clearing they paused. Tarrant was burning up the remains of a dead tree, felled some time ago, judging by the weathered look of the exposed end of the trunk. Stripped to the waist, he was working like a man demented, and his body glistened with sweat. The frenetic energy with which he was attacking a

recalcitrant branch, the leaping flames and billowing smoke
all combined to impart to the scene a disturbing air of
violence, of passion unleashed. A picture of Tarrant as he had
first seen him, the suave, sophisticated man of the world,
flashed across Thanet's mind. It was difficult to reconcile the
two images.

Thanet stepped forward. "Mr. Tarrant?" he called.

Tarrant gave a final wrench at the branch before glancing
over his shoulder, staggering a little as it finally parted
company with the trunk. Then he laid it on the ground and
wiped his forehead with the back of his arm before slowly
straightening up. He was breathing heavily, his sparse fair
hair dark with sweat.

Thanet advanced, holding up a hand to shield his face from
the intense heat. He was conscious of sweat breaking out all
over his body. "Could we have a word?"

"Is it Damon?"

Thanet shook his head. "No further news yet, I'm afraid."

Now that Thanet's impetus was broken, the energy seemed
suddenly to drain out of him, and he put out a hand to steady
himself against one of the few remaining branches of the
dead tree. Then, body sagging with fatigue, he walked heavily
to the edge of the clearing and picked up a checked shirt
lying on the ground. He pulled it on.

"Perhaps we could find somewhere cooler?" suggested
Thanet.

"We'll go indoors."

Tarrant led the way to the back door of the house and then
to the study, pausing in the kitchen to ask Vicky to bring a jug
of iced lemonade. He slumped into his chair behind the desk
and indicated that Thanet and Lineham should sit down.

"What is it now?" he said wearily, taking a red spotted
handkerchief from his pocket and mopping at his forehead
again.

What had driven Tarrant to that bout of frenetic activity?
Thanet wondered. Had he been trying to blot out misery, or
guilt?

Thanet didn't want to believe that this man had killed his
wife. Tarrant, he was convinced, had loved her deeply. But
he had to acknowledge that the surgeon was one of the prime
candidates. Over the years Thanet had seen many a reasonable man or woman ultimately driven to violence, the trigger
factor sometimes so apparently trivial that others gaped in

disbelief that so minor an offence should have such disastrous consequences. If Tarrant had realised that the man in his wife's room wasn't Speed...Well, Nerine might well have taken one lover too many. Thanet knew that if this man were innocent he should be allowed to mourn in peace, that it would be inhuman to cause him further, unnecessary pain. But he might be guilty and the professional in Thanet knew that he had no choice. Much as he hated the idea, it was his duty to get at the truth. And if Tarrant had lied...

"You remember, when we spoke to you last, you told us that when you came back to the house at lunchtime on the day your wife died, you heard a man's voice from her bedroom?"

Tarrant's lips tightened. "Yes."

"You told us that it was Mr. Speed."

"That's right."

"You'll have had more time to think about it, by now. Would you care to amend that statement in any way?"

Tarrant caught the flicker of a glance from Lineham. *You're being too soft with him. Sir.*

There was a knock at the door and Vicky entered with a tray, ice-cubes chinking. She set it down on a side table and poured three tall glasses and handed them around. Thanet would have preferred not to accept the drink. In the circumstances he didn't feel comfortable about enjoying Tarrant's hospitality. But it would have been churlish to refuse and besides, it looked like fresh lemonade. Thanet could see the bits of lemon floating around in the cloudy liquid. His throat suddenly ached for the delicious coolness of it.

He smiled up at Vicky. "Thank you."

Tarrant had already drained his glass and was holding it out for more. "God, I needed that. Delicious, Vicky."

"Good." Vicky refilled his glass then held up the jug, raising her eyebrows at Thanet and Lineham.

They shook their heads.

"I'll leave it here and you can help yourselves if you change your minds."

Thanet waited until the door had closed behind her before saying, "Well?"

"I'm sorry, I've forgotten what the question was."

"I asked if you'd care to amend your statement in any way...That you'd heard Mr. Speed's voice in your wife's room."

"That's what I thought you said. I don't know what you mean. How could I 'amend' it, as you put it?"

"You're sure, that it was Mr. Speed's voice?"

"I told you, yes." Tarrant was impatient now, and Thanet was pretty sure that he was sincere.

"What are you getting at, Inspector?"

Thanet sighed. There was no going back. "I'm afraid it couldn't have been Speed."

"But . . ."

"Mr. Speed tells us that he did intend to visit your wife that lunchtime, but that he didn't do so because he saw your car turn into the drive ahead of him. That was at twelve thirty-five. You did say you got here just after half past twelve, didn't you?"

"Yes. But . . . Just a minute. Let me get this quite straight. You're saying that he arrived *after* me?" Tarrant paused, his eyes going blank as he focused on the next, inevitable question. "But in that case," he said slowly, "who . . . ?"

"Exactly, Mr. Tarrant. In that case, who was with your wife?"

Tarrant gave an uncomprehending shake of the head, then rubbed his hands over his face as if to erase his confusion. "I have no idea. None."

"Any conjectures?"

"No!" It was almost a shout. "Look here, Inspector, there must be some mistake. You must have got this wrong."

"I'm afraid not, sir. We have an independent witness who confirms that Mr. Speed was definitely not in this house at twelve thirty-five that day."

Tarrant swivelled his chair to look out of the window, and Thanet wondered what he was thinking. If he was innocent, his thoughts must be bitter indeed. Even after her death, it seemed, Nerine's promiscuity had the power to reach out and turn the knife in the wound which had given him so much pain all his married life. And if he was guilty . . . Well, thought Thanet, if Tarrant was guilty he deserved an Oscar.

Tarrant shook his head and his voice was tight with suppressed emotion as he said, "I'm afraid I can't help you, Inspector. So if you don't mind . . ."

Outside, Lineham said, "What d'you think, sir?"

Thanet shrugged. "For what it's worth, I'd say he was telling the truth. But I've been wrong before and no doubt I'll be wrong again. What did you think?"

"Same as you. What now?"

"Another word with Miss Barnes, I think. She saw Tarrant knock on his wife's door that lunchtime, remember. And I distinctly recall feeling that she was holding something back."

"You mean, she might know who the new man was?"

"Well, she's around the house all day, isn't she? We don't know how long the new affair had been going on, and even if she didn't see him on that occasion, she might have seen him on another."

"True. There is one odd thing, though . . ."

"What?"

"Well, everyone seems to agree that Mrs. Tarrant never tried to hide her affairs, so why the secrecy surrounding this one?"

"Perhaps she wanted to be sure of the new lover before casting off the old? Or perhaps . . ." Thanet came to an abrupt halt. Suddenly, all was clear to him. And yes, it would explain so much . . .

"Perhaps what?" said Lineham.

"Come on. Let's go and see Miss Barnes."

But finding her took a little time. Eventually a murmur of voices led them to the room next door to the sitting room in which they had interviewed old Mrs. Tarrant that morning. The old lady's bedroom? wondered Thanet as he knocked.

"Just a minute." Marilyn's voice. A moment or two later the door opened a few inches. "Yes? Oh . . . Sorry, you can't come in. Lavinia's in one of her dressing-up moods and she's changing."

"Could you spare us just a few moments?"

Marilyn glanced back over her shoulder. "If you'd wait, I'll be as quick as I can."

Thanet nodded. "Fine."

The door closed. Lineham leaned against the wall beside it, gazing into space and whistling tunelessly between his teeth. Thanet strolled along the corridor to a window at the far end. Daphne and Beatrix Haywood were standing at the door of the coach house, deep in conversation. Beatrix was carrying a wicker basket over one arm and as he watched she set off purposefully down the drive. Going to the village, presumably. Shopping, perhaps? Or possibly to help prepare for the jumble sale this afternoon. He and Lineham had seen the notice outside the church hall as they had driven past, earlier. Daphne stayed watching the older woman until she was out of sight, then turned back into the house, closing the door behind her. They certainly seemed to get on well, thought Thanet. But then, their needs dovetailed beautifully. Daphne needed someone to run her home and Beatrix needed a home to run. But in addition they were linked by a powerful emotional tie: Daphne's only lover had been Beatrix's only son.

"Sir," called Lineham.

Marilyn Barnes came out into the corridor, closing the door behind her as Thanet hurried back.

"She'll be all right for a few minutes now," she said. "What did you want to ask me?"

No point in wasting time. "It seems that Mrs. Tarrant had taken a new lover," said Thanet. "Could you tell us who he is?"

Marilyn gave him a long, considering look. "Who told you that?"

"Shall we just say that it has...emerged, during the course of our investigation."

She sighed, shook her head, lips compressed. "Have you talked to Mr. Tarrant about this?"

"Yes."

"And what did he say?"

"He denies all knowledge of it. He seemed distressed."

"He didn't know. I was hoping he wouldn't find out."

"You're sure he knew nothing about it?"

"Pretty sure, yes. Mr. Tarrant rarely comes home in the middle of the day."

"So who...?"

The bedroom door opened and Lavinia Tarrant stood dramatically framed in the opening, posing with one foot forward, like a fashion model.

"Is that you, Jack?"

Thanet suppressed a gasp. Could this really be the sweet old lady they had talked to the previous day? She was heavily made-up and might have stepped straight from the fashion pages of the late nineteen twenties. Her dress was of pale orange crêpe, with a low, boat-shaped neckline, a very short, gathered, two-tier skirt and a low-waisted, tubular bodice decorated with a geometric design of brightly coloured sequins. Pointed shoes, dangling earrings, and a waist-long string of pearls completed the flapper image. But once again the effect was merely grotesque, the contrast between the bright young clothes and the shrunken body within them a tragic reminder of mortality. Thanet remembered a conversation he'd had once with an old lady in her nineties. "The sad thing is," she'd said, "I still feel sixteen inside." Would Lavinia Tarrant say the same? he wondered.

"No, Lavinia," said Marilyn. "Jack's not here yet." Then, in an undertone, to Thanet. "Jack was her husband." She turned back to the old lady. "You said he wouldn't be here until this evening, remember?"

Lavinia frowned, eyes clouded with the effort to resurrect the memory. She shook her head. "Did I? I don't remember."

Marilyn took her arm. "Why don't we go into the sitting room?" She began to steer her charge along the corridor.

"Miss Barnes," said Thanet urgently. "You still haven't told me who he is."

She paused, glancing back at him, her expression wry.

"It was *Tim* Speed," she said.

FIFTEEN

Thanet raised a hand in a gesture of acknowledgement, then hustled Lineham away. At times like this, even after all these years in the force, the sergeant's streak of puritanism tended to surface. Sure enough, as soon as the door had closed behind Marilyn Barnes and Lavinia, Lineham hissed, "But she was old enough to be his *mother*!"

Thanet glanced around, then frowned at Lineham and shook his head. Lineham took the hint and remained silent as they went down the stairs, across the hall and through the front door into the sunshine.

They both blinked and screwed up their eyes against the sudden transition to brilliant light.

"What's the time, Mike?"

Lineham squinted at his watch. "Quarter past twelve, sir."

"Right. Speed starts his lunch hour at twelve thirty. There's time for a sandwich and a quick pint at the Dog and Pheasant before seeing what he has to say for himself."

"OK, sir." Lineham set off across the gravel.

"Where are you off to, Mike?"

"The car."

"Mike, do you realise how far away the Dog and Pheasant is?"

Lineham shrugged. "Four hundred yards, sir? But I thought we were going on to Mr. Speed's house after that."

"We are. And that's another four hundred yards or so. Half a mile in all. You'll lose the use of your legs one of these days." And Thanet set off at a brisk pace for the gate.

"I just like driving, that's all," Lineham protested, falling in beside him.

"There's more to life than a gleaming bonnet and a powerful engine, Mike. Anyway, we'll have time to talk."

"He's only eighteen," said Lineham, instantly slipping back into gear again. "And her son's friend."

"Not unheard of," said Thanet. "Come on, Mike, don't be naive. You've come across far worse than this. They're both consenting adults, after all. He's a good-looking young man and she was a very beautiful woman."

"You don't seem too surprised, I must say. You'd already guessed, I suppose."

"The possibility did cross my mind, I must admit, while we were talking after seeing Mr. Tarrant just now. I could kick myself for not seeing it before. No, what I find much more interesting are the implications."

"You mean, how the other people involved would have reacted if they knew."

"Yes. I rather think that's the crux of the matter. Did they know?"

The two men walked in silence for a few moments, then Lineham said, "I'm not sure about Mr. Tarrant. I think I believed him, but . . . I suppose, if he did know, it would be understandable if he hoped it wouldn't get out. It would make his wife's reputation sink to an all-time low, if it was generally known she'd been cradle-snatching."

"Quite. But as far as the Speeds are concerned, I'd guess they do know, wouldn't you agree? And I shouldn't think they'd want it to get out, either. It would certainly explain why they were so touchy every time Tim was mentioned."

"I bet they only found out that lunchtime," said Lineham. "Yes," he went on excitedly, "if you think about it, it all fits. Remember the family row the neighbour overheard, and the atmosphere between Speed and Tim which PC Driver noticed, that afternoon? And if Speed had known before then, why would he have been lurking in those bushes? No, I'd guess he suspected she'd found someone else—perhaps because she'd put him off once or twice, whatever—and wanted to find out who it was. So he hung about until Tim came out and then . . ."

"What?"

Another silence, while they speculated.

"It must have been an awful shock for him," said Lineham. "It's one thing to suspect you're being given the push, another to know you've been supplanted by your own son. I should think he'd have gone after him there and then, caught him up in the garden."

"That neighbour of the Speeds, Mrs. Shrimpton . . . What time did she say she heard them having that row?"

"One fifteen I think, sir. And she saw Tim leave ten minutes later."

"Yet his lunch hour is supposed to be from twelve to one. It looks as though they both went straight home from High Gables."

"They didn't leave together in the car, though, sir. That witness who saw Speed park in the field would surely have mentioned it, if he had arrived alone and left with someone else."

"But as we were saying a few minutes ago, it's only a short distance to the Speeds' bungalow. Perhaps Speed didn't want to get into the car with Tim after what he'd just learned, and told him to walk home."

"And he did! Pretty obedient of him, don't you think?"

"Perhaps he thought he might as well face the music and get it over with. What are you drinking?"

On this lovely summer Saturday the Dog and Pheasant was crowded with weekend drinkers. Lineham spotted a sign to a rear garden and they carried their beer and sandwiches outside. The tables under their striped umbrellas were well spaced out, affording more privacy.

All the same, they automatically lowered their voices, leaned together like conspirators.

"Well," said Thanet, "it would certainly strengthen Speed's motive, that's for sure. He must have been in a real turmoil, that afternoon."

"I bet he was mad with Mrs. Tarrant, for choosing Tim of all people . . . It wouldn't be in the least surprising if he grabbed the first chance he had and slipped back to the house during that test drive, to give her a piece of his mind."

"And what about Mrs. Speed, Mike? This would give her a much stronger motive too."

"Yes. But wait a minute. That's a thought. Don't you think it's a bit odd, that Mr. Speed would have chosen to have it out with Tim at home, when he knew his wife would be there?"

"He probably wasn't thinking straight. As you say, he'd just had a pretty nasty shock. The garage would have been a bit public, too, for the sort of conversation he would have had in mind. Customers could have kept walking in and interrupting them."

"True. I suppose, in the heat of the moment, he could even have forgotten his wife would be there. Or maybe he did remember, and deliberately chose to have it out with Tim at home, knowing that she'd be as outraged as he was, if for a different reason, and would back him up."

"She would certainly have been furiously angry with Nerine. First of all stealing her husband and then seducing her son . . . During the afternoon she must have been plucking up the courage to go and tell her what she thought of her. If you remember, she was first seen hesitating outside the gates of High Gables just after four. Obviously her nerve failed, on that occasion. But later, at about ten past five, she was actually seen going up the drive . . ." Thanet drained his glass. He was eager to hear what the Speeds had to say about all this. "Ready, Mike?"

The hall of Shangri-la smelled of boiled cauliflower. Mrs. Speed reluctantly invited them in. She was wearing a pink nylon overall and looked hot, her plump cheeks mottled an unhealthy shade of red. She showed them into the living room and left to fetch her husband. By daylight the garish colours of the carpet, upholstery and curtains could not conceal the fact that the room was shabby and much in need of refurbishment. When she returned with Speed she had shed her overall. They were both looking apprehensive.

As they sat down Speed pointedly consulted his watch. "I've got to be back at work in half an hour."

"We'll try not to keep you too long."

Thanet had been trying to make up his mind over which tactics to employ: the shock approach or the more subtle one? Which would be most effective with these people? On the surface they appeared ordinary, inoffensive types, but Thanet had long ago discovered just how deceptive appearances can be. It is always difficult to tell how people will react in a crisis, and the situation in this house both now and last Thursday could certainly be described as that. If they were both innocent what they now needed was a period of calm in which to regain their equilibrium. Unfortunately this was just what he could not allow them. If one of them were guilty . . . It was the same old dilemma and he knew that once again he had no choice in the matter. He had to find out the truth, and to do so he would have to press as hard as was necessary. But, how best to do it?

He looked at them sitting side by side on the settee staring at him, Mrs. Speed perched uncomfortably on the edge, Speed even now a prey to vanity, running a hand over his balding head to check that the thinning strands were evenly spread out. It was difficult to visualise either of them pushing Nerine off that balcony, and even if one of them had, Thanet was prepared to believe that it was in the heat of the moment rather than in cold blood. But the fact remained that each of them had a classic motive for murder. Revenge and jealousy are emotions which only too easily get out of hand.

Unfortunately, if one of them were his quarry, there was so far not a single scrap of evidence to prove it. He had to hope for a confession. If he tried the shock approach and failed, there would be nothing left to fall back on. But if he proceeded cautiously, eroding their defences bit by bit, he might in the end succeed in winkling the truth out of them.

Thanet was not perturbed that the silence had become uncomfortably protracted. The Speeds were obviously finding it difficult to cope with and were showing signs of tension. Speed was smoking a cigarette with quick, nervous puffs, and now he stubbed it out, cleared his throat and opened his mouth to speak. Mrs. Speed shot him a quick glance and caught his eye. The message that passed between them was clear: *wait*.

But after only another minute or two Speed couldn't stand it. With a defiant look at his wife he burst out, "Well? How much longer're we going to have to sit here like a couple of lemons?"

"We were just waiting for you to begin, Mr. Speed." Thanet's tone was conversational, courteous.

"Me, begin? Why should I begin? This is your idea, not mine." Speed lit another cigarette and sucked the smoke in greedily.

"We thought you might have something to tell us," said Lineham.

The belligerence drained out of Speed's face and although he and his wife did not so much as glance at each other Thanet picked up their unspoken thought. *Oh God, how much do they know?* He had noticed it many times before, this telepathy between married couples in times of stress.

"We've told you all we know," said Mrs. Speed. But her attempt at firmness was a dismal failure and the statement almost became a question.

"Really?" Thanet sat back, folding his arm and looking from

one to the other and back again, as if searching for something he failed to find. "I really don't understand it, Sergeant, do you?"

"Understand what?" Speed was sweating now and the reek of motor oil was growing stronger as his body temperature rose, an emanation as distinctive as a fingerprint.

Suddenly Thanet remembered: the first time he had entered Nerine Tarrant's bedroom he had caught an elusive whiff of something incongruous. Now he realised what it was. It is notoriously difficult to recognise smells out of context and he supposed that he might be excused for not having been able to identify motor oil in all that silken, feminine elegance. Although Tim had only been working at the pump and in the office garage his clothes must have picked up the smell and left that almost undetectable imprint upon the air.

"Why is it, do you think, Sergeant, that when people wish they hadn't been in a certain place at a certain time, they seem to manage to convince themselves that they were invisible?"

"Beats me, sir."

"Invisible? What do you mean? What are you talking about?"

But they had both understood him. Thanet could read it in the flare of a nostril, an averted eye, a whitening of the knuckles.

"Oh, I think you know what I mean, Mr. Speed." Abruptly Thanet abandoned his jocular, almost benign tone and leaning forward said accusingly, "Don't you?"

"No!" Speed glanced at his wife for support. "No, we don't, do we, Ceel?"

Celia Speed did not reply for a moment. She gave Thanet a level, assessing look, then said, "I think we'd better hear what the Inspector has to say, don't you? I think he's rather angry with us."

"Yes," said Thanet. "You could say that. I'm angry because this is a murder investigation and I don't like people wasting my time. Both of you, I find, have lied to us. No," and he raised a hand as they both made to speak, "don't say anything at the moment. Just hear me out. Now it's always very difficult, when people do lie to us, to work out their motives in doing so. They might be innocent of the crime we are investigating and merely trying to conceal some little family secret they don't want broadcast—no, I'm sorry, you really will have to wait until I've finished, you had your opportunity to speak and you didn't take it—or, *or* they might be lying because they are up to their necks in the crime in question and are trying to wriggle out of being suspected. I'm not sure which it is, in your case."

"The first," they said together, and stopped.

"But naturally, you would say that, wouldn't you?" said Thanet. "Being the lesser of two evils."

"But it's true!" said Speed. "I did explain to you, at the garage . . ."

"Oh no, Mr. Speed," said Lineham. "We're not talking about that. This is something else."

"Something else . . . ?"

"Suppose you come right out and tell us what we are supposed to have done, Inspector," said Celia Speed.

"No. Suppose you try to set the record straight. Suppose *you* tell *us* anything you 'forgot' to tell us the first—or in the case of Mr. Speed, the second—time around."

Mrs. Speed made as if to rise. "Do you mind if I get a glass of water?"

"Sergeant Lineham will get you one."

While they waited for Lineham to return Thanet said, "Let me just say this. If you are innocent of this crime, you have nothing to fear. Unless what you tell me is relevant to the investigation and eventually has to be used in court, I assure you that it is not going to become a matter of gossip amongst the neighbours through any indiscretion on our part. I think you understand me."

They exchanged glances. *They do know about Tim.*

"But," Thanet went on, "this time I really want the whole truth and nothing but. Otherwise . . ."

There was no need to spell it out. *Otherwise you'll find yourselves in deep water indeed.*

Lineham returned with a cup of water. "Sorry, I couldn't find the glasses."

Mrs. Speed took the cup with a murmur of thanks and drained it at a draught.

"So who's going to begin? Mr. Speed, perhaps?"

SIXTEEN

"Let's start from the moment you parked your car in that field, shall we, Mr. Speed? And remember, we're not just guessing at all this. We do have witnesses."

Mrs. Speed closed her eyes tightly, as if to shut out the view of a too harsh reality, and swallowed hard. But this did not succeed in stopping the tears which now began to force themselves between her closed eyelids. With an exclamation of impatience she flicked them away with the back of her forefinger, groped in her pocket for a handkerchief and failed to find one. "Sorry," she said. "There are some tissues in the kitchen..." And again she dashed away the tears with her finger.

Thanet waited until Lineham had fetched the tissues and she was rather more composed, then said, "Look, Mrs. Speed, I can guess how painful all this is for you. There's absolutely no need for you to be here while we're talking to Mr. Speed. Why don't you go and lie down for a little while? Your husband will call you for us, when we need to see you... And if you're not feeling well enough, then we'll leave it until another day."

Long before he had finished his little speech she was shaking her head.

"No, I'd rather stay, thank you. Really."

Thanet guessed that she would prefer to know exactly what was going on in here than lie on her bed in a torment of uncertainty and speculation. He gave a slight shrug. "As you

wish." He glanced from wife to husband and then said,
"Perhaps it might help and perhaps hurry things along a little
if I openly state what I hinted at just now. We do know about
Mrs. Tarrant and your son."

He had guessed that this would produce more tears, and
he was right. Mrs. Speed briefly turned her face into her
husband's shoulder and he put his arm around her. After a
moment she sat up again, blew her nose and whispered, "I'm
sorry. It's just that . . . I can't . . ." And she shook her head, at
a loss for words. Finally she raised her head and looked
directly at Thanet. "I still find it difficult to believe."

"I can imagine. I'm sorry."

She studied his face, and after a moment said with a note of
surprise, "Yes, I believe you are."

"It must have been a tremendous shock to you."

"Yes." She glanced at her husband and added bitterly, "To
both of us, in different ways."

"There was a row, I believe," said Thanet.

"Yes." She frowned at the memory, and blew her nose
again. "Tim . . ."

Thanet said nothing, waited.

She gave a little shrug. "Tim says it was *her* doing. That
the idea would never have entered his head, if she hadn't
made the first move. To him she was just Damon's mother,
that's all. And then . . . But I don't want to go into all that. It
happened, that's all, and somehow I'm going to have to learn
to accept it."

"How long had it been going on?"

She was studiously avoiding looking at her husband now. "A
couple of weeks, so far as I can gather."

"And you suspected something of the sort, Mr. Speed?"

"Yes. But . . ." His voice was hoarse and he paused to clear
his throat. "But not that it was . . . him, of course." He
obviously couldn't bring himself to say his son's name in this
context.

"So you decided to try to find out who had supplanted
you."

Speed nodded.

It had been exactly as they thought. Speed became suspicious when Nerine started putting him off. He knew her
routine for entertaining her lovers over the lunch hour and on
the day of the murder he decided to spy on her, to try to find
out who his rival was. In the normal way of things Tarrant

never returned home during the day and Speed had been disconcerted to see his Mercedes turn into the drive. But it had occurred to him that Tarrant's return home might have been unexpected. If Nerine were entertaining a lover it would be interesting to see what transpired. And he might yet learn who his rival was.

So he had carried out his plan, parking in the field and entering the garden via the back gate as usual, then hiding in the rhododendron bushes, a vantage point which gave him a good view of both front and side entrances.

He had been there only a minute or so when Tarrant came out in a hurry, jumped into his car and drove off. He had looked upset and Speed wondered what had happened in the house. He knew that Nerine always locked her bedroom door when entertaining, and thought that Tarrant had perhaps heard voices inside and jumped to the obvious conclusion.

"You didn't think that in that case he might have forced some sort of confrontation? Hammered on the door? Gone around onto the balcony and tried to get in through the french windows?"

Speed shook his head. "No." He shifted uncomfortably. "He . . . His attitude to Nerine's boyfriends was very peculiar. I mean, he used to behave as though it wasn't happening, even when it obviously was, right under his nose! I could never understand it."

Mrs. Speed was sitting tight-lipped, nostrils pinched as though there were a bad smell in the room.

Speed cast her an apologetic glance, then said, "Anyway, I thought it was worth hanging on a bit longer, just in case there was someone with her. And then, about ten minutes later . . ."

"All right," said Thanet. There was no point in rubbing salt into the wound. "We can guess what happened next. You saw Tim come out, realised you couldn't have a shouting match there and then in Mrs. Tarrant's garden, and ordered him home. Why? You knew your wife would be here. I should have thought she'd be the last person you'd want around, in the circumstances."

"She wasn't supposed to be here," said Speed sullenly. "I'd told her I wouldn't be back, dinnertime, and she said in that case she'd ring up a friend of hers, go shopping with her in Sturrenden and have a bite to eat in the town."

"But Betty had already made other arrangements," put in Mrs. Speed, "so I didn't go."

"I see." *More lies*, said his tone. He distinctly remembered both of them giving the impression that Speed had all along intended going home for lunch that day.

"So what happened?"

Speed was studiously avoiding looking at his wife. "She could see something was wrong, straight away."

'Lance! I thought you said you weren't coming home? I haven't got anything ready for . . . What's the matter? What is it?'

'I . . . Oh God.'

'Lance. Tell me.'

'It's Tim.'

'Tim? What's happened to him? Has there been an accident? He's not . . . He's not . . . dead?'

'No, nothing like that. He's all right. But . . .'

'But what? Lance, just tell me, will you?'

'I don't know how to. I've just found out . . .'

'WHAT?'

'That's he's been . . . having it off, with Mrs. Tarrant. Oh God, Ceel, I'm sorry. Don't look at me like that. He'll be here any minute. I sent him home. I thought you'd be out.'

"And then Tim came home," said Speed, "and there was the most almighty row. He'd didn't stay long, walked out in the middle of it."

"I'm surprised he went back to work in the garage that afternoon, after all that."

"I said he'd bloody better, or he could say goodbye to his nice little holiday job, and they don't grow on trees these days, you know. I stayed behind with Ceel for a while. She was in a bit of a state."

Scarcely surprising, thought Thanet, after that little bombshell had landed in her lap. "And then what?"

The staccato question made them exchange a look of surprised alarm.

"What do you mean?" said Speed. "You know what happened then. We told you, last time you was here."

"You mean, you went back to the garage as if nothing had happened, worked there all afternoon, took a car out for a test drive for twenty minutes at around a quarter past five, then shut up shop and came home as usual."

"Yes. Yes!"

"No little detours to High Gables, to see Mrs. Tarrant?"

"No! Look, Inspector, you wanted the whole truth and now you've got it."

"Have I? How do I know you're not lying, Mr. Speed?"

"Because I'm not! I swear it."

"That's what you said last time. And the time before. That's the trouble with telling lies, you see, Mr. Speed. You destroy your own credibility."

This was unanswerable. Speed's lips tightened, but he said nothing.

Thanet turned to Speed's wife. "And you, Mrs. Speed?"

Without looking at her husband, Celia Speed said calmly, "After the row with Tim I was furious with Mrs. Tarrant." Her chin lifted a little "I had every reason to be, I think you'll agree. First my husband, then my son... I decided I'd go and tell her exactly what I thought of her."

Speed obviously knew all this. He shook his head in resigned exasperation. His wife ignored him but there was a note of defiance as she continued.

"I couldn't go straight away because of the meeting in the village hall. I'd been asked to give the vote of thanks, to the speaker. Afterwards, well, I wanted to get it over with and in fact I walked as far as the gates of High Gables... But old Mr. Parkin was expecting me. He's got arthritis and we all take it in turns to give him a hand. I always go on Thursday afternoons, and I was already late because of the meeting. So I visited him first, then went back to High Gables again. This time I actually got as far as walking up the drive."

"And then?"

Mrs. Speed's plump cheeks quivered as she shook her head. "I couldn't do it. I... I'm not the sort of person who goes in for rows, and I was still feeling all churned up after the one at dinnertime. And, well..."

She gave her husband an uncertain, embarrassed glance, and Thanet wondered what was coming. "You may think me stupid, Inspector, but people like Mrs. Tarrant always make me feel nervous. Well, inferior, I suppose. I mean, she was so beautiful, always so elegant, so confident... I just lost my nerve. I told myself I hadn't given up the idea, but I'd do it another day, when I was feeling better, and, you know, had got myself ready."

Had had her hair done, armoured herself in her smartest clothes, and was feeling her unconfident best, Thanet supposed. He winced at the thought of such a confrontation and was glad that Celia Speed had at least been spared that. There was no doubt in his mind as to who would have come off best.

"And then . . ." She shrugged. "I just came home."

And nothing could shake either of them. These were their stories and they were sticking to them. After a while Thanet decided that it was pointless to continue.

He and Lineham walked back to High Gables to pick up the car. It was very hot, the sun high in a sky of the purest cerulean blue. The cottage gardens were a brilliant kaleidoscope of colour, canvases crowded with the strawberry pink of foxgloves creamy-white at the throat, the frothy gold of alchemilla, the sprawling mauve of catmint and everywhere the pinks and reds, yellows and apricots of roses in full bloom.

"Well, if either of the Speeds did it, it looks as though we're going to have to produce some pretty cast-iron evidence before they'll admit it," said Lineham.

"Mmm." Thanet paused to inhale the fragrance of a clump of sweet rocket growing through a white picket fence. "Let's hope forensic come up with something useful. Let's see, it's Saturday. With any luck we might have something through from fingerprints on Monday. And the PM should be finished by now, so I expect Doc Mallard will give us a verbal report this afternoon. Not that I'm expecting too much from that."

It was just before two o'clock and outside the village hall a little queue had formed.

"Didn't know jumble sales were so popular," said Lineham.

Thanet grinned. "Quite a lot of people become addicted, I believe. Joan tells me that lots of dealers comb the local paper for jumble sale ads and get in there fast, in the hope of bargains. She usually runs the white elephant stall at our church bazaar and the second the doors open people come streaming in as if it were the first day of Harrods' sale. They know exactly what they want. There's one chap who always hunts for brass, makes for her stall like a homing pigeon, turns everything over, grabs what he wants and is off, presumably to his next target, within a matter of minutes."

"Scavengers."

"Quite."

"Look, I bet that's one, sir."

Among the straggle of determined women with carrier bags

was a seedy-looking character in stained corduroys, a grubby checked shirt and greasy anorak.

"No prize for that observation, Mike."

"There's Mrs. Haywood."

Beatrix Haywood was approaching from the other direction, scarves a-flutter. She spotted them, raised a hand in greeting and came to ask if there were any news of Damon before pushing past the queue. She knocked on the door and was admitted.

"Helping on one of the stalls, I expect," said Lineham.

"Mmm." Thanet was trying to decide what to do next, but he needn't have bothered; over the car radio they learned that Halo Buzzard had been picked up and brought in for questioning.

"Who knows?" said Thanet as they sped back to Sturrenden. "We could have been running around in circles for nothing. Buzzard is, after all, the only person known to have uttered threats against her."

In most murder cases, as Thanet knew well, the most obvious suspect usually turns out to be the murderer. He had had just such a case himself, only last year. This might well turn out to be another.

"Yes, ten years ago! That's why I doubt if it'll come to anything. For one thing, ten years is a long time to cool off. For another, no one who has spent ten years inside is going to risk spending another ten unless there's a pretty hefty profit in it."

"It's also a long time to brood over a grievance."

"I know. But still . . ."

Buzzard was in a belligerent mood. As soon as Thanet entered the room he jumped to his feet.

"'Ere, what the 'ell's going on? There was I, behaving meself, 'aving a nice quiet drink with me mates and in come you lot and before I know where I am I'm stuck in 'ere and left to cool me 'eels for an hour. I got better things to do with me time, you know."

"And so have I. So let's get on with it, shall we, Buzzard?"

The reason for the man's nickname was immediately obvious. Thanet knew that "Halo" was thirty-two, but his face had the unmarked smoothness and texture of youth, and his blue eyes and fair curls gave him a deceptive air of innocence. It was all wrong, Thanet thought, that a man who had been convicted of armed robbery and grievous bodily harm should look so angelic.

"Get on with what? I'm not getting on with nothing. I know my rights and I demand my phone call and my solicitor."

"Don't worry, you'll get your rights. All in good time. If that's what you want. But don't you think you might be overreacting a bit? I merely wanted to have a little chat with you. Afterwards, if you're in the clear, you can go."

"A little chat!" Buzzard almost spat the words. "Very cosy, I'm sure. Oh, no, you ain't catching me out like that. I ain't saying a word until my brief is here."

"Pity. You could have been away in a matter of minutes. Still, it's up to you. As it is, I'm afraid you'll just have to accept our hospitality for a bit longer."

"Why? I told you, I ain't done nothing."

"I seem to have heard that song before," said Thanet. "And you ought to know by now that we don't pick people up without good reason."

"Pull the other one. Once you've been inside you can't even crap without the rozzers breathing down your neck... Anyway, what good reason? Go on, you tell me that. What good reason?"

"You were seen in the area where a crime was committed, on Thursday afternoon."

"So what? What crime? Where?"

Had there been an overtone of unease, there? Of fear, even?

"On the outskirts of Sturrenden."

"Mistaken identity."

"No mistake. The witness is reliable."

"I don't care if the Pope hisself swears he saw me. He's lying."

"You were somewhere else, of course."

"Of course. Playing poker with some mates."

"Time, place, names, addresses?" said Thanet wearily.

Lineham took them down.

Thanet stood up. "We'll have to check these out of course." He turned to go.

"'Ere! You're not going to leave me twiddling me thumbs while you check all that lot? It's Saturday. They could be anywhere... football match, taking the kids to the seaside... They could even be away for the weekend!"

"That's just too bad, I'm afraid. Come on, Buzzard. You're

not seriously suggesting we let you go so that you can rush off and contact these mates of yours, make sure they back up your story? You must be joking."

"It's harassment, that's what it is. Harassment. Dragging me in off the street and interrogating me..."

"You weren't dragged, and a five-minute conversation can scarcely be called interrogation."

"You haven't even told me what I'm supposed to have done!"

Thanet had reached the door, and he turned to face Buzzard.

"Murder," he said quietly. "That's what."

Buzzard's expression changed. His eyes narrowed and his mouth pinched up in apparent disbelief. "Murder? What the 'ell you on about? Whose murder? When? Where?"

"If you're telling the truth," said Thanet, "you don't need to know, do you? You've got an alibi, remember?" And he turned and walked out. As Lineham closed the door behind them he heard Buzzard say, "'Ere, 'ang on a minute...!"

"We'll leave him to stew for a while," said Thanet. "You'd better get a team onto checking on these 'mates' of his. I've no doubt they'll back him up, but we'd better go through the motions."

"What d'you think, sir? D'you think he's our man?"

Thanet sighed. "I doubt it, worse luck. But there was something... Underneath all the bluster I thought I detected a distinct note of nervousness."

"I agree. I was wondering... Even if he's not involved in our case, it's possible he was up to something else that afternoon."

"Let me see... Thursday... Thursday... Of course! The burglary out at Nettleton Grange! Mike, I bet that's it. And if so... Look, go and have a word with Bristow, he's in charge, tell him what we think and suggest it might be worth getting a search warrant sworn out, while we've got Buzzard safely tucked up here. It's a long shot, but we might just be lucky."

Thanet knew from past experience that a criminal pulled in on suspicion of one crime might well prove guilty of another.

"Surely he wouldn't have stashed any stuff in his room? He's too old a hand for that."

"You never know. He hasn't been out of prison that long, he might not have built up enough contacts yet to have been able to dispose of everything. It's a long shot, of course, but worth a try."

"I'll get on to it right away."

On the way up to his office Thanet ran into Doc Mallard, coming down.

"Ah, Luke. I heard you were back. I've just been looking for you."

"The PM results?"

"Verbal report, yes."

"Come along to my office."

Someone had come in and shut the window while Thanet and Lineham were out, and the room was stifling, airless. With an exclamation of annoyance Thanet went to open it. "Place is like an oven." He took off his jacket and slung it on the back of his chair. "Well Doc, what's the news?"

SEVENTEEN

Mallard perched on the corner of Thanet's desk, picked up a report and began to fan himself with it. "If you're hoping for a sensation you're going to be disappointed. We didn't learn anything we hadn't already guessed. She was in very good shape, vital organs all healthy. Cause of death, as we thought, fracture-dislocation of the cervical spine—or, to put it in layman's terms, a broken neck."

"No signs of a previous struggle?"

" 'Fraid not. Sorry to be so unhelpful."

Thanet sighed. He was longing to flex his back, which was beginning to ache again, but he tried never to draw attention to his weakness in front of other people. "Not your fault. Ah, well . . . Not that I really expected anything, but still . . ."

"How's the case going?"

"So-so. It's early days yet, of course."

"Has the boy turned up yet? What's his name? Damon? Damon! What an outlandish name. Fancy saddling any child with a handle like that."

"No, I'm afraid not. There's been not a sight nor sound of him."

"But you're not worried about him, are you? In the sense that he could be in danger? I understood he was seen leaving of his own accord."

"That's right, yes, he was. But I'd give a lot to know *why* he went. He's not in any of his usual haunts."

"Didn't you say he was up on a drugs charge, recently? You've talked to his probation officer, of course."

"Yes, we have."

Malland frowned at Thanet's tone. "Sorry, I didn't mean to tell you how to do your job."

"Oh no, Doc, please don't misunderstand me. It's just that... well, his probation officer is Joan."

There was a brief silence while Mallard took in the implications. "Ah," he said at last, heavily. "I can see that that might cause... complications."

So there it was, the opportunity Thanet needed, to unburden himself. Should he take it?

Thanet himself had often been the recipient of confidences. He liked people and it showed. He was approachable, sympathetic and percipient and inevitably he had found himself in the position of having to try to sort out the all-too-frequent marital difficulties of his men. Despite his apparent openness, however, he was really a very private person and the prospect of discussing his relationship with Joan with an outsider, however trustworthy, appalled him. Over and over again, presented with an apparently insoluble marriage problem, he had given the same advice: talk about it with her (or him), as honestly as you can. Sooner or later, he realised, he and Joan were going to have to do just that.

"It is a bit tricky, yes. We've never encountered this particular problem before. In the circumstances, I suppose we're lucky to have escaped up to now. Still, we'll cope, no doubt."

Mallard took the hint. "Yes." He put down the report with which he had been fanning himself and slid off the edge of the desk. "Well, I'm sorry I couldn't have been more help. Let me know, if there's anything I can do."

Left alone, Thanet stood up, crossed to a filing cabinet and grasped it firmly with both hands, at shoulder level. Then, feet apart, he raised himself on his toes and slowly, carefully, arched his back, clenching his teeth as the dull ache sharpened into the edge of pain. Then he straightened up, relaxed. He repeated the exercise five times and returned to his chair, careful to sit upright, with the base of his spine hard against the back of the seat. Then he lit his pipe, closed his eyes and began to think.

He was convinced that Damon was somehow at the root of the problem. What had caused him to shoot off like that, "like a bat out of hell," as one witness had put it? It was possible, of course, that there was some perfectly innocent explanation, that he had gone away by previous arrangement and had left in haste because he was late. But with every day that passed this possibility seemed less and less likely and in any case smacked too much of coincidence for Thanet's liking. There was that missed appointment, too.

The other explanation was that something had happened to make him run away.

But what?

Thanet ran over the alternatives. One (the most obvious): Damon had killed his mother and was in hiding from the police. But if so, what could have driven him to it? There must have been a quarrel, obviously, but what about? Any of the usual things, Thanet supposed: late nights, loud music, girls, rudeness, inconsideration... But a row over any of these would escalate into violence only if there had been a long, accelerating history of clashes, and surely somebody, at some point, would have let slip a hint if Damon's relationship with his mother had been as stormy as that. No, if there had been a quarrel, it must have been about one specific issue.

What?

Of course! Thanet's eyes snapped open as a possible explanation occurred to him. Damon had been in the house all day. Which presumably meant over the lunch hour. What if, by chance, he had happened to come downstairs at the wrong moment and had seen Tim, his friend, emerging from his mother's bedroom?

Thanet considered the idea. How would Damon have felt? Knowing so little about him, it was difficult to tell. Would he have been shocked, censorious, disgusted, or amused, resigned, even titillated?

In any case, Thanet simply couldn't believe that the shock would have been enough to cause an eighteen-year-old to leave home and to stay away despite the considerable publicity surrounding the murder. Nor would he have hung around for hours before departing in a hurry.

So what would Damon have done? Thanet felt that his most likely reaction would have been to say nothing. Or, if he decided he must speak, to have blurted it out immediately.

But just say, for the sake of argument, that Damon decided to tell his mother what he thought of her behaviour but found he needed time in which to pluck up his courage to do so. Why take so long about it?

Tim had left High Gables at around ten to one. Nerine had been in the house for another hour before leaving for the hairdresser's, had returned at half past three and had been around for another couple of hours (dead or alive) before Damon's departure. Surely the most likely time for Damon to have tackled Nerine would be as soon as she got back from the hairdresser's. Why wait a further two hours? And if Damon had in fact killed his mother soon after her return at half past three, surely he wouldn't have hung about so long before departing in such a hurry?

No, Thanet decided. It hadn't been such a brilliant idea after all. The timings were all wrong. If Damon had had a quarrel with Nerine, it must have been about something else.

But what?

There was no way of telling.

Thanet abandoned this line of thought and moved on.

Why else might the boy have run away? Thanet couldn't imagine that it was simply because he had found his mother's body. In that case he would have been shocked, yes, but surely his natural reaction would have been to assume an accident and call for help? No, if Damon had not committed the murder himself, and if he yet knew that a murder had been committed, the only possible reason why he could have disappeared was because he knew who had killed his mother *and wanted to protect that person*.

So, who would Damon wish to protect?

His father?

If Roland Tarrant had committed the murder, it must have been later on in the afternoon. Nerine had certainly been alive and well until half past three and there were witnesses enough to confirm that Tarrant had been fully occupied at the hospital until he left at a quarter past five. No, if Tarrant had done it, it must have been after his return home at twenty to six, and Damon couldn't have known; he had left the house just before his father arrived. Did this mean that Tarrant was in the clear? Not necessarily. Thanet still had to allow for the fact that Damon's departure might have nothing to do with the murder.

So who else might the lad have been trying to protect? Certainly there was one obvious person, much as Thanet disliked the idea: Damon's grandmother. She had had both motive and opportunity. And it sounded as though during that second rest period from four thirty to five thirty the old lady had seen something, heard something, done something that had frightened her badly. Why else, when Marilyn went to get her up from her rest, should she have been crouching in the corner of her bedroom, like a terrified child? Had she just returned from her daughter-in-law's room after a quarrel which had got out of hand and resulted in an outburst of senile frenzy?

Thanet's neck prickled as he remembered Lavinia's face when she had whispered, *"Death."*

Thanet shook his head. So much speculation, so much frustration, in not being able to follow up essential lines of enquiry. If only Damon were available, if only Lavinia were rational, her memory undimmed by the disease gnawing away at her brain... But if it was a sense of loyalty which had driven Damon away, there was no doubt about it, Lavinia was the most likely candidate to have inspired it.

Who else had been on the premises during the afternoon? Thanet mentally checked them off.

Beatrix Haywood had been in the attic sorting out things for the jumble sale, until just after the quarrel between Nerine and Lavinia over the mess in Nerine's bedroom, at half past three.

Vicky Cunningham had returned from her shopping trip at three and had been working the kitchen until four.

Daphne Linacre had arrived back at the coach house at twenty to five and claimed to have gone straight to bed, with a migraine.

Then there was Marilyn Barnes, who had been in the house all afternoon. There was, too, Thanet reminded himself, one other person: Nicky, Marilyn's ten-year-old son. Perhaps he should be questioned again. Children were astonishingly observant and Nicky had been in the house or out in the garden from a quarter to four right up until the time the murder was discovered.

Thanet considered the list. Of all these, the only other person he thought Damon might have been tempted to protect was his aunt, Daphne Linacre. She seemed to be fond of the boy...

The door opened and Lineham came in, glowing with satisfaction.

"All fixed, sir. DS Bristow was very keen to cooperate. As

he said, we've nothing to lose by taking a look and maybe a lot to gain. We managed to contact a JP and she's satisfied that there are sufficient grounds for a search warrant." He plumped down at his desk, and looked eagerly at Thanet. "Anything new? Have we heard about the PM yet?"

"Yes, but there's nothing of any use to us. Cause of death a broken neck."

Lineham pulled a face. "Pity. So where do we go from here?"

"I think it's time we put our heads together, tried to thrash things out."

"OK. Where do we start?"

"Well, I've been thinking about Damon." Briefly, Thanet summarised his conclusions.

Lineham said slowly, "You could well be right, about him disappearing so that he couldn't be questioned. But it's a pretty short-sighted thing to do, surely? I mean, he couldn't hope to vanish permanently."

"Maybe not. But that hasty departure smacks of impulse, of panic, even. And if he had in fact seen his mother murdered by someone he knew and loved, his grandmother for instance, he would have been in a state of shock. But he'd know that if he stayed he'd be questioned and might well have felt that he wouldn't be able to lie convincingly. Perhaps he hoped we'd simply accept that it was an accidental fall. In any case he'd have hoped that if he kept out of the way long enough the thing would be resolved without his evidence being instrumental in bringing about the arrest of someone close to him. In which case he's lying low until it's all over."

"If that's what happened we ought to be concentrating on the latter part of the afternoon. I can't see him hanging about for hours after witnessing a murder, before taking off in that kind of a hurry."

"If." Thanet sighed. "The trouble is, it's all speculation and doesn't get us any further."

"And there's still a possibility that he took off for some reason unconnected with the murder."

"Quite."

"Well, the one thing that seems pretty certain, unless Buzzard did it, and I think we both tend to agree that that's unlikely, is that it was an unplanned murder. Someone with a grievance against Mrs. Tarrant had a quarrel with her and it got out of hand."

"That seems the most likely explanation, Mike, I agree."

"The trouble is, there are so many candidates. If it was old Mrs. Tarrant, it must have been because of the threat either to put her in a nursing home or to get rid of Miss Barnes.

"If it was Marilyn Barnes, it was either because she wanted Roland Tarrant for herself or because she was afraid of losing her job—which in her case means losing her home, too. And she has her son to think of.

"If it was Mr. Tarrant, it was because he'd finally snapped, after overhearing his wife entertaining her lover—especially if he realised it was Tim Speed in there. Tim is Damon's friend. Mr. Tarrant might well have recognised his voice."

"I don't know, Mike. I'm inclined to believe him, when he says he thought it was Tim's father. Their voices are very alike, you know."

"True. All the same, I'm still not convinced about all this turning-a-blind-eye stuff. And it's one thing to know it's going on, another to have your nose rubbed in it.

"Then there are the Speeds. Now there are two juicy motives, if you like. It can't be easy for an ageing Romeo like Speed to realise he's been chucked out of his mistress's bed by his own son. And as for Mrs. Speed . . . Well, I know she seems inoffensive enough, and she's generally well liked and all that, but even if she managed to come to terms with the fact that her husband was having it off with Mrs. Tarrant, when it came to finding out that the woman had now got her claws into young Tim . . . Mrs. Speed's only got the one chick, sir, and it's generally accepted that even the mildest of mothers can turn into a tigress when defending her young. We only have her word that she didn't actually go into the house and see Mrs. Tarrant, that second time. I'm not saying she necessarily went there intending to kill her, but I can just imagine the sort of a scene there might have been between them, can't you?"

"Yes." Thanet could imagine it, quite clearly: Nerine, cool, elegant, amused, scornful, and Celia Speed, dowdy, hot with anger, frustration, humiliation . . . "There's Nerine's sister Daphne, too, don't forget, Mike. We might yet turn up some reason why she could have done it."

Lineham frowned. "It's difficult to see what could have triggered it off in her case. She wasn't even there until late afternoon. And she and Mrs. Tarrant did seem to live pretty separate lives. Unless we're wrong about thinking it was an unplanned murder, and Daphne Linacre had just been waiting for the right opportunity to come along. Bit of a coincidence though, in that case, that she just happened to hit upon the very afternoon when her sister had seriously upset a whole lot of other people, don't you think?"

"I suppose so." Thanet felt dispirited. All that seemed to be happening at the moment was that the list of suspects was growing longer and the chances of nailing any one of them seemed to be becoming more remote. "What we really need is just one little bit of hard evidence, Mike."

"Well, we'll just have to keep hoping forensic come up with something."

"Yes. Meanwhile, I think we ought to have a word with Nicky Barnes. It occurs to me that he was around in either the house or the garden from a quarter to four right up to when the body was discovered."

"Carson seemed satisfied that the boy hadn't seen anything suspicious."

"I'm aware of that. All the same, you never know. It might not have seemed suspicious to Nicky, but with what we now know about the comings and goings in the house that afternoon . . ."

"You think we ought to try and talk to him today, sir?"

"Might as well. Come to think of it, it's odd that we didn't see him around earlier on, when we were out at the house. It's Saturday, he wouldn't be at school."

"Perhaps Miss Barnes is still keeping him out of the way, sir."

Thanet grinned. "If so, I can't imagine he'll be very pleased about it. If he's anything like Ben he'd want to be where the action is."

But apparently Nicky had gone on a school trip to Windsor Safari Park and wouldn't be back until late. Marilyn Barnes was not keen on the idea of the boy being interviewed at the end of such a long day.

Lineham arranged to see him at ten next morning.

EIGHTEEN

Talk it over with her.

All the way home snatches of Thanet's own advice to those with marital problems kept coming back to him. He'd always known, of course, that it is far easier to give counsel than to follow it. Now, for the first time, he was on the receiving end and a very uncomfortable sensation it was.

It was a quarter to midnight and in the centre of town there were still people about. It was, after all, Saturday night. But the suburban streets through which Thanet was now driving were virtually deserted, most of their windows in darkness. He turned left, catching up with an old Vauxhall which was limping along at twenty-five miles an hour. Thanet was about to overtake when without warning it swung out in a curve before turning into a narrow driveway. He considered stopping, to remonstrate, but couldn't be bothered. He was too tired, too preoccupied, too engrossed in his private dilemma to have any energy to spare for minor misdemeanours. He drove on.

Pick your moment. Don't, above all, choose a time when you're both upset, in the middle of an argument. Easier said than done. If you were working long hours, as he was, time with your wife was at a premium, especially time alone with her. If you were tired after a heavy day, and she was already in bed and asleep when you got home, she was scarcely going to appreciate being woken up and asked to have a serious discussion, in the middle of the night. And mornings were

169

always such a rush, with both of them getting ready to go to work, and the children around... But I must *make* time, he told himself fiercely. We can't go on like this.

All day, whenever he had allowed his concentration to slip, a wave of misery had washed over him at the memory of the rift between them. There had been arguments before, of course, times when one or the other of them—sometimes both—had been tired, contentious or on edge. But except for those distant, premonitory rumblings seven years ago, when Joan had chosen probation as her career, there had never been anything as serious as this. He could certainly never remember a time when she had gone off to bed without even saying good night to him—it had always been a matter of principle with them to follow the advice from Ephesians 4:26 drummed into them by both sets of parents: *Let not the sun go down upon your wrath.* It had, they found, never failed to work.

I can't let this happen, he thought. There must be some way around it.

But if there was, he couldn't see it. Perhaps he should simply climb down, make an abject apology and leave it at that?

But why should he?

If a man close to the victim disappears virtually at the same time as a murder is committed, the inference is obvious: there is a strong possibility that in some way he is involved. Surely Joan ought to be able to see that, after giving Damon twenty-four hours' grace, Thanet had had no option but to publicise the boy's disappearance?

He had arrived home. Joan usually liked to be in bed by half past eleven, but the muted glow behind the curtained window of the living room told him that she was still up. Thanet got out of the car, locked it, then stood for a moment, hesitating. Despite his eagerness for a reconciliation he found that he was reluctant to go in and face her.

It was very quiet; only the occasional roar of a distant car and the orange globes of the street lamps punctuated the wan midsummer darkness. The full moon was encircled by a band of milky, opalescent cloud and even as he watched a few high, ragged wisps drifted across it. Rain tomorrow?

Light suddenly spilled across the front lawn as a curtain in the living room was pulled back, and Joan peered out. She must have heard the car and was checking that it was indeed her husband out there, not thieves on the prowl. She drew the curtain again and a few moments later the front door opened.

"Luke?"

"Coming."

She was wearing the blue silk kimono he had given her for her last birthday. As he came up to her she said, "I wondered who it was, lurking about out there."

Good resolutions were at once swamped by an irrational uprush of indignation. "I was not 'lurking'!" He brushed past her.

"Sorry! Lingering, then." She followed him into the kitchen. "D'you want anything to eat?"

"No, thanks. I picked something up in the canteen." He took a can of lager out of the fridge, held it up. "D'you want one?" The note of forced politeness in his voice gave him a jolt. What was he doing? Here he was, presented with the very opportunity for which he had been hoping. The fact that Joan had waited up for him showed that she must be in a conciliatory mood.

She was shaking her head. "I had a cup of tea, half an hour ago."

He put the can down on the table and reached for her hands. "Joan?"

She returned his gaze steadily, defiantly, almost. "Yes?"

"We've got to talk."

"I know."

"Sorry I was so bad-tempered just now."

A little shrug, a barely perceptible movement of her shoulders. "That's OK." She attempted a smile. "You've had a long day."

"No reason why I should take it out on you... Truce?"

The smile was warmer now. "Truce."

He tugged her towards him and gave her a brief hug. "Let's go into the other room, shall we?"

He kept his arm around her as they crossed the hall. Surely, with goodwill on both sides they ought to be able to sort this out? Suddenly he felt more optimistic than he had all day. They sat down side by side, his arm falling from her shoulders as she curled away from him into her favourite position in the corner of the settee, legs tucked beneath her. The coffee table nearby was littered with photographs.

She gestured towards them. "I really must get around to sticking them into an album."

"Mmm." He took a long, grateful drink of lager and leaned forward to set the can down on the table. There it was, spread out before him, a pictorial record of their married life together: their summer wedding, honeymoon in the Dordogne, Bridget's christening, Ben's, holiday photographs, children's parties, family gatherings at Christmas... He picked a photograph out at random: Ben and himself, in the garden. He was squatting beside his son, who was holding a bright red balloon on the end of a string. It had been taken on Ben's second birthday, he remembered. What had made Joan indulge in this orgy of nostalgia? he wondered. Regret for happier days gone by, fear of the future, or a need to reassure herself that with so much shared happiness they had a solid foundation on which to build a bridge over the chasm that now yawned between them?

He risked a glance at her. She was watching him solemnly. What was she thinking? She was as apprehensive as he, he realised. How best to begin?

"I don't know where to start," he said helplessly.

She shrugged. "There's no point in beating about the bush. Let's start with the TVS appeal, shall we?"

"Why not. All right. Let's. You first."

"I just don't know why you acted so... precipitately." Her tone was reasonable, unaccusatory. "I should have thought it could easily have waited another twenty-four hours, if not longer."

She was, he could see, trying very hard to follow all the precepts he had been laying down for himself. His own voice echoed in his head. *Try to see her point of view.* "I don't see that I had any choice. I couldn't—I still can't—believe that it was sheer coincidence that Damon disappeared on the very afternoon his mother was murdered. I'm convinced there must be some connection."

"But as it turned out, the appeal had no effect. He still hasn't turned up."

"That's beside the point. We couldn't know that. The point is, we had to try."

"I'm not saying you didn't have to try, but why then, at that particular moment? Why not give him a little more time?"

"But why should I have?" In spite of himself a note of indignation, of belligerence, almost, was creeping back into his voice. "Look, Joan, I think what you're really saying is that I should have treated him differently simply because he was—is—your client."

Her frown deepened. "That's not true."

"Isn't it?"

She hesitated. She was, he could see, making a real effort to be honest with herself. "I'm not sure," she admitted at last.

"You see, what I had to ask myself was, if Damon was not your client, would I have put out that appeal when I did? And the answer was yes, I would."

"Are you sure, Luke?"

"Yes. Yes! Of course I am." But, was he? He glanced at Joan. She was frowning down at her lap, rolling the sash of her kimono round and round her forefinger. "You don't believe me."

A tight little shake of the head. "It's just that..."

"What?"

She looked up, met his accusatory gaze. "Oh never mind. Forget it."

"No!"

There was a brief silence. Thanet told himself that nothing would be achieved and everything might be lost if he couldn't control his irritation, and he took a deep calming breath before saying, "Look, I'm sorry, love. We'll get nowhere if we just stop talking every time things are getting sticky. Maybe you're right and I just can't see it yet. So tell me what you think, and we'll take it from there."

She looked at him doubtfully, then said, "Well, there wasn't any reason to believe that he might have committed the crime, was there?"

"No." He tried hard to be fair. "There still isn't, for that matter."

"So... Did you feel that you were stuck without his evidence?"

"No, not exactly."

"That you couldn't progress any further without talking to him?"

"No, but..."

Joan shook her head. "Then I'm sorry, I still can't see why you couldn't have waited a little longer. It's not like you, Luke. You knew the boy might not know his mother had been killed... What a way to hear news like that! With the implication that he might somehow be involved."

"There was no such implication!"

"Oh, come on, darling. What do you think people think, when that sort of appeal goes out? 'The police are anxious to talk to . . .' It's the first thing they think of, that that person is under suspicion."

"I can't help it, if people misinterpret."

"Luke," said Joan softly. "A minute ago you asked me if what I was saying was that I thought you should have treated him differently because he was my client. I'm still not sure of the answer to that. Now I would like to ask you . . . Do you think you *did* treat him differently because he was my client?"

Thanet recognised the prickle of shock which ran through him in reaction to her question; he had experienced it before, in facing an unpalatable truth. He suppressed the instinctive "No!" which sprang to his lips. He owed it to Joan, to himself, to both of them, to try to match his honesty with hers.

"Perhaps," he said at last. "But if so, I certainly wasn't aware of it, at the time."

"I didn't suppose for a moment that you were. But," and her tone was gentle, "that isn't quite the point, is it, darling?"

"What is, then?"

"The point is, that—assuming that he did in fact hear of the appeal—it's Damon who's been the loser, as a result of our private . . . war, conflict, disagreement . . . whatever you like to call it."

That was true. The thought pained him. He had acted unprofessionally and an innocent boy might have suffered. But why had he really gone ahead when he did? It wasn't enough, simply to say that he had overreacted. If Joan had been a little more forthcoming, in the first place, it might never have happened, he thought defensively. He said so.

"You mean on Thursday night, when you wanted me to talk to you about Damon?"

"Well I did feel you could have been a little more helpful." Thanet's sense of grievance had returned in full force. "After all, I've always talked freely about my cases to you, knowing that I could trust you implicitly never to talk about them. Surely you could have done the same?"

"But it wasn't the same, was it?"

"Why not?"

"Our cases have never overlapped before. I've never needed to use any of the things you've told me, in my work."

"But this was a murder case. A woman had been *killed*..."

"I know. D'you think it was easy for me, to withhold information which could have been useful to you? But I had to, don't you see? I couldn't betray my client. It's a question of... well, of loyalty, I suppose."

"And what about your loyalty to me?" The words were out before Thanet could stop them.

"But that's different, isn't it?"

"Is it?"

"Of course it is!" Joan was beginning to get angry too, now. "Have you ever had any reason to doubt my loyalty to you, in our private life?"

"No, of course not."

"Then just tell me this. I said a minute ago that I've never needed to use any of the things you've told me, in my work. If I had, if a client of mine had been involved in one of your cases as a prime suspect, would you then have been prepared to talk to me so freely? Have you in fact talked to me as freely, in this case, even though Damon is not seriously under suspicion?"

"I've scarcely seen you."

"Maybe not. But even if you had, I bet you would have edited what you'd told me."

Thanet didn't answer. She was right and they both knew it.

"And tell me this too. If, on Thursday, I had in fact given you any information about Damon upon which you could act, would you have acted upon it?"

He had to admit that he would. And Joan would have known that he had betrayed her confidence. There seemed to be no end to the complications and ramifications of this issue. Perhaps, after all, hers was the wisest course.

"I suppose I would." He wasn't proud of the grudging reluctance in his tone, but at least he had managed to admit that he was wrong. He forced himself to say it. "You're right, it could have caused all sorts of difficulties."

She sank back against the settee, as if the argument had sapped her energy. "I've always dreaded this happening, you know."

"What, in particular?"

"Clashing, over our work. You warned me, didn't you, right at the beginning. And I was so confident we could handle it, so . . ." She shrugged. "So naive, I suppose. The truth was, I wanted so much to go into probation that I just didn't want to listen to anything that might put me off."

"And have you ever regretted it?" But he knew the answer.

"No, never. I really enjoy it—though 'enjoy' isn't perhaps the right word. I find it satisfying, fulfilling."

And that, thought Thanet, with a sudden spurt of insight, was what he had never really been able to accept: that his wife should need anything beside himself, their children and their home, to feel fulfilled. Was he really so egocentric? He professed to love Joan, but if he truly loved her he would want above all to enable her to develop every aspect of her potential. True, he had paid lip-service to the idea, but even his capitulation had been brought about by selfish motives: he had known that, if he didn't give in, he would bring about a breach between them that would never be healed.

Was this, then, the root cause of their difficulty? Not that she was wilful, lacking in loyalty or understanding, but that he was childishly self-centred, jealous and spiteful. He saw now that it was he, not she, who had erected that barrier between them. From the moment he realised, on Thursday, that one of Joan's clients was a possible suspect in this case, he had anticipated trouble. Worse, it was almost as though, deep down inside, he had welcomed it.

Had he needed so much to be proved right in warning Joan against her choice of profession that after all these years he had seized the first opportunity of trying to force her to admit that it had been a mistake?

The thought made him squirm.

She was watching him apprehensively, as if she were aware of the private struggle going on inside him and were nervous of the outcome. He felt deeply ashamed that he, who had always prided himself on his tolerance, his compassion, his understanding of others, could have been so prejudiced, so punitive, so blinkered in this, the most important area of his life. Humble, too, that Joan, who was so wise, had continued to love him despite it all.

It wasn't enough, he realised, to attempt to come to terms with this unwelcome insight himself. He owed it to her to bring it out into the open. Perhaps, then, they might at last attain the peace which had always eluded them over this issue before. He turned to her, took her hand.

"I know you do. Find your work fulfilling, I mean. And I

suppose . . ." Oh, God, it was hard, very hard, to expose one's weaknesses to anyone, especially hard when all along he had felt that he was the one with the grievance. He tried again. "I suppose that's what I've found so hard to accept. That I—we—weren't enough for you."

He could tell that she knew how much the admission had cost him.

"Yes. Men do find that difficult, I think. Women have always accepted the importance of a man's work, made allowances for it."

As she had, he thought—all those late nights, broken promises, last-minute phone calls, cancelled excursions . . . A policeman's wife was called upon to make more sacrifices than most. To think that he had always prided himself on overcoming this problem by talking about his work to her, thinking that this would compensate for the demands it made upon her. How condescending could you get! Why should she, an intelligent woman with so much to offer, have been expected to be satisfied with the crumbs that fell from his table?

"I think," Joan was saying, "that the next generation will find it easier. Ours was brought up in the transition period, and there have been a lot of casualties along the way."

And we could well have been one of them. It was a chilling thought.

"I'm sorry. Can you forgive me?"

She opened her arms to him. "Need you ask?"

NINETEEN

Thanet set the tray down on the dressing table and drew back the curtains, frowning at the dismal scene outside. The ring around the moon had fulfilled its promise and it was raining heavily, a continuous drenching downpour discharged by an unbroken ceiling of leaden cloud. But this morning not even this dreary prospect could lower his spirits for long. Their reconciliation last night had been sweet indeed, and today he was glowing with the well-being of a man restored to full health after a long and serious illness.

Joan stirred and opened one eye. Quickly, Thanet picked up the tray and crossed to stand at attention beside the bed.

"Room service, madam."

She blinked and looked up at him, taking in his pose, the tray. She shot up in bed. "Darling!" And as he lowered it onto her lap, "Breakfast in bed! What a luxury! Thank you." She raised her face for a kiss and Thanet obliged with alacrity, breathing in the warm, sleepy smell of her skin and regretting the impulse that had driven him early out of bed to prepare her breakfast before leaving for work. But the appreciation on Joan's face as she surveyed the carefully laid tray reassured him that it had been the right thing to do, and he surveyed his handiwork with satisfaction: flowered traycloth, best bone china, chilled orange juice, a pot of freshly ground coffee (decaffeinated, Joan's latest fad) and a hot croissant.

"No red rose in single holder, I'm afraid," he said in mock apology. "It would have dripped all over the place."

She glanced at the rain streaming down the window-panes. "A wet Sunday. Horrid. Still, at least it makes it not quite so bad that you've got to go to work."

"True."

"Are the children up?"

"Still asleep, I think."

"They can have a lie-in. As long as they're up in time for church . . ."

Thanet kissed her goodbye and peeped into the children's rooms. Humped shapes slumbered on. He smiled indulgently, closing the doors softly behind him. It would do them good to sleep late for once.

As he drove through the deserted streets he remembered what it was that had woken him up so early: the knowledge that in his sleep he had been dreaming, and that the dream had been trying to tell him something important, something to do with the Tarrant case. He had struggled to reach back into it, to fix it in his memory before it faded, but he was already too late, it had gone. What had it been about? He frowned, trying to remember. Briefly, a green image flickered across his mind, and was gone. What had it been? Garden, field, wood, park, landscape? Mentally, he shrugged. Perhaps it would come back later, when he wasn't thinking about it.

On the way up to his office he ran into DS Bristow.

"Thanks for the tip, sir. We nailed him!"

"Buzzard?"

"Yes. Would you believe it, one or two juicy little items from Thursday's robbery tucked away under a loose floor-board! They never learn."

"Good. That's excellent. Make sure some credit goes to the PC from traffic, who spotted him in the first place."

"Of course, sir."

"What time was the robbery committed?"

"Between four and half past, on Thursday afternoon. Does that clear him, as far as your case is concerned?"

"I doubt it. The trouble is, we still haven't been able to pinpoint the exact time of the murder."

The phone was ringing as Thanet entered his office: Tarrant, again enquiring for news of Damon. It was obvious that by now the surgeon was really worried about his son.

"Isn't there anything else you can do?"

"I assure you, sir, that everything that can be done is being done. And I promise that the moment we have any news of him, we'll let you know."

By now Thanet was himself becoming concerned about the boy. Considering the amount of publicity it really was becoming very difficult to believe that Damon hadn't heard of his mother's death. And if so, why hadn't he been in touch?

Thanet was still studying a large-scale map of the area when Lineham arrived.

"Morning, Mike."

"Morning, sir. You're looking very cheerful today. Don't tell me you've had one of your bright ideas overnight."

"No such luck, I'm afraid."

The phone again. Daphne Linacre, this time, also enquiring about Damon.

"Still no news of him, then?" said Lineham, when Thanet had crashed the receiver down in a thoroughly disgruntled mood at having had to communicate the same bad news twice in ten minutes to anxious relatives.

Thanet shook his head.

Lineham evidently considered it politic to change the subject. "What are you doing with that?" He nodded at the map.

Thanet told him, and for a while they discussed whether or not it might have been possible for Buzzard to have committed the murder either before or after his foray to Nettleton. On balance, Thanet was inclined to dismiss him as a suspect.

"I can't really see him committing a murder, then calmly going on to do a robbery ten miles away. Or vice versa. I should have thought his main aim would have been to put as much distance as possible as quickly as possible, between himself and the scene of either crime."

"I agree."

"Anyway, it's time we were leaving for Ribbleden, to see Nicky Barnes. I've arranged for WPC Fernley to come with us."

A woman police officer has to be present when a child is interviewed.

"Right, sir."

Even on the main road there was very little traffic about and after turning off into the country lanes they had the drowned countryside to themselves. Ribbleden looked as though it had decided to turn its back on the weather; doors and windows were firmly shut and apart from a bedraggled paper boy there was not a soul about. Not everyone was lying in bed late, though; a number of cars lined the road outside the church.

"Must have an early service," said Lineham.

"They have to stagger them. The vicar has four parishes to look after, I believe."

"How on earth does he manage at festivals?"

"With difficulty, I imagine. I was talking to one country parson last year and he told me he'd conducted ten harvest festivals at different churches, schools and organisations."

"I should think he was ploughing the fields and scattering in his sleep," said Lineham with a grin.

They drew up at the gates of High Gables but before Lineham could get out to open them a small wet figure emerged from the shelter of a tall shrub and performed the task for him.

"Nicky, I presume," said Thanet. "Waiting for us, obviously. Stop when we're inside."

The car drove in and Thanet wound down his window, waited for the boy to approach. "You must be Nicky. I'm Inspector Thanet, and this is Woman Police-Constable Fernley and Detective-Sergeant Lineham. Want a ride?"

Nicky nodded eagerly. He was well equipped for the weather in hooded anorak and wellington boots. He clambered into the back and leaned into the gap between the front seats, dripping water everywhere.

"Ever been in a police car before?"

"No."

Thanet explained how the radio worked. "There are two frequencies, one for transmitting, the other for reception. Those pips you hear mean that someone in another patrol car is talking to the control room..."

After they drew up outside the back door Thanet spent several more minutes chatting to the boy. If the ice was broken it would be far easier to get Nicky to open up to him, if there was anything to tell. Besides, he liked boys, was used to having them around. Ben's friends were always in and out of each other's houses. Not, he thought, that there were any signs of this one being difficult to handle. His expression was open, alert, and he was clearly storing up every word in order to impress his friends.

"We'd better go in, I suppose," Thanet said at last. "I expect your mum will have seen us arrive and she'll be wondering where we've got to."

"OK." Nicky scrambled out, reluctantly.

They had arranged that Lineham would wait in the car; three police officers, they agreed, might be a little over-whelming for the boy. Nicky led them into the kitchen where Thanet had first met the old lady and her companion.

Marilyn Barnes was alone. "I've arranged for Lavinia to have coffee with Mr. Tarrant," she said, noticing Thanet's enquiring glance around the room. "I thought it would be easier."

"Good idea."

"I made some for us. You'd like a cup, I expect."

"Thank you." Thanet introduced Jessica Fernley and they all sat down. He waited until the coffee had been poured and then turned to Nicky, who was watching him expectantly.

"Now then, Nicky, I expect your mum's told you what we want to talk about."

"Thursday afternoon," said the boy promptly.

He was of average height for his age, and rather thin, with bony elbows and narrow wrists, his very short hair emphasising the shape of skull and jawline. The brown eyes so like his mother's were eager and intelligent.

"That's right. Now I know one of my men has interviewed you already, so I'll just explain why it is I need to talk to you again. As I'm sure you know, after a major crime like this, we have to spend a lot of time building up a picture of exactly what happened in the period leading up to it. It's very painstaking work, rather like putting together a huge jigsaw puzzle, and the pieces are supplied by all the people we talk to. The trouble is, some of them can be pretty vague, but in the end, by checking one person's version with another's we usually manage to fit it all together. But it is often necessary to see people more than once—take your mother, for in-stance." He glanced at Marilyn. "I've talked to you several times, haven't I?"

She nodded. "To most of us, I should think."

"The other thing, of course, is we often find that after people have had time to think they remember things they didn't the first time around."

Nicky was nodding sagely.

"But I must emphasise that I want you to try to remember everything, every single thing, that you saw and did on Thursday afternoon after you got home from school, from the moment you walked through the gate—I assume you came in the back way, along the footpath?—right up to the time you left to stay with your friends."

"Everything?"

"Everything. Step by step. I'll try not to interrupt too much. Close your eyes, if you like, if it would make it easier."

But that wouldn't be necessary, Thanet could tell. Already Nicky's eyes were glazing in recollection.

"Now, you got home at about a quarter to four, I believe?" He waited for the boy's nod. "And it was very hot. Was there anyone about, in the garden?"

"No. I came along the footpath and in through the gate in the back fence, like you said, then through the garden and across the drive to the back door. I was thirsty . . . Is this the sort of thing you mean?"

"Yes, exactly. Go on."

"There was no one in here, so I made myself a drink of squash. Then Mum came in, with Mrs. Tarrant—old Mrs. Tarrant, that is. She, Mrs. Tarrant, was in a state and Mum was trying to calm her down, so I grabbed an apple and went out to play."

"Did you go to a friend's house, or stay in the garden?"

"I stayed in the garden."

The flow of information seemed to have come to an abrupt halt. Why?

"So what did you do, in the garden?"

Nicky glanced at his mother. "I . . . er . . ."

"Well?" said Marilyn, breaking in impatiently. "You what?"

"I went to my den," he mumbled.

At once Thanet understood. This was the boy's secret place and he didn't want his mother to know about it. A glance at Marilyn Barnes told him that she had also cottoned on.

She rose. "I think I'd better just pop along to see Lavinia for a moment, Nicky. You'll be all right?"

He couldn't hide his relief. "Yeah, sure."

As soon as the door had closed behind her Thanet said, "I had a den, too, when I was a boy. It was crammed in between the back of the garden shed and the hedge—our garden wasn't anything like as big as yours. I got hold of some old planks, and a bit of corrugated iron for the roof . . . No one was allowed in there unless they were invited. It was my own special, private place . . . I expect yours is the same."

"Yes." Nicky lowered his voice, glanced at the door. "Mum doesn't even know where it is."

I shouldn't be too sure of that, thought Thanet. "Look, Nicky, I don't want to pry into your secrets, I really don't. And I promise that if you tell me roughly where it is, I won't tell a soul, neither of us will, not without your permission, anyway."

He glanced at WPC Fernley, who shook her head vigorously. "Of course not."

Nicky shrugged. "OK. It's over behind the coach house, in some big bushes."

"Far behind?"

"A fair way. A hundred yards or so, I suppose."

Thanet wasn't sure if this estimate could be trusted. Distances are difficult to estimate, especially where there are trees and shrubs about.

"Can you hear any sounds from the coach house?"

"Not really, no. Unless there are people talking in the garden at the back."

"And were there?"

"No. Miss Linacre was at work, anyway, till later."

"We're getting a bit ahead of ourselves. Can we go back to when you first went out, just before four o'clock. You went straight across to your den?"

"Yes."

"Did you see anyone on the way?"

"Only Mrs. Haywood. She was just going into the coach house as I came out of our back door."

That fitted, Thanet thought. Beatrix Haywood had told them that after overhearing the row between Nerine and her mother-in-law she had hung about in the attic for a further ten minutes or so before returning to the coach house, for fear of meeting either of the protagonists.

"Did she see you?"

"No. She had her back to me."

"Then what? Go on. You're doing very well."

Nicky looked pleased. "The next thing was that just as I got to my den I heard Vicky drive away."

Vicky of the Benetton jeans. "How did you know it was Vicky if you were that far away?" Thanet could guess the answer, but it was best to take nothing for granted.

"I know the sound of her Fiesta."

"Right. So then what did you do?"

"I've been trying to construct the walls—you know, weaving branches in and out." He pulled a face. "It's not as easy as it sounds."

Thanet grinned. "I know, I've tried it myself... So you were moving about, I expect, fetching branches... Or did you have a pile already gathered?"

"No, I was moving about, like you said."

"So, and I want you to think very carefully, did you see anyone about, at any point, while you were working?"

Nicky shook his head regretfully. "No, sorry."

"Never mind. What happened next?"

"I heard the bell, for tea... The garden's so big I often didn't hear Mum when she used to call me, so now she comes to the back door and rings that." Nicky nodded at an old-fashioned hand-bell which stood on the windowsill by the sink. "No, hang on... Was it before, or after...?" His forehead creased as he tried to remember. "No, it was before, I remember now... A few minutes before the bell rang I heard Miss Linacre arrive home—I know the sound of all the cars."

"That would have been at about twenty to five?"

"Yes."

Again, it fitted.

"And a few minutes afterwards, you heard your mother ring the bell. Did you go in straight away?"

"No. I was in the middle of a tricky bit, and I wanted to get it finished."

"And that would have taken how long?"

"Another five minutes or so. Then I came back to the house. I saw Miss Linacre going into the coach house as I came out onto the drive."

Suppressing the sudden flare of excitement Thanet kept his tone carefully casual as he said, "Going in, you say?"

Nicky nodded. "I thought she must have gone to fetch something she'd left in the car."

"You saw her come away from the car?"

"Oh, no, just go into the house. Anyway, then I came back here and had my tea." He grinned. "It was hamburgers."

"Your favourite, by the sound of it... Then what?"

"Mum went to get Mrs. Tarrant up from her rest, and," he grimaced, "I washed up the tea things. While I was at the sink I saw Damon go across to the coach house."

Again, this was news but once more Thanet betrayed no special interest. "That would have been at what time?"

Nicky frowned. "Twenty, twenty-five past five, I suppose."

"Did he go in?"

"Yes. The front door was open. They often leave it open in the hot weather."

"Did he seem in a hurry? I'm only asking, because as you know, Damon's disappearance is a bit of a mystery, and very few people seem to have seen him that afternoon."

"You don't think...?"

"That he had anything to do with his mother's death? No, not for a moment. But we are afraid that he might be rather upset, and we're anxious to find him."

"No, he didn't seem to be in a hurry. He didn't stay, though. He was only in there a minute or two and he came out again, back to the house."

"How did he seem?"

Nicky shrugged. "On the way back he was walking slowly, with his hands in his pockets, looking at the ground. Then, as he got nearer the house, he suddenly speeded up. Mum and Mrs. Tarrant came in then and I'd finished my washing up, so I went back out to the den. Not long afterwards I heard Damon drive off—his car makes a terrific din—and then, only a minute or two later, Mr. Tarrant came home. Soon after that all the fuss began, and Mum rang Mrs. Rice and she came to fetch me."

Thanet nodded with satisfaction. "Well Nicky, all I can say is that I wish all witnesses were as concise and as helpful as you."

On cue the door opened and Marilyn came in. Perhaps she had been waiting tactfully outside? Thanet turned to her. "I was just saying how helpful Nicky has been, Miss Barnes. Thank you for letting me talk to him."

"Oh, good." But she didn't sound too sure. "You've finished, now?"

"Yes, we have." Thanet rose and WPC Fernley closed her notebook and followed suit.

"Oh, just one small point, Miss Barnes. Could we confirm the time at which you called Nicky in for tea?"

"A quarter to five," she said promptly. "I always call him at a quarter to five."

"Thank you."

Outside, it was still raining hard and they made a dash for the car, flung themselves in. All the windows were steamed up, giving the illusion of total privacy and isolation.

"Well?" said Lineham. "Any luck?"

"Some." Thanet glanced at Lineham's impatient face and grinned. He knew the sergeant hated being kept in the dark.

"There were two interesting points. One: Nicky heard Daphne Linacre's car arrive at twenty to five. He was playing in his den, in the garden, and didn't actually see her at that point. Five minutes later, at a quarter to five, his mother called him in for tea, but he was busy doing something and didn't actually go in for another five minutes or so. But when he did, he saw Daphne Linacre going into the coach house. He assumed she'd left something in her car, and had gone out to fetch it, and of course, there might be some perfectly innocent explanation, but..."

"She gave us the impression she was so prostrated by migraine that she could scarcely totter up the stairs to bed!"

"Precisely. And if she did have a migraine I can't see her running any trivial errands herself. It seemed to me that Miss Haywood was only too willing to be at her beck and call."

"I agree... Yes, that is interesting. What was the other thing?"

Thanet related what Nicky had told him about Damon.

"I wonder why he went across to the coach house? Sir, you don't think..."

Thanet recognised the dawning sparkle in Lineham's eyes. A theory was being born. "What?"

"Well, you know what you were saying about Damon disappearing because he wanted to protect someone? And one of the people you thought he might have wanted to protect was his aunt? Just suppose that earlier, soon after Daphne Linacre got home, he overheard a quarrel between her and his mother? And that for whatever reason he decided to go and see his mother half an hour later? He goes into her room, finds it empty, and walks out onto the balcony, calling her. She's not there, but he crosses to the rail to see if she's in the garden and sees her lying on the terrace. He rushes down, finds that she's stone dead and comes to the conclusion his aunt must have shoved her over during the quarrel. He's very shocked, naturally, and he goes straight across to the coach house, to tackle her. But Mrs. Haywood says his aunt is ill, she's got a severe migraine, and can't be disturbed. He doesn't know what to do, so when he comes out he's in a bit of a daze, walking slowly, as Nicky said. Then, on the way back to the house, he makes up his mind. If his aunt has killed his mother he doesn't want to be any part of the uproar that's bound to follow. He'll keep well out of the way for a few days until the fuss has died down. He rushes up to his flat, throws a few things in a bag and takes off."

Lineham folded his arms and sat back with an air of satisfaction. "What d'you think, sir?"

"Could be. Of course, he could have gone across to the coach house for a dozen different reasons, none of them anything to do with the murder: he could have wanted to confirm an arrangement, borrow some money, return a book, ask a favour . . . He might simply have wondered why his aunt was home from work so early, gone across out of curiosity."

"You'll be suggesting he went across to take afternoon tea with them, next. Sir."

"No need to be sarcastic, Mike. It could well have been as innocent as that. They were on pretty good terms. Look at the way she and Mrs. Haywood keep ringing up to enquire about him."

"And I suppose he only stayed a minute or two because Mrs. Haywood was busy looking after Miss Linacre and wouldn't have had time to talk to him."

"Quite." Thanet enjoyed baiting Lineham occasionally. "Actually . . ."

"What?"

"Well, let's say, for the sake of argument, that it did happen as you suggest, that the two sisters had a quarrel which got out of hand . . . I suppose that the strain and the shock might well have brought on a genuine migraine—or the beginnings of one, anyway, by the time Damon went across, half an hour later."

"If you ask me, she never had one at all."

"And the vomiting we heard from upstairs, when we went across that first evening?"

"Emotional reaction," said Lineham triumphantly. "From having committed a murder."

"There's still something you haven't explained, in this neat little theory of yours, Mike."

"What's that?"

"Motive, Mike, motive. Why, in the middle of a sunny June afternoon, should Daphne Linacre suddenly rush home from work and kill her sister? Any suggestions?"

"I'm sure I can come up with something, given time."

"I've got a better idea than that."

"What?"

"We'll go across to the coach house and ask her."

TWENTY

Daphne Linacre answered the door herself.

"You've got news of Damon?" she said, apprehensively.

Without her sunglasses she looked older, perhaps more vulnerable, Thanet thought. Her eyes were a bleak pebble-grey, flecked with brown. Once again she was smartly dressed in crisp cream linen skirt and matching blouse, with a soft, caramel-coloured cardigan slung loosely around her shoulders.

Thanet shook his head. "Sorry, no. We'd like another word with you, if we may."

She stood back without a word, silently waiting while they removed their dripping raincoats.

"You can hang them there." She nodded at a row of hooks behind the front door. Then she led them into the sitting room.

Sunday newspapers were scattered around the armchair in which she had sat last time they were here, and a half-empty cup of coffee stood on a small table nearby.

"I've been having a lazy time, as you can see. Nothing much else to do on a morning like this. Do sit down. Would you like some coffee?"

"We've just had some, thanks."

Where was Beatrix Haywood? Thanet wondered.

As if she had picked up his unspoken thought Daphne Linacre said, "Bea's at church. I told her she was crazy to go out in this weather if she didn't have to, but she insisted."

Her concern evidently hadn't extended to offering Mrs. Haywood a lift, Thanet thought.

"Well, how can I help you?"

"A minor point," said Thanet. "A small discrepancy. We thought you could clear it up."

Despite his dramatic announcement to Lineham that they would go and ask Daphne Linacre why she might have killed her sister, Thanet was well aware that it would be pointless to do so. She would simply deny it, or laugh it off, as she had last time. And they would have revealed more than they wished of their suspicions.

She smiled. "Oh dear, the third degree. What have I done, I ask myself? Do go on."

"Perhaps you could bear with us and tell us once more exactly what you did when you got home on Thursday afternoon."

She gave him an assessing look. "Why should I? I've been through it once, that should be enough, surely."

Thanet sighed. "Often, when people have had time to think, they remember details they forgot the first time around. It's understandable. Nobody thinks very clearly, in a state of shock."

There, he had given her a way out, if she needed one. Would she take it?

Apparently not.

"I'm afraid I have nothing to add." Then, noting his waiting silence she said irritably, "Oh, very well, then, if I must. I came home from work with a migraine. When I got here all I wanted to do was go upstairs, undress and lie down in a darkened room. Which was precisely what I did."

"You came through the door and went straight up the stairs?"

"Got it in one, Inspector."

"You're sure you didn't, for instance, talk to Mrs. Haywood for a minute or two?" Thanet persisted.

"No."

"Or go into the kitchen, for a drink of water, perhaps?"

"No, I did not! Look, when I drove up Bea was waiting at the door. She knew I was feeling ill, we'd spoken on the telephone earlier. She helped me up the stairs. I went to the bathroom to pee—if we must have the sordid details—then into my bedroom, where I undressed, got into bed and closed my eyes with a huge sigh of relief. Does that satisfy you?"

"According to a witness you were seen entering this house some ten minutes after you got home."

She raised one eyebrow and said with amusement, "Really? Well, all I can say is, he's either mistaken—to put the charitable interpretation on it—or he's lying in his teeth. And if it's the latter, I should say his motives require investigation, Inspector."

"You deny it, then."

"I certainly do! Surely I can't spell it out any more clearly than I already have!" She folded her hands and cracked her knuckles, a habit which Thanet had always abhorred. But he refused to allow himself to be distracted. He was trying to make up his mind if she was lying. Sometimes it was easy to tell—a facial expression, a false note in the voice, certain gestures such as rubbing the side of the nose, but at others it was well-nigh impossible and this, he decided reluctantly, was one of those occasions. Daphne Linacre met his gaze stare for stare and it was obvious that nothing was going to make her change her story in even the slightest detail.

He was certain that Nicky hadn't been lying, but was it possible that the boy had been mistaken? Thanet didn't think so. But there was no way at present to prove or disprove his story.

They would have to leave it there.

"Very well." He stood up. "But if you should suddenly recall . . ."

"I shan't." The extent of her resentment showed in the sudden surge of energy with which she swung herself up out of her chair. "Who is this . . . informant, anyway? I have a right to know, don't you agree?"

Thanet shook his head. "I'm sorry, I can't tell you that." The last thing Thanet wanted was to expose Nicky to ill will.

"Then there's nothing more to be said."

Back in the car Thanet looked at Lineham and grinned. "Well? Still as keen on your latest theory?"

The sergeant grimaced. "I still think it could have happened like that."

"That's the trouble with this case, Mike, there are too many credible possibilities, too many suspects with means, motive, opportunity, and no way at present of proving anything against any of them."

"Miss Linacre doesn't seem to have a motive, as you so rightly pointed out. And as far as she's concerned we keep coming up against the same old question: why on earth should she suddenly decide to come home from work one afternoon and kill her sister?"

"If she did do it, something must have happened, to make her. But what?"

"And why? What possible reason could she have?"

What possible reason?

The windows had misted up again and Thanet stretched out a finger and absentmindedly cleared a small space on the glass. A small cameo appeared, of a young beech tree, its fresh green summer foliage drooping with the weight of unshed water. Something flickered at the back of Thanet's mind. What was it? He cleared a little more space on the glass, his finger switching from a circular movement to straight lines. The picture was larger now, revealing a rosebed encircled by grass and a line of trees in the background, their tossing, heaving branches a mass of greens in every shade and tone.

Again there was that flicker at the back of his mind.

This time the sensation was unmistakable. Thanet had experienced it before, not frequently, but sufficiently often for him to recognise it when it happened. His unconscious mind had, quite independently, been sifting, weighing, sorting, assessing and had come up with a conclusion of its own. It was now in the process of passing it on, up through the layers of his consciousness to the point where he was able to acknowledge it. He closed his eyes and sat quite still, trying to blank out the sound of the rain drumming on the roof, the awareness of Lineham tactfully silent in the seat beside him . . . He had a brief, vivid image of the picture he had seen through the window just now, and then, without warning, he was seeing another picture, himself and Ben, in the photograph he had held last night—and then another, and another . . . Illumination came, bringing elation and a sense of triumph. Already, in his dream last night, he had made the connection . . . His eyes snapped open.

Lineham was watching him eagerly.

"Of course, Mike!"

"What?"

"Her motive. Daphne Linacre's motive. I think I've got it!"

"Well, are you going to tell me or not?"

"Naturally."

Thanet explained, enjoying the dawning comprehension in Lineham's face. He had just finished when his bleeper went.

"There's a phone box near the village hall," said Lineham.

It was a message from Joan. She'd had an idea where Damon might be and had decided to follow it up herself. She had taken the children to her mother's for the day.

"Did she say where she was going?"

"No, sir. It can't be too far away, though. She said that all being well she hoped to be back by mid-afternoon."

All being well.

"She said it was a long shot, sir, but that if she found him and managed to persuade him to come back with her, they'd go straight to your office. She said not to raise your hopes too high, though."

Thanet looked at his watch. Eleven o'clock.

At least four hours to go, then.

TWENTY-ONE

Thanet glanced at his watch. Twenty to four. Only three minutes had passed since the last time he looked. Time was crawling along so slowly it seemed virtually to have stopped.

Where was she?

His eagerness to talk to Damon was overshadowed by his anxiety about his wife. He knew that this was irrational, that Joan spent much of her working life dealing with criminals of every kind, but he didn't like not knowing where she had gone or what sort of a situation she might have walked into.

It was impossible to concentrate, and he tossed the papers he had been pretending to study onto his desk and got up, walked restlessly across to the window. The rain had stopped about an hour ago and the cloud ceiling was breaking up, the first patches of blue sky appearing.

"We should hear something soon, sir."

Thanet gave a tight nod.

"In fact, I'd say it was looking quite hopeful. If she'd had a fruitless journey she'd have been back by now."

"We can't say that if we don't know where she's gone."

"No, but she did say mid-afternoon. She must have had some idea of how long it would take."

"Mid-afternoon is so vague. It could mean anything, from two thirty to four thirty."

"Even if it meant four thirty, at the outside, if she hasn't managed to find him we should hear from her before long. In that case she'd probably go straight back to your mother-in-law's and ring from there."

"I imagine so. There'd be no point in coming here if she hadn't had any luck."

"But if she did manage to find him, we might have to wait a good while longer. It could take some time to persuade him to come back with her."

"Impossible to tell." Thanet swung away from the window and returned to his desk. He picked up a report, riffled through it, put it down. His hand strayed to his pocket and came out holding his pipe. He didn't usually smoke in the middle of the afternoon but he felt that the occasion warranted a relaxation of the rules.

Lineham watched resignedly as Thanet filled his pipe and got it going.

"Anyway, she must have thought there was a good chance of finding him, sir, or she wouldn't have gone off like that."

"True. Though she did say it was a long shot."

They were going around in circles. Thanet stood up. "Come on, Mike. There's no point it sitting around speculating like this. A change of scene will do us good. Let's go up to the canteen and have some tea. We can easily be contacted there."

They were carrying the cups across to a table when the message came through.

"I've been told to tell you your wife has arrived, sir."

Relief was sweet. "Is she by herself?"

"I don't know, sir. I haven't actually seen her."

"Where is she? Downstairs?"

"Yes, in the entrance hall. Shall I bring her up to your office?"

"No, I'll go down myself."

Thanet sent Lineham back upstairs and went down alone. Outside the glass doors leading into the entrance hall he paused for a moment. Joan hadn't seen him yet. She looked tired. She was sitting with her eyes closed, leaning her head back against the wall. There was a young man beside her whom Thanet recognised immediately from the photographs released to the media. So she had brought it off. He experienced an uprush of pride and excitement. Damon, too, looked tired. He was sitting forward, elbows on both knees, clasped hands dangling loosely between.

Thanet pushed open the door and entered the hall. Damon must have seen him heading towards them and stirred because Joan opened her eyes. She smiled up at him.

"Ah, there you are. This is Damon Tarrant. Damon, my husband, Detective-Inspector Thanet."

Damon nodded but did not respond to Thanet's smile. His photograph hadn't done him justice. His resemblance to his mother was striking, her dark beauty translated here into masculine planes and angles. He looked strained, apprehensive and slightly dazed.

Thanet wondered if Damon had indeed learnt of his mother's death only a few hours ago. If so he must still be in a state of shock.

"Damon would like to make a statement," said Joan.

"Good." He looked at the boy. "But are you sure you're up to it?"

Damon glanced at Joan, who said, "You could leave it until tomorrow, you know."

The boy shook his head. "I'd only lie awake all night worrying about it. I'd rather get it over with."

"All right. We'll go up to my office, then, shall we?" His office would be less impersonal than an interview room. "This way."

Joan rose too, but Damon said, "There's no need for you to come, Mrs. Thanet."

"You're sure? I'm very happy to be present during the interview, if you'd like me to."

"No. Really. I'll be fine."

"I'll wait here, then, in case you want to see me afterwards."

"That's not necessary, really."

"If you're sure, Damon," said Thanet. Secretly he was relieved. Questioning a witness with Joan present as the probation officer was not a prospect he relished. Then, to Joan, "I think it would be a good idea if you went home. You're looking tired."

"I am, a bit. All right, then, if you're sure, Damon."

"I'll be fine," Damon insisted.

Thanet and Damon set off towards the glass doors, then Thanet turned back with a murmured word of apology. He had to speak to Joan privately. Damon nodded and stood waiting, listlessly. Thanet cast a worried glance back over his shoulder as he said to Joan, "Are you sure he's fit to be questioned?"

Joan shrugged. "You saw for yourself. He's adamant that he wants to get it over with. I think he'll feel a lot better, if he does."

"Did he know his mother was dead?"

"No. No radio, television or newspapers. He'll explain."

"Did he tell you why he ran away?"

Joan pulled a face. "Yes. He's going to tell you that himself."

"Legitimate reason?"

She nodded sadly. "Oh yes, only too legitimate."

Thanet took her arm and gave it a quick squeeze. "Don't worry, I'll be gentle with him."

"I know."

"Bye then, darling, and thanks."

Thanet arranged for some tea to be brought up to his office. It arrived almost immediately and Damon cupped his hands around the mug as if to warm himself.

Where to begin?

"We've been very worried about you, you know."

Damon attempted a cynical smile. "Nice to know someone is."

"Everyone is. You must know that, surely. Your father, your. . ."

"My father." It was a sneer.

Thanet knew why the boy was taking this attitude, but he wasn't going to say so, at this point.

"Yes. He's very fond of you."

Damon said nothing, merely jerked his head sideways in a gesture of repudiation.

It was time to tackle the first hurdle. "My wife tells me you didn't know of your mother's death until this afternoon."

"No." For a moment Damon's self-control hovered in precarious balance, then he put the mug clumsily down on the edge of Thanet's desk and covered his face with his hands. "Oh, God. . ."

Thanet and Lineham exchanged glances.

"Look, Damon—if I may call you that—I'm really not sure that this is the best time for us to talk to you. You've had a pretty severe shock. Are you sure you wouldn't prefer to wait until tomorrow?"

"No!" Damon rubbed his hands over his face, as if to clear

his mind, pressing thumb and forefinger into his closed
eyelids. Then he raised his head and met Thanet's eye.
"Sorry. I'm all right, really. Go ahead."

Thanet waited a moment, then said, "As you wish. Well,
we couldn't understand, you see, how you could have avoided
hearing the news. It's been in all the papers, on the radio and
television..."

"We didn't have any of those, where I was." Damon gave a
reminiscent sigh and shook his head, as if in disbelief that
such a place existed. "It was great. So peaceful, so cut off
from everything..."

"Where was this?"

"It's a commune, down on the Surrey/Hampshire border.
One of my friends went off to live there, last year. They're
into self-sufficiency, that sort of thing."

"A religious community?"

"No. Unless you call believing in peace and sharing everything in common a religion... It was the only place I could
think of, to run to, where no questions would be asked and
I'd have time to..."

"To what?" said Thanet gently.

Damon shrugged. "To sort myself out."

Thanet waited, but the boy was silent.

"What was it that needed sorting out, Damon?"

No reply.

Thanet decided to try a different tack. "From our point of
view, the problem was that we couldn't think why you had
taken off like that. We guessed you might not have known
about your mother's death, of course. We assumed that if you
had, you would have called for an ambulance. Unless..."

Damon glanced up sharply. "Unless what?"

Thanet hesitated. "Did Mrs. Thanet tell you that it wasn't
an accident?"

Damon swallowed, nodded.

"Then you must appreciate that we are trying to find out
who was responsible." Thanet was picking his words carefully,
trying to avoid emotive words like "murder" and "killed." "So
we did wonder if one possible reason why you disappeared
was because you were trying to protect someone."

Damon stared at him. "Trying to... Are you saying that
someone in the family might have done it?"

"We have to take that possibility into consideration."

Damon was shaking his head slowly, in disbelief. "That's impossible! I assumed it was an outsider. A burglar, a tramp . . ."

"I'm afraid it doesn't look that way, Damon. So you see, we thought that it was just possible you might have witnessed the crime and run away because you couldn't face being questioned about it. Especially if it had been committed by someone you were fond of."

Damon was shaking his head again, vigorously this time. "You're saying you really thought I might have seen my mother killed and done nothing about it?" He gave a disbelieving laugh. "That's crazy. That really is absolutely crazy."

"It may seem so now that we've met you. But you must remember we didn't know you, or anything about you . . ."

"Mrs. Thanet did."

"Mrs. Thanet knows her job. Without your permission she wouldn't tell us anything about you which we couldn't easily learn from someone else."

"Even when it's her husband in charge of the case!"

"Even then, Damon. I mean it."

There was a brief silence while Thanet gave the boy time to digest this, then said, "Anyway, to get back to the point I was making, it was very difficult at first for us to think of any other reason why you should suddenly just drop out of sight like that."

Silence.

"So, why did you?"

"I don't have to tell you that."

"No."

Damon was gazing miserably into space.

Thanet waited a moment, then added gently, "You don't have to tell me, Damon, because I already know."

The boy's attention snapped back with an almost audible twang. "That's not possible!"

"Yes, it is. All sorts of things come to light in the type of investigation we've been conducting."

"In that case, there's no need to talk about it, is there?"

"But there is. I have no way of knowing for sure, of course, but I have a feeling that in some way your reason for leaving home on Thursday is very important to our understanding of this crime."

"But how can it be? It concerns no one but myself."

"Does it? Does it, really? If you think for a moment, I believe you'll see that that simply isn't true. There are other people who are bound to be affected by the fact that this information has come to light, several of them."

Damon was silent for a while, gazing down at the floor. Finally, he shrugged. "I suppose you're right."

"In that case, would you tell me the whole story? It really would help. I gather you only found out about this on the afternoon of your mother's death?"

Damon nodded. "Yes." He hesitated, shrugged. "OK. If you already know... Where d'you want me to begin?"

TWENTY-TWO

From the corner of his eye Thanet saw Lineham give an anticipatory stir. The sergeant was as eager to hear Damon's story as he was. Thanet knew the What but he very much wanted to know the Where, the When and the Who. He must be careful not to rush things, now that Damon had at last capitulated.

"You could start by telling me how you spent the day."

"OK." He paused, thinking back. "I slept late. Some friends of mine had finished their A levels the day before and I went out with them in the evening, to celebrate. I didn't get up till around eleven, then I had some breakfast and went out to do some work on my car. I was out there for about an hour, then I went back up to my flat, had a beer, and crashed out on my bed. When I woke up it was well after three and I was hungry. I made myself some scrambled eggs, then I, well, just bummed around doing nothing much—played some tapes, looked at some motor magazines, that sort of thing . . ."

"Usually, when you were at home during the day, you didn't go down for lunch with your mother?"

"No. She doesn't eat lunch, just has a pot of yoghurt or something. Sometimes I go down to the kitchen and eat with Vicky, but on Thursdays she goes into Sturrenden for the weekly shop, and has lunch with a friend."

"I see. Go on." Thanet was filled with compassion for the strange, isolated life this boy had led, but he was careful not to show it. Damon might have had every material luxury but he had been sadly lacking in the warmth and support that only a close family can give.

"By late afternoon I was getting a bit fed up with hanging around, so I thought I'd go along and see a friend of mine who lives in the village, get something fixed up for the evening."

"That would be Tim Speed?"

"That's right, yes."

"And this would have been at what time?"

"Around a quarter past five, I should think."

"Right. Go on. No. Just a minute. Didn't you have an appointment with my wife, on Thursday afternoon?"

Damon looked sheepish. "Yes, I did. I forgot it, I'm afraid. Normally, of course, I'd have rung her as soon as I realised, but in the circumstances it went clean out of my mind."

So it was as simple as that. He had fogotten.

"Anyway, when I went out of the back door I saw my aunt's car outside the coach house. I was a bit surprised, because she doesn't usually get home until around a quarter to six. Anyway, I'd promised to fix a new aerial on for her—her old one was snapped off by vandals last week—so I thought I'd pop in and arrange a time to do it. The front door was open, so I went in. The sitting room door was ajar and she and Mrs. Haywood were talking. I was about to walk in when I heard my name.

'I still can't believe that Damon is my grandson.'

'Even though you're holding the proof in your hand? I can. Oh yes, I can believe it all right. I ought to have known that, with me out of the way, my dear sister wouldn't have been able to resist the opportunity of seducing my fiancé.'

'D'you think Roland knows, Daphne?'

'If anyone does, he should! I bet he was so besotted with her he just turned a blind eye to the fact that Damon arrived well ahead of schedule.'

'But why didn't you guess? You knew Roland had been away in Australia for a couple of months before they got engaged. You could have worked it out for yourself.'

'I agree, I could. I was a fool, that's why. At the time I couldn't think of anything but the fact that Jocelyn was dead. It never even entered my head to think that he might have been having it off with Nerine while I was safely tucked up in hospital. God, what an innocent I was.'

'Do stop pacing about like that, Daphne. You're giving me a headache.'

'Oh, shut up, Bea, for God's sake. I'm trying to think. I've got to work out what to do now.'

"I didn't wait to hear any more," Damon said, miserably. "I just backed out, as quietly as I could, and went back up to my flat."

A wounded animal seeking sanctuary, thought Thanet.

"But when I got there, I felt I was going to suffocate. It was as if the walls were... sort of closing in on me." He looked at Thanet with mild surprise. "Funny really. It's a big room with lots of light... I don't know what I did next. Paced about a bit, I think, trying to take it in... that I was a..." He shook his head, unable to say the word. "I wasn't really thinking straight. I kept hearing their voices—my aunt's and Mrs. Haywood's in my head. Suddenly I couldn't stand it any longer. I felt I had to get out, right away from there. But where could I go? I threw a few things in a bag, and all the time I was trying to think of somewhere. Then I remembered the commune. So I just... took off."

"You didn't leave a note, or try to tell anyone where you were going?"

"Why should I? I didn't owe them anything, I reckoned, not after what they'd done to me."

"What had they done to you, Damon?"

"Lied to me!" the boy shouted. He put his head in his hands. "The lot of them," he mumbled.

It was obvious that, much as Damon might have enjoyed his stay in Surrey, it had done nothing to restore his peace of mind. Thanet was now regretting having persuaded Joan to go home. She and Damon had driven back in separate cars, and she would have had no opportunity to talk to him at length, try to enable him to come to terms with what had happened.

Perhaps I should ring her, Thanet thought, ask her to come back, so that she can spend some time with Damon after the interview is over. He had a vivid mental image of her in the waiting room, eyes closed, head leaning back against the wall. She had looked so tired... No, he really didn't want to bring her back if he could help it. On the other hand, he certainly couldn't allow the boy to leave in this state. Many of his colleagues, Thanet knew, would have had no qualms about doing so, but he knew, too, that he wouldn't be able to live with himself if he did.

Thanet glanced at Lineham and nodded towards the door. The sergeant got up and went out. The sound of the door closing softly behind him made Damon glance over his shoulder and, Thanet hoped, register that they were now alone.

Thanet abandoned his chair and went to perch on the edge of his desk.

"That isn't true, you know. Your aunt and Mrs. Haywood, for instance. They didn't lie to you. It's obvious that they'd only just heard the news themselves."

But how? Thanet wondered. How, after all this time, had they stumbled upon this long-buried secret?

Damon shook his head dismissively. "I wasn't thinking of them."

"Your mother, you mean?"

"For one, yes."

"Could you really have expected her to tell you the truth, in the circumstances?"

Damon was silent for a moment. Then he shrugged. "Maybe not. Though it does explain one thing."

"What?"

"Why she couldn't stand the sight of me."

"I'm sure that's not true."

"No? In that case, why did she avoid me? Why didn't she ever spend time with me? Or take me on outings, like other mothers do? Or come to sports days and speechdays and . . ." Damon shook his head, hard, as if to suppress the unruly emotions which were threatening to swamp him. "Oh, no, don't try to make me believe she cared about me, because I wouldn't believe you, not in a million years."

"Damon," said Thanet quietly.

His tone brought the boy's head up with a jerk.

"I'm going to tell you something about your mother, something that I think might help you to understand her better. You see, in the course of an investigation such as this we learn a great deal about the people involved, and especially about the person at the heart of it, the victim. Now I'm not going to try and pretend your mother cared about you, because by all accounts she didn't. But," he went on quickly as the boy flinched, "I do want you to understand this. *It was nothing to do with you.*"

Damon frowned. "What do you mean?"

"I mean that it wasn't that she found you unlikeable, or unlovable or personally repulsive or anything like that, but that she was incapable of caring, really caring for anyone. Even for someone who loved her as deeply as your father."

The boy was silent, trying to absorb this new and unfamiliar interpretation of a situation he had always understood differently.

"I know that when people don't seem to like us much we always take it for granted that it's because of something we've said or done, or not said or not done, or just because of the way we are, but the fact of the matter is that quite often it's nothing to do with us at all, but with the person himself—or, as in this case, herself. You see, your mother was so badly hurt when she was a little child, that I think she built a wall around herself so that she would never have to suffer in the same way again. I'm not saying that she said to herself consciously, I shall never allow myself to love someone for fear that they will hurt me, because small children just don't think in those terms. But I'm convinced that, deep down, unconsciously, she decided never to allow herself to become vulnerable again—and that meant not allowing herself to care. The trouble is, of course, that people like that can do a great deal of harm to the people around them, especially to those who are dependent on them, like children . . . Like, in this case, you. May I make a suggestion?"

Damon nodded dumbly.

"Have you ever heard of Mrs. Glass?"

"My aunt goes to see her sometimes. Wasn't she their housekeeper when they were children, she and my mother?"

"Yes. She knew them both well, virtually brought them up. I think if you heard the way she speaks of your mother, and the things she could tell you about her, you may come to feel very differently about the way she treated you. After all, you know yourself, from your experiences of the last few days, how shattering it can be when your world falls apart . . . Just think how much worse it is if you're little more than a toddler, and can't begin to understand what's going on . . . Go and talk to Mrs. Glass, Damon. She'd be delighted to see you, I'm sure. She's a very interesting old lady and loves having visitors . . ."

Thanet paused for a moment and then said, "But I have a feeling that the person you were really talking about, when you mentioned people lying to you, was your father, wasn't it?"

Damon's subdued mood was at once swept away by a gust of anger. "Don't call him that! He's not my father! My father was someone I never knew, someone I'd scarcely heard of!"

"Jocelyn Haywood might have been your natural father, but Roland Tarrant was—is—your real father, and you know it."

"Do I? Then why didn't he tell me the truth?"

"For two reasons, I think. First of all, he loves you, and he wouldn't have wanted to hurt you..."

"Loves me," said Damon scornfully.

"Yes, loves you. He's been very worried indeed since it became evident that you hadn't just gone to spend the night with friends. He's rung up every day, twice or three times, to ask if there was any news of you..."

Damon was listening as if he would like to believe what Thanet was saying but found it impossible to do so. "If he loves me why wasn't he honest with me from the beginning? Surely he must have known I'd find out some time. It's like when you're adopted. Everyone knows it's best to tell kids they're adopted right from the start."

"Maybe. But you weren't adopted, were you? Your situation was a bit more... delicate than that. What would you have wanted him to tell you? That your mother became pregnant by another man but he married her just the same? Also, he had to consider the other people involved, people who might be deeply hurt by the knowledge, like your aunt. If he'd told you from the start, as you suggest, how could he be sure that you wouldn't have let slip the truth inadvertently? And you can hardly swear a small boy to eternal silence, can you?"

"It's all very well for you to say that! You can't know what it's like, to find out that no one is who you thought they were. Your father isn't your father, your grandmother isn't your grandmother... And, worst of all, you yourself are not the same person, but someone else..."

"That's not true, Damon. You are not someone else. You are yourself, you have the same genes, the same personality, the same appearance, the same mind, as you've always had. Oh look, I'm not saying this new knowledge doesn't change things, of course it does, but it need not change them for the worse if you don't let it. Your relationship with some of the other people around you will be different, yes, but maybe, and I'm thinking especially of your father, maybe things will be even better between you, now that this is out in the open. Just think how worried he must have been, that somehow you would find out, that it might drive you away from him."

Had Roland Tarrant even suspected that this might have been what had happened on Thursday? Thanet wondered. Surely not. After eighteen years he must have thought the secret was buried for ever. And yet... the clues had been there, scattered about, for anyone to read, as Thanet had read them...

"I think, you know, that the best thing you could do would be to talk to him about it, as honestly as you can."

Damon was shaking his head. "I can't do that."

"Why not? Because it would be difficult, uncomfortable, embarrassing? Maybe it would be all those things, but one thing's certain, it wouldn't be nearly as difficult, uncomfortable or embarrassing as living the rest of your life saying nothing about it and trying to pretend none of this had ever happened. Because it has happened and nothing's going to change that. You can't wave a magic wand and make everything as it was before."

Damon was silent.

"Won't you at least give it a try? After all, what have you got to lose? And just think what you have to gain! I haven't exaggerated his feelings for you, you know, as I think you'll see when you discover how relieved he is to see you back. What's more, with your mother gone, he'll need you more than ever."

The boy glanced up, a gleam in his eye. "That's true." His eyes glazed and he looked away, over Thanet's shoulder, perhaps into a distant place where he and Tarrant encountered each other as equals for the first time. "I suppose you're right," he said slowly. "What have I got to lose?"

The battle, it seemed, was won. Thanet breathed an inward sigh of relief and then said carefully, "If you like, I could give you a lift. I have to go out to Ribbleden anyway... Ah, no, I suppose you have your car."

"Yes... But I think, if you don't mind, I'd prefer to go with you." Damon shook his head in disbelief. "You're not like any other policeman I ever met."

"Policemen are people, like everyone else." Thanet slid off the desk, rubbing his buttocks, which had gone numb. "We even get pins and needles," he said with a grin.

Damon grinned back at him. The smile transformed him, making him look much younger and, for the first time, carefree.

Thanet felt a warm glow of satisfaction. Social-worker Thanet, he told himself wryly. Perhaps I've missed my vocation.

TWENTY-THREE

Beatrix Haywood had come to the door. "She's in the garden. If you go around the side of the house..."

It was six o'clock and a perfect June evening. The last of the clouds had rolled away and the sun had come out. Even though it was late in the day there had been enough heat to dry roads and pavements, roofs and driveways. Vegetation was another matter and gauzy veils of mist hung over the saturated landscape.

After delivering Damon to a delighted and relieved Tarrant, Thanet and Lineham had come direct to the coach house. Now they followed the narrow stone path which ran along the side of the house towards the back garden. Backed by tall shrubs, its edges were softened by an overhanging tapestry of foliage plants in gold and silver and many shades of green. Over the end of the path, at the back corner of the house, was a trellised archway spangled with the shimmering white stars of clematis.

At first the vista through the archway was blurred, indistinct, like the glimpse of a garden through a wrought-iron gate in an impressionist painting, but as they drew closer the view became more defined, blurs of colour resolving themselves into individual bushes or clumps of herbaceous plants. Even so, Thanet caught his breath as he stepped through the arch.

It was, quite simply, the most beautiful garden he had ever seen. It was deceptively small and Thanet could not have analysed its charm, but it was obvious that nothing short of genius and an instinctive love of plants and knowledge of how to use them had shaped the magical harmony of form and habit, foliage and flower which lay about them. He had taken it for granted that Daphne Linacre must be knowledgeable about plants; despite the fact that she had had no formal training, the nursery was, after all, her living. But there had been no hint of the creative talent beneath that brusque, business-like exterior.

She was bent double over a flower border, pulling out weeds. "Oh, no, not again", she said as she became aware of the two policemen. She was wearing faded jeans and a cotton shirt, its sleeves rolled up above the elbows, and her face was flushed with exertion. She wiped her forehead with the back of her wrist and put her hands on her hips, squinting at their faces against the slanting sunlight. "What is it this time?"

"We thought you'd like to know that Damon is safe and sound," said Thanet.

"Really? Oh, that's wonderful! He really is all right?"

"Yes, he's fine." Thanet gestured at a white-painted table and some chairs set out on a small paved patio near the back door. "Shall we sit down?"

As he turned he caught a flicker of movement behind the open kitchen window. Beatrix Haywood was obviously anxious to know what was going on. He had every intention of ensuring that she did.

There was a tray on the table with two glasses and a half-empty jug of lemonade.

"Would either of you like a drink?" said Daphne, raising the jug, obviously wishing to make amends for their rather cool reception. "I could easily get some more glasses. Or you could have something stronger, if you like."

Both men shook their heads and she poured a glass for herself and drank it off in one draught.

"Phoo, that's better. Gardening's hot work in this weather."

"It's beautiful," said Thanet, gazing around. "The most beautiful garden I have ever seen."

She looked pleased. "I'm glad. But I'm sure you didn't come here just to discuss horticulture, Inspector, much as I should be delighted to do so. You were saying about Damon..."

"We've just brought him home. He's with his...father."

If Daphne had been aware of that deliberate hesitation she didn't show it.

"Where's he been?"

"Staying on a commune, in Surrey, apparently."

The heavy eyebrows went up. "A *commune*? How on earth . . . ?"

"He'd heard about it from a friend of his."

"But why did he go off like that, without telling anyone?"

"Ah," said Thanet. "Now we come to it." He paused, then said, slowly and deliberately, "He went because of a conversation he overheard between you and Mrs. Haywood."

He was certain he hadn't imagined the alarm in her eyes as they flickered towards the open window behind them.

But she must have prepared herself for this moment and her expression was merely of amused disbelief as she said, "Really, what an improbable story, Inspector! I'm afraid he's been having you on. He's rather good at that."

"I believe not, Miss Linacre. He was most specific. And what he told me merely served to confirm what I had already worked out for myself."

"I haven't the faintest idea what you're talking about."

"Oh, I think you have, Miss Linacre. In fact, I'm certain of it. And I think it was as much of a shock to you as it was to him . . . to find out that his father was not Mr. Tarrant, as he has naturally always assumed, but Jocelyn Haywood, your former fiancé."

Despite her carefully maintained façade the bald statement affected her, as he had hoped it might; briefly, the lines of her face sharpened as her jaw clenched. Then she said, "What a ridiculous idea! I don't know what fairy stories you've been listening to, Inspector, but I think it's thoroughly irresponsible of you to come here making wild accusations without an atom of proof."

Unfortunately, she had hit the nail right on the head. He had no tangible evidence that Damon's story was true. He was certain that it existed, in some shape or another—unless, of course, it had already been destroyed—and by now he had a shrewd idea of how they had happened to stumble upon it, but the fact remained that his only real weapon against her was subtlety. Somehow he had to extract a confession, and it was obvious that this wasn't going to be easy. She had had several days now in which to plan her strategy and it was clear what it was going to be: denial and more denial. It was, after all, only Damon's word against hers and that, in the final account, would not be enough.

"Accusation, Miss Linacre?" He kept his tone, too, light and amused. Two could play at that game, he thought. "What accusation?"

Briefly, she looked disconcerted. But she quickly recovered. "That it was my fault that Damon went away like that, of course."

"So you deny that any such conversation ever took place?"

"Categorically."

"Strange." Thanet seemed to muse. "First we have one witness whose evidence suggests that you have been lying to us, now we have another . . . How many more people are you going to claim are 'mistaken' before you admit the truth?"

"Which is what?"

He had to admire her nerve. She was actually trying to force him to a premature accusation! He considered: should he allow her to appear to do so? He came to a decision and sat back in his chair with every appearance of relaxation, aware that Lineham was watching him. The sergeant knew from past experience that when Thanet looked at his most relaxed, he was at his most devious.

"Very well. I'll tell you the truth as I see it. Please feel free to interrupt, whenever you wish."

"Last Thursday, the day your sister was killed, Mrs. Haywood spent the afternoon up in the attic of the main house, sorting out stuff for the jumble sale yesterday. Now your sister, as we all know, was a compulsive hoarder, and my guess is that when she got married all her stuff from your former home came with her, and that much of it was never even unpacked but put, still in its boxes, up in the attic."

Thanet paused, expecting a denial, but it didn't come. Daphne Linacre was listening with a tolerant, almost indulgent expression. He sent up a little prayer that his strategy was going to work and that he wasn't making a humiliating mistake.

"You've already told me that it was only after much persuasion and with considerable reluctance that your sister finally agreed to part with some of her discarded clothes, and that she stipulated which boxes Mrs. Haywood was allowed to sort through.

"Now my guess is that those were the oldest boxes, and that at least one of them contained stuff which dated from before she was married. And that in that box was something, I don't know what—a letter, perhaps—which gave away the secret that Mrs. Tarrant had carried for so long—the fact that her son Damon had been fathered not by her husband, but by another man, Jocelyn Haywood, her sister's fiancé. Not a very pleasant thing to have happened, especially as her sister—you—had been away in hospital at the time, recovering from a perforated appendix.

"And of course, the point is that Beatrix Haywood, who found this evidence, whatever it was, was the young man's mother. She's getting on a bit now, and this was all a tremendous shock to her. She'd had no idea that her son had had an affair with his fiancée's sister, and certainly no suspicion that all these years she'd had a grandchild of whose existence she had been unaware. Also, of course, she was very angry on your behalf—you've been extremely kind to her, taking her in when she was homeless and generally treating her as the mother-in-law she would have been if her son had not died long ago."

Daphne was leaning back in her chair, apparently as relaxed as he, her fingers steepled across her stomach. Now Thanet noticed that the tips had gone white and that her hands were trembling slightly with the pressure she was exerting. Encouraged, he continued.

"So, once Mrs. Haywood had recovered from that initial shock her first instinct was to tell you what she had discovered. She came back here and rang you at work. I'm pretty certain she told you the news then and there, because you at once made an excuse for leaving work early and all the way home you brooded on what you'd learnt, working yourself up into a fury against your sister. Jocelyn Haywood had been the only man you ever loved, whereas Nerine had had countless admirers, serious or otherwise. For her to have stolen him from you, in your enforced absence, was betrayal of the worst kind. And for him to have given her the child that should have been yours by right... You simply couldn't bear the idea.

"You reached here at twenty to five, went indoors and demanded further details from Mrs. Haywood, who showed you the evidence she had found in the attic. As soon as you had satisfied yourself that the story was true you stormed across to the main house, determined to have it out with your sister. You quarrelled, and during the course of that quarrel you lost control of yourself and threw her from the balcony."

Thanet paused, breath held, alert for the slightest sound from behind him. Was it going to work, was his gamble going to pay off?

He prepared to play his last card. If this failed . . . He nodded at Lineham, who stood up.

"Daphne Linacre, you are not obliged to say anything unless you wish to do so but what you say may be put into writing and given in evidence."

The kitchen door flew open with such force that it rebounded against the wall, and Beatrix Haywood came rushing out. "No!" she cried. "No! You've got it all wrong."

Daphne was out of her chair in a flash. "Bea, shut up!"

Mrs. Haywood squirmed away from the arm which Daphne had flung around her shoulders. "No, I won't. I can't let you . . ."

"Bea, stop. They've no proof, I tell you."

"I don't care!" It was a cry of total despair. "I can't go on like this, not for ever. It . . . I . . ." She took a long, ragged breath and once again freeing herself from Daphne's constraining arm turned to face Thanet. "It was me," she said. "I did it."

"What nonsense!" cried Daphne. "She's overwrought, she doesn't know what she's saying. Bea, you must go and lie down." Daphne took Mrs. Haywood by the arm, presumably with the intention of propelling her towards the house, but yet again the older woman shrugged her off.

"Daphne, it's no good, can't you see? They'd be bound to find out sooner or later, and in any case I couldn't go on living like this for the rest of my life, I simply couldn't."

Daphne shook her head in despair. "She doesn't know what she's saying. It's all been too much for her." But there was no conviction in her voice now.

There was a brief, exhausted silence.

Then Beatrix Haywood sank down on one of the chairs, limbs splayed like a rag doll. "You have to believe me," she said. "Daphne had nothing to do with it."

"Would you like to make a verbal statement now?"

She nodded, and once again Lineham delivered the caution. Then he sat down and opened his notebook.

Beatrix was looking down at her lap, fingers plucking nervously at a loose thread protruding from a seam of the same flounced, flowery skirt in which Thanet had first seen her, topped today by a heavily embroidered white peasant blouse with long sleeves and draw-string neck. Her hair, as usual, was escaping from its bun. Eventually she said, as if it were all the explanation necessary, "She laughed at me, you see."

"Nerine did? When you went to see her?"

A nod.

"When was that?"

"Just after she had that row with Lavinia. I'd found the letter not long before. It was in the pocket of a yellow dress, and the envelope was still stuck down, it hadn't even been opened. She hadn't even cared enough to open it...

"I recognised Jocelyn's handwriting and although I knew I shouldn't, I couldn't resist reading it..." She shook her head and rubbed her hand wearily across her forehead. "I'd give anything to turn the clock back and leave that letter unread, so that we could go on the way we always were, not knowing." She gave Thanet a despairing look. "They say that knowledge is power, but power can be evil..."

"What did the letter say?"

"That she killed my son," said Beatrix Haywood simply.

Thanet nodded.

"You guessed?" she said sharply.

"Shall we say I put two and two together? Though I confess I wouldn't have put it in quite those terms."

"How else could you put it?" Little by little she was recovering. She was already looking more composed and now she sat up in her chair, straightening her shoulders, crossing her legs and folding her hands in her lap. "She was a bad woman, an evil, wicked woman, and Jocelyn would be alive today if he hadn't got tangled up with her."

"Could you tell me what the letter said, exactly?"

"You can have a look at it, if you like."

Daphne sat up with a jerk. "You told me you'd destroyed it!"

Beatrix shook her head sadly. "I know. I'm sorry. I was going to, but... It's the only letter I've ever had from him."

"But it wasn't even written to you, it was written to Nerine!"

"It's no good, Daphne, I just couldn't do it." She reached into her pocket, took out an envelope and handed it, almost reverently, to Thanet.

It was addressed to Miss Nerine Linacre, and had an old fourpenny stamp on it. Thanet extracted the single, folded sheet of paper inside. It was covered with myriad creases as though someone—Beatrix? Daphne?—had savagely scrumpled it up and then smoothed it out again. The handwriting was sprawling, unformed, immature.

Wed. March 20th '69

My darling Nerine,

I've been so worried about you. Every time I've called or phoned for the last couple of days, you've been out, and you were so upset the last time I saw you...Please, try not to be. I hope you're not still angry with me for suggesting an abortion, I was only thinking of you and honestly, truly, I'm glad you feel the way you do.

I'm writing because we really must talk before Daphne comes home on Friday. We have to decide what—and when—to tell her about us. Because we do have to tell her, don't we, now that we'll be getting married as soon as possible? I promise I shall try to be the best husband and father in the world.

Please, my darling, get in touch with me soon. A day when I don't hear your voice is a day wasted, and life without you would not be worth living. If I don't hear from you before then I'll call round at 7:30 tomorrow (Thursday) evening.

All my love, for ever and ever,
Jocelyn

Thanet handed the letter to Lineham, then asked the question which had been puzzling him ever since he first worked out what had happened.

"I wonder why she didn't have an abortion." He couldn't see Nerine refusing the easy way out on moral grounds.

Daphne gave a cynical laugh. "That's easy. She was scared stiff. One of her schoolfriends got pregnant when she was sixteen, had an abortion and died. She always swore she'd never take the same risk herself."

"I see..."

"But you can see now what happened, can't you?" Beatrix Haywood leant forward in her chair in her eagerness to make sure he understood. "Daphne and I have worked it all out. While Roland was away in Australia and Daphne was in hospital Nerine got bored and thought she'd amuse herself with Jocelyn. Then she discovered she was pregnant. She would have had no intention of tying herself for life to a struggling artist, so she took the obvious way out and when

Roland got back and proposed to her again, she accepted. No doubt that's why Jocelyn couldn't get hold of her, she was out with Roland. And when Jocelyn's letter arrived she didn't even bother to open it, just shoved it in her pocket and forgot about it.

"So, when Jocelyn turned up to see her on the Thursday evening, the day before Daphne was due back from hospital, he was greeted by the news that she and Roland were engaged."

Thanet remembered the scene as it had been so graphically described by Mrs. Glass who, in her innocence, had misinterpreted the whole incident: Jocelyn's arrival with the red roses meant for Nerine, not Daphne; and Nerine's cruel welcome: "Oh, Jocelyn. Come along in and have a glass of champagne. Roland and I are celebrating our engagement." Then the hand held out to display the ring, and Jocelyn's reaction: a white face and "No, thanks. I wouldn't want to intrude."

"It was on the way home that he was killed." Mrs. Haywood's face was pinched. "His car ran into a tree and exploded. He was burnt to death." Her fists clenched in vicarious pain.

"You think he did it deliberately?"

She shook her head. "Suicide, accident, it makes no difference. She was responsible, as surely as if she had been at the wheel herself. A pity she wasn't."

Lineham handed the letter back to Thanet, who folded it carefully and put it back into the envelope.

"So after finding this and realising its significance, you went to see Nerine?"

"Not immediately. By that time she was in the middle of the row with Lavinia. I obviously couldn't tackle her then and there, so I waited until everything had quieted down and Marilyn and Lavinia had gone down downstairs. Then I went along to Nerine's sitting room.

'Oh, it's you, Beatrix. Have you finished upstairs yet . . . What's the matter? You look as though you've seen a ghost.'

'I have.'

'What is this, some kind of joke? Why are you looking at me like that?'

'If you read this, you'll find out. Even if it is eighteen years too late.'

'What on earth are you talking about? What is it? It's

addressed to me . . . It's from . . . from Jocelyn. Where did you get this? How dare you read my private correspondence!'

'Never mind where. You never even opened it, did you, at the time?'

'So what? Surely I have the right to open or not open letters that are addressed to me? Look, I've had enough of this. I see no reason why I should be interrogated in my own sitting room. I'd like you to leave, now, if you don't mind.'

'Oh, but I do mind. I mind very much. I have no intention of leaving until this is sorted out.'

'Until what's sorted out? I really don't know what you're going on about, Beatrix.'

'Don't you? Don't you really? Look at the date on that letter.'

'Oh, very well. Right, I've looked. So what?'

'So it was written the day before Jocelyn died. And the Thursday he was referring to was the day before Daphne was due home from hospital.'

'So?'

'It was also the day you and Roland got engaged, I believe?'

'What about it?'

'And the day Jocelyn had his accident.'

'I really don't . . .'

'The day my son was burnt to death.'

'You're not suggesting . . . Oh, now look, wait a minute. I think you're getting things a bit out of proportion here. I know Jocelyn and I had a bit of a fling . . .'

'A bit of a fling? A bit of a fling? A fling that ended in one person's death and another person's birth. You call that a bit of a fling?'

'Well, what else was it? I certainly wasn't serious, Joss knew that . . .'

'Don't call him Joss. His name was Jocelyn, and he was never called anything else.'

'Well he was by me. I'll call him what I damn well like. For God's sake, Beatrix, he's been dead for eighteen years.'

'Yes. And I've only just learned that, but for you, he'd be alive today.'

'You can't be serious.'

'Oh, but I am. Deadly serious. Jocelyn had a serious nature too, he took after me. And when he said life wouldn't be worth living without you, he meant it.'

'So you're suggesting . . . My God, you are, aren't you?

You're suggesting that it wasn't an accident at all. That it was suicide. That Jocelyn killed himself because of me . . . You're crazy, d'you know that? Crazy. Getting worked up like this over something that happened nearly twenty years ago. Just look at you! Honestly, Beatrix, if you could only see your face . . .

"Then she began to laugh," said Mrs. Haywood grimly. "She just went on and on, louder and louder, till tears ran down her face, she couldn't stop. We were out on the balcony. She'd stalked out there earlier, when she asked me to leave, and I'd followed her. She was laughing so much she had to cling on to the rail for support, and she sort of doubled up over it, so that the upper part of her body was hanging over. She went on and on laughing until my head felt as though it was gong to explode." Beatrix put her hands over her ears as if to shut out the sound of it, echoing down the days. "I can still hear it, now," she whispered. "I couldn't stand it. I took hold of her shoulders and shouted at her at stop, but she wouldn't. So I . . . I bent down, swung up her legs and . . . gave her a little push."

She shook her head wonderingly. "That's all it took, just one little push."

TWENTY-FOUR

The village of Biddenden, with its broad cobbled pavements and black-and-white timbered weavers' cottages, is one of the most picturesque in Kent. The sign which hangs outside "Ye Maydes," Thanet and Joan's favourite restaurant, perpetuates the memory of Eliza and Mary Chalkhurst, a celebrated pair of Siamese twins, unique in that they survived, joined at the hip, well into middle age—a notion over which Thanet's imagination always turned somersaults. How was it possible to live in such indissoluble intimacy with another person? he wondered. Never to be able to take even the smallest independent action without the full consent and cooperation of somebody else . . . ?

"Just one little push?" said Joan as they parked opposite "Ye Maydes" and got out of the car. "Mrs. Haywood is deceiving herself, surely. It would take a lot more than that to tip a grown woman over a rail three foot six high."

"Not necessarily. She says that Nerine was 'doubled up over the rail' in a bout of hysterical laughter. The rail could therefore have acted as a fulcrum, and very little force indeed would have been necessary, to tip the balance one way or the other. Think of a see-saw."

"Yes, I see."

"Good evening Mr. Thanet, Mrs. Thanet."

Mrs. Daniels, the owner, came forward to greet them as they stepped into the heavily beamed exterior and turned left into the little bar, where in winter a log fire always burned in the huge inglenook fireplace.

Supplied with drinks they settled down to a serious study of the menu and, orders given, Joan sank back into her chair with a sigh of contentment. "I love celebrations," she said.

"Me too." And on this occasion there was more than one reason to celebrate. It was an immense relief to have brought out into the open and satisfactorily resolved the issue which for years had been festering away beneath the surface of their marriage.

After they had chatted for a while Joan said, "Anyway, there are a million things I want to ask you."

This was their first opportunity to talk at length. Thanet had no desire to spend the evening discussing the Tarrant case, but he didn't want to disappoint Joan. He resigned himself to their usual "post mortem."

"Such as?"

"Well, before we got bogged down in complicated explanations, just tell me first what you think frightened old Mrs. Tarrant so much?"

"Almost certainly she went along to Nerine's sitting room, wandered out onto the balcony and saw Nerine lying on the terrace below, very obviously dead."

Joan grimaced. "Poor old thing. I suppose it's one of the few occasions when she can be grateful for her erratic powers of recall."

"True."

Joan sipped at her drink and grinned. "Now comes the tricky bit. I want you to explain how you managed to put two and two together and come up with four."

"Tricky is the word. The answer is, I didn't, at first. In fact, to begin with, I began to wonder if I ever would. There seemed to be so many people with legitimate reasons for quarrelling with Nerine—her husband, both the Speeds, her mother-in-law, Marilyn Barnes..."

"You say, 'quarrelling with,' not 'killing.' You thought from the beginning, then, that it wasn't a premeditated murder."

"Yes. It did look very much like an unplanned attack. Anyway, it was you who eventually put me on the right track."

Joan's eyebrows went up. "Me?"

"Yes. And talking about you . . . Did I tell you how beautiful you are looking this evening?"

Joan was wearing a dress in misty greens scattered with wild flowers—buttercups, ox-eyed daisies and cornflowers. It conjured up visions of long, lazy summer afternoons in the country. Thanet said so.

She smiled back at him and squeezed his hand. "Romantic!"

"Have I ever denied it?"

Mrs. Daniels approached. "Your table is ready now, when you are."

"Thank you."

They were shown to a table for two near the window and Joan gazed about with satisfaction at the red-and-white colour scheme which contrasted so effectively with the abundance of dark beams. "I love this place."

"It's the nicest we've ever found, I agree."

Their first course arrived: a fanned avocado topped with Atlantic prawns marinaded in a blue-cheese dressing, for Joan. And for Thanet, melt-in-the-mouth deep-fried bread-crumbed slivers of veal served with three different dips: horseradish, tomato and garlic, and chive. For a while there was complete silence punctuated only by murmurs of appreciation.

"Anyway," said Joan eventually, "what did you mean, when you said that it was me who put you on the right track?"

"Well, you remember when I got home on Saturday, you'd been looking at photographs? There was one that I picked up, of Ben and myself in the garden . . . I didn't realise at the time, but it was that photograph that started to make things come together."

"In what way?"

"Well, there were two particular photographs amongst those I'd seen at High Gables . . . One of them, a wedding photograph of Nerine and Roland Tarrant, was in Nerine Tarrant's sitting room. The second, which was really rather similar to the one of Ben and me, was in her mother-in-law's room, a photograph of Roland Tarrant and Damon in the garden, on Damon's first birthday."

"So?"

"So, the first had been taken in the spring, because the daffodils were out, the second in the autumn. And when I got Lineham to check Damon's date of birth we learnt that he had been born only six months after his parents' marriage, and there'd been no whispers of his being a premature baby. I knew that Roland Tarrant had been away in Australia from soon after Christmas until the middle of March that year, so the conclusion was obvious: someone else was Damon's father."

"Jocelyn Haywood, her sister's fiancé."

"That's right. Daphne was in hospital, remember, and Nerine didn't seem to have had any other man in tow at the time. I checked with Mrs. Glass—the woman who more or less brought Nerine and Daphne up. She's an amazing old dear. Still icing wedding cakes at the age of eighty-one!"

Joan laughed. "Really?"

"She's a curious mixture of wisdom and naivety—she seemed to understand the girls very well indeed, but when it came to their relationships with men . . . She confirmed that Jocelyn had been around a lot while Daphne was in hospital, but put it down to the fact that he was lonely—that he had no family down here and with Daphne away naturally turned to Nerine for company."

"I gather you think that Jocelyn meant no more to Nerine than someone to amuse herself with, at a time when she was at a loose end."

"Yes, I do. Though that makes her sound very cold-blooded, and I don't think she was. I think that she just had a driving need to feel important to somebody—anybody, to reassure herself of her own worth."

"You wouldn't say she was a nymphomaniac, then?"

"Oh, no, definitely not, though I daresay a lot of people thought she was. No, I'm inclined to agree with her husband, who saw her as so damaged by the sudden and total withdrawal of love she suffered as a small child, that she spent the rest of her life looking for it, without being able to commit herself completely to any one person for fear of being hurt again. He told me he'd always hoped that one day she would wake up and see that she could find all she wanted or needed right there in her own home, in him. He really did love her, you know, darling. He was prepared to put up with anything as long as she stayed with him, convinced that in the end she'd come to her senses and find him waiting."

"Poor man. He must be absolutely shattered by all this."

Thanet had a brief, vivid image of Tarrant, sweat running down his body, attacking the dead tree with an axe in a vain attempt to exorcise the demons of pain and loss which were his constant companions. "Yes, he is."

"What I don't understand is why nobody else, at the time, seemed to have realised that he couldn't have been Damon's father."

"Oh, I think they must have. But Nerine's father wouldn't have cared enough to make much of a fuss about it, as long as his daughter was respectably married, and Roland Tarrant certainly wouldn't have let the fact that Nerine was pregnant by another man deter him from marrying her. He would have taken Nerine on any terms. And his mother . . . Well, I think Lavinia Tarrant would have been glad to see Roland get the woman he wanted, but bitterly resentful of the fact that he had been cheated. Not that she seems to have held it against Damon, she seems very fond of him, but I suspect that she might well rather have enjoyed being a thorn in Nerine's flesh. Those little forays to create chaos in Nerine's private territory, for instance, I'm not sure they were as innocent as Marilyn chose to make out . . . No, the one person who would have been deeply hurt by the knowledge was Daphne, and I think she was too upset by Jocelyn's death to give any thought to the matter. I imagine she simply took it for granted that Roland was the father. I don't suppose she ever knew that Roland was away in Australia for quite so long. The latter part of his absence coincided with her stay in hospital and for much of that time she was very ill indeed, almost died from that perforated appendix, I gather . . . Anyway, to get back to what we were saying, I think looking at that photograph of Ben and me set me off. I remember waking up the next morning knowing that something had clicked, and not being able to put my finger on it. That came later on in the day."

"Why? What happened then?"

"I talked to Nicky Barnes. I think I told you, he's the son of the woman who looks after old Mrs. Tarrant. He's ten . . . Children are often remarkable witnesses. They seem to see things with an uncluttered vision most of us lose as experience piles on the preconceptions and prejudices . . . And it's usually easy to tell when they're lying."

"And Nicky wasn't?"

"Oh, no. He's bright, and observant, too. Now Daphne Linacre had told us that the reason why she came home from work early that afternoon was because she had a migraine. She also said that when she got there she could think of nothing but lying down in a cool, dark room and had gone straight up to bed. But when I talked to Nicky he told me that he heard her car drive up and that ten minutes later, when he went across to the house for tea, he saw her going back into the coach house. When I challenged her about this, she flatly denied it, and I couldn't see why, unless she had something to hide."

"You thought she might have been coming back from seeing Nerine—from killing her, in fact."

"I certainly thought it possible, yes. But what I couldn't understand—which was why I hadn't seriously considered Daphne as a suspect up to that point—was why, after living next door to Nerine in reasonable harmony all those years, she should suddenly take it into her head to leave work early, come home and kill her. It seemed such a wildly improbable thing to do. Now I realised that there could be a proviso—*unless she had just learnt something which completely changed her attitude towards Nerine*.

"That was when it clicked, about the photographs. If Nerine and Jocelyn had had an affair while Daphne was in hospital, if Damon was their son and Daphne had only just found out... At first I couldn't imagine how she could have found out, but then I remembered that it was after receiving a phone call from Beatrix Haywood that she suddenly decided to go home—and Beatrix had been up in the attic of High Gables that afternoon, sorting through boxes of Nerine's old belongings for stuff to send to a jumble sale..."

"So you suspected she might have come across something, a letter, some papers, that told her the truth... But wait a minute... Why wouldn't Mrs. Haywood have guessed at the time, when Damon was born?"

"I checked on that. Apparently she was living up north then, so she wasn't involved with the Tarrant family—she didn't know anything about Roland being away while Daphne was in hospital, and so on. And in fact it wasn't until several years later that she moved down here. She'd kept in touch with Daphne and when the house she was renting was pulled down to make way for a motorway project Daphne offered her a home."

"Kind of her."

"Yes. Though I suspect her motives weren't entirely altruistic. Daphne doesn't exactly strike me as the domesticated type, and she gained a devoted, unpaid housekeeper for the duration."

"Cynic!"

Thanet grinned. "Realist, I'd say." He smiled at the waitress who had come to clear away the first course. "That was delicious."

They waited until the girl had gone, then Joan said, "So at that point you thought that it must have been Daphne who had killed Nerine?"

"To begin with, yes."

"So what made you change your mind?"

"I didn't change my mind, exactly... It was just that, when I really started to think about it, work out what must have happened if Daphne were guilty, it didn't make sense."

"Why not?"

"Daphne got home at twenty to five—several people have verified this. Allow five minutes for her to hear Beatrix's story, two minutes to gét over to the house, another two to get back... Nicky saw her when he went in to tea at ten to five, and his mother confirms the time. So that would have given Daphne just one minute in which to quarrel with Nerine and push her over the balcony."

"It only takes a second to push someone off a balcony..."

"Yes, I know. But I couldn't see Daphne rushing over to the main house having made up her mind in advance to kill her sister. I think she'd have gone because she wanted to verify the story, hear the truth of it from Nerine herself... She would have wanted to *know*, as much detail as possible. Wouldn't you agree?"

"Yes, I think that's true. Most women would."

Thanet shrugged. "So I began to have doubts whether she could have done it."

"You didn't discount her entirely, then?"

"Oh no, I couldn't afford to do that. But I did think that it was much more likely to have happened as in fact it did happen."

Their main course arrived. Joan had chosen sautéd pieces of beef fillet topped with caramelised Dijon mustard, and Thanet was having Paillard de Saumon a l'oseille—a flattened piece of Scotch salmon quickly pan fried and served with a wine and sorrel sauce. His mouth watered as the delectable aroma drifted up to his nostrils, and once again there was a reverent silence as they savoured the first mouthfuls of food.

"How was that?" said Joan eventually.

"Mmm?" They had been married long enough for Thanet

to know at once that she was simply picking up the conversation again as if there had been no hiatus. "Ah, yes, well it was very simple, really." He briefly narrated Beatrix Haywood's story. "When she realised what she had done she went straight back to the coach house and rang Daphne. She can't remember a single word of the conversation, but according to Daphne she simply said, "Daphne, something really terrible has happened. Please come home at once," and put the phone down. Daphne knew that Beatrix would never make such an appeal unless there was something seriously wrong, so she left immediately. When she got home Beatrix poured out the whole story and Daphne hurried over to check for herself that Nerine really was dead—she didn't go into the main house at all, just around to the terrace. Then she went back to the coach house and spent some time planning what they should do and say when the inevitable investigation began, confident that any strangeness in Beatrix's behaviour would be put down to shock over the murder—as, indeed, it was. On the face of it, you see, there was nothing to connect Nerine and Beatrix other than that they were next-door neighbours. Later on, of course, Daphne had a delayed reaction. Mike and I heard her being sick upstairs when we were there talking to Beatrix Haywood—who, incidentally, after the initial panic, remained remarkably cool and level-headed for someone who usually gives the impression of being a bit scatterbrained. It had all been a terrible shock to Daphne, of course, learning of Jocelyn and Nerine's betrayal and the baby, then discovering that Beatrix had actually killed Nerine..."

"But why didn't she report the murder? After all, she'd had nothing to do with it, and now she's made herself into an accessory after the fact."

"I know... I think it was partly because she's genuinely fond of Beatrix—they're both a bit odd, and they suit each other; partly because Beatrix is Jocelyn's mother, and over the years Daphne has come to think of her as family; and partly, I think, because Daphne felt no loyalty to Nerine after what she had just learned about her. Also, of course, I think she accepted that it was an accident, in the sense that Beatrix hadn't gone to see Nerine with the intention of killing her, and that Beatrix therefore didn't deserve to go through all the pain and suffering that an arrest for murder would entail."

"It was very strange, don't you think, the way it happened?"

"You mean, why Nerine should have had that bout of hysterical laughter? Yes, it was. Disastrous, too, of course, in that Beatrix just couldn't take the idea that Nerine should think any of this funny. In fact, I don't think she did. I think she was still in a state of considerable tension after the row with Lavinia, which had taken place immediately before. Then Beatrix stalked in like an avenging angel and, well, as I said, Beatrix is a bit odd—hair always escaping from a bun and arty, peasant-style clothes most inappropriate to a woman of nearly seventy... I can quite see she might have looked a bit comic, and I suspect that what was initially no more than a mildly amused reaction turned into one of those bouts of uncontrollable laughter we all experience from time to time— you know, the more inappropriate it seems, the harder it is to stop."

"Like getting the giggles in church, you mean."

"That sort of thing, yes."

"So you're saying that when you finally went to see Daphne, you really weren't sure which of them had done it?"

"If either of them had! I tell you, Joan, I was taking a most almighty risk. Looking back, now, I go cold when I think about it. You see, as I said, there were a number of other people who had equally strong motives and opportunities, and there was no logical reason why one of them shouldn't have done it."

"So why take that risk? Why not just wait, and see if anything more conclusive emerged?"

Thanet grinned. "It's good to live dangerously, sometimes. And the longer I considered Beatrix as a suspect, the more likely it seemed that she was the culprit."

"Why?"

"Well, she's pretty obsessive about Jocelyn, still, even after all these years—convinced that if he'd lived he would have been another Picasso. You should see their sitting room—it's like a third-rate art gallery."

"You don't seem to have a very high opinion of his talent."

"I don't know much about art, as you know, you're the expert there, but I must admit I wasn't impressed, no... Anyway, as I say, Mrs. Haywood didn't see it that way. And of course, he was her only son. The point is that people with obsessions can be dangerous—it often doesn't take much to tip them over the edge, if they're in a highly emotional state at the time."

"As she was, because she was convinced that it was Nerine's fault that Jocelyn died."

"That's right, yes."

Their plates were cleared away and the pudding trolley appeared, loaded with tempting dishes.

"I honestly don't think I can manage anything else," said Joan.

"What about a sorbet? You could make space for that, surely," said Thanet.

"Well . . . possibly, yes. Orange, perhaps?"

Thanet chose trifle, always his favourite, and Joan's sorbet arrived in the hollowed-out shell of an orange, with a little lid of orange peel on top.

"And was it?" said Joan. "Nerine's fault, that Jocelyn died?"

"Perhaps not in the sense that Mrs. Haywood meant. She was convinced—still is, for that matter—that he killed himself because of the shock of learning of Nerine's engagement."

"You don't agree, though?"

"I just don't know. It could well have been an accident. The weather was bad that night—heavy rain, and a strong, gusting wind . . . But in the sense that after such a shock he might have been driving carelessly then, yes, perhaps Nerine was at least partly responsible."

"What will happen to his mother, now that she's confessed?"

"Well, she's been charged with murder, but my guess is that it will be reduced to manslaughter by reason of provocation and she'll probably get a two-year suspended sentence."

"Let's hope so, anyway."

"Yes. Certainly the jury will be able to see that she's appalled by what she did. The trial will be a pretty nasty experience for her, but I think she'll come through it all right. Then, all being well, she'll be able to sink gently back into obscurity as Daphne's housekeeper. Though I suppose they'll have to move. I can't really see them wanting to go on living in Roland Tarrant's back garden."

"No. How's he reacted to all this?"

"Shocked—stunned, in fact. I don't think he's taken it in properly yet . . ."

"I can imagine . . . Mmm. This is really delicious," said Joan. "Would you like to try some?"

She held out a loaded spoon, and Thanet tasted.

"Yes, it is good. Cointreau in it, d'you think?"

Joan tasted again, considered. "Yes, I think you're right."

"I hope you're remembering all these culinary details for Bridget. She'll want chapter and verse tomorrow."

"As usual."

They grinned at each other, and for a few minutes discussed Bridget's prospects of getting a positive response from the *Kent Messenger*. Then Joan said, "All right. So for one reason and another you became convinced that it was Beatrix who had killed Nerine. But why, in that case, did you choose to accuse Daphne?"

"As a matter of fact, I didn't actually accuse her. I admit I gave the impression of accusing her, but that's quite different. And I did it with the express intention of trying to manipulate Beatrix Haywood into a confession."

"But why not tackle Beatrix? Daphne sounds much less likely to cave in."

"Ah, it was all rather subtle, really. I thought that Beatrix would be much more likely to 'cave in,' as you put it, if she thought Daphne was going to be arrested for a crime she, Beatrix, had committed. I made sure she could hear the interview, and I knew how hard she would find it to stand by, saying absolutely nothing, while it seemed that Daphne was getting in deeper and deeper. Whereas if I'd accused her directly all she'd have had to do was keep on flatly denying it."

"How devious can you get!"

Thanet grinned. "But of course, it was you who really helped me to bring it off, by finding Damon like that."

"Sounds to me as though you had it all worked out without him."

"Maybe, but that isn't the same as *knowing*. I couldn't possibly have talked to Daphne as I did on the basis of mere speculation. Having Damon's confirmation made all the difference. I was convinced all along that his disappearance was somehow central to the case, and of course it was. And I was very grateful indeed to you, for producing him."

"I wasn't at all sure it would come off."

"But it did. And although, at the moment, he's naturally in a bit of a state, I have a feeling that he'll settle down, in time. Have you had a chance to talk to him yet?"

"Yes, I saw him today. He'd had quite a long talk with his father, I gather. And if we're handing out bouquets, I think you deserve one, for persuading him to do so."

Thanet smiled. "Social-worker Thanet in action. I thought

at the time perhaps I'd missed my vocation. You would have been proud of me."

"Oh, I am," said Joan. "Make no mistake about that, I am."

Their eyes met in a lingering, loving look which saluted the value of each to the other.

"Mutual admiration society, then," said Thanet.

They raised their glasses and drank the last of the wine in a silent toast.

ABOUT THE AUTHOR

DOROTHY SIMPSON, winner of Britain's Silver Dagger Award, is the author of six previous Luke Thanet novels, most recently *Suspicious Death*. A contributor to *Ellery Queen's Mystery Magazine* and *Alfred Hitchcock's Mystery Magazine*, she lives in Kent, England.

NERO WOLFE STEPS OUT

Every Wolfe Watcher knows that the world's largest detective wouldn't dream of leaving the brownstone on 35th street, with Fritz's three star meals, his beloved orchids and the only chair that actually suits him. But when an ultra-conservative college professor winds up dead and Archie winds up in jail, Wolfe is forced to brave the wilds of upstate New York to find a murderer.

THE BLOODIED IVY
by Robert Goldsborough
A Bantam Hardcover
05281 $15.95

and don't miss these other Nero Wolfe mysteries by Robert Goldsborough:

THE MYSTERIOUS WORLD OF AGATHA CHRISTIE

Acknowledged as the world's most popular mystery writer of all time, Dame Agatha Christie's books have thrilled millions of readers for generations. With her care and attention to characters, the intriguing situations and the breathtaking final deduction, it's no wonder that Agatha Christie is the world's best-selling mystery writer.